SUPREME JUSTICE

A THRILLER

BOOK 3

IN

THE BODY MAN SERIES

ALSO BY ERIC P. BISHOP

THE BODY MAN SERIES:
The Body Man
Breach Of Trust
Supreme Justice
Downfall (Summer 2026)

THE OMEGA GROUP SERIES:
Ransomed Daughter
Babylon Will Rise
Untitled Troy Evans Origin Story (2026)

SUPREME JUSTICE

BOOK 3 IN THE BODY MAN SERIES

ERIC P. BISHOP

BRUNOE MEDIA PUBLISHING

eBook ISBN-979-8-9917666-2-3

Paperback ISBN-979-8-9917666-3-0

Hardcover ISBN-979-8-9917666-4-7

Library of Congress Cataloging-in-Publication Identifiers: LCCN: 2025911585

Book Cover by Momir Borocki

Book Formatting by Atticus

First Edition July 2025

Printed in The United States of America

10 9 8 7 6 5 4 3 2 1

DEDICATION

Donald (Donnie) Cheshire Jr

1975 - 2016

For the lips of an adulteress drip honey,

and smoother than oil is her speech;

But in the end, she is bitter as wormwood,

sharp as a two-edged sword.

Her feet go down to death,

Her steps take hold of Sheol.

Proverbs 5:3-5

CHAPTER ONE

ASHEVILLE, NORTH CAROLINA

THE GROVE PARK INN

Merci de Atta's legs compressed the torso of the overweight man and squeezed with the ferocity of a serpent as it crushed the life from a helpless prey.

The man gasped for breath, but his vain attempt to inhale life-giving oxygen only resulted in more intense pain as Merci exuded compounding pressure on his chest. Careful not to break any ribs or leave visible signs of a struggle, she positioned her body in such a way as to deliver maximum stress with minimum effort.

The deviant wedged between her thighs liked it rough. Merci intended to deliver on what he paid for, even if it didn't result in the happy ending he expected.

Lying in the center of the bed, the man's sole focus became a struggle to breathe. With her thighs like a vice around the side of his chest, her knees pinned his arms into the mattress. The move immobilized his arms. He struggled for sixty seconds and tried to throw her from atop, using his bent legs and waist as leverage. But to no avail. Years of poor diet and a lack of motivation to exercise caught up to him as his mid-section girth prevented his thrusts from effectively dislodging the petite woman, less than half his weight.

Merci weighed one hundred and twenty-five pounds, but what she lacked in body mass she made up for in lean muscle, agility, and innate skill. Her toned body was sculpted over years of focused work and dedication to her craft. She used her figure as a weapon, both the physical strength it exuded and the shapely features which enticed weak-minded men to fall into her traps.

Her skill set allowed her to administer death wherever and whenever necessary. For the right price.

The man's eyes scanned the hotel room. The cherry-colored bedside nightstand and brass lamp caught his eye as he entered a death spiral. Although life slowly left his body, his gaze stopped at Merci's glossy black bra. Her pert, overflowing breasts, in a two-size-too-small bra, momentarily distracted his fight-or-flight struggle for life.

She used the weakness of the opposite sex to her advantage countless times. In fact, she counted on it to not only extinguish life, but to save hers.

Merci noticed him focusing on her breasts. She smiled, then gave him a not-so-subtle wink. She leaned close to his ear. "Men are weak," she said in a sultry tone. "Pathetic."

The man gasped a large gulp of stale hotel room air, exhaling with a strained voice as he uttered "Omaha," just loud enough to be heard over the sound of the room's air conditioning.

He had spoken their pre-arranged safe word.

Merci's face contorted to a frown. "You know you're not Peyton Manning, right?" Seconds later, she climbed off his chest.

The man nodded, grabbed at his sternum once she got off, and the pressure abated. "That ... was ... intense." He spoke between gasps of precious air. "I thought ... you ... were actually ... gonna suffocate me." The words cut in and out between jagged breaths.

Merci smiled as she slid off the bed. "You're so funny, and you got off easy that time. The exciting stuff hasn't even started, big guy."

He coughed up a bit of phlegm. "I ... I can't wait." A devious grin spread across his red hued face.

"Want a drink?" Merci asked as she walked toward the bar in the corner of the room.

"Of course." He nodded and wiped the perspiration from his forehead.

Merci smiled warmly. "Pick your poison."

He let out an elongated breath. "I'm a Jack man."

Before she got behind the mahogany bar, Merci turned to see him staring at her pert ass, covered in black laced panties. "One Doctor Jack to cure your ills on the way, Mr. Omaha."

"Pour one for yourself, darlin'," he replied in out-of-breath gasps.

"Don't mind if I do."

The man adjusted the oversized pillows and straightened the down comforter on the bed as he re-positioned where he lay.

Merci used the brief interlude to remove two shot glasses from under the bar, carefully pouring a small vial of clear liquid she hid in the back corner of the shelf into the man's glass before she filled the rest with Jack Daniels.

She carried both shot glasses back to the bed, his in her left hand. Before she reached the side of the bed, she tossed down the amber liquid in her right hand in one quick motion, licked her lips, then tucked the other shot glass between her voluptuous breasts. It proved to be a tight fit in the way-too-small bra.

Merci climbed up and slowly maneuvered across the bed. She was careful not to spill a drop of the liquid as her body glided over the bedspread like a viper. She climbed atop him, slowly rubbed her body on his before saying, "Bottoms up."

He sat up and buried his face between her breasts.

She leaned over and allowed him to shoot down every drop within the glass. The man fell back onto a fluffy pillow. A contented look spread over his face as his eyes slowly closed, and he almost appeared to drift off to sleep.

Merci counted to ten using the old one Mississippi, two Mississippi methodology before she climbed off him.

He lay there motionless for several seconds before his eyes popped open. A look of terror replaced the contented expression as his body convulsed. The tremors started slowly, like the motion of a mixer on the lowest setting. Within seconds, the jerking movements became intense as his body flailed about all over the bed.

As quickly as it started, he went still, and his eyes rolled back in his head.

Merci waited two more minutes and watched his chest intently. She then checked his pulse.

Nothing.

She dressed, put the same black cocktail dress on that she had slipped off thirty minutes earlier, and then donned surgical gloves. It took her twenty minutes to wipe the room down and erase any DNA she may have left in the room or on his body.

Before leaving, she removed the hair samples and fingerprints from her handbag and staged the scene as instructed by her employer.

The vial of clear liquid she administered contained a chemical that triggered a massive heart attack. Within hours, the manufactured chemical would leave little trace, but what remained would display the same compound as cocaine. Most coroners would take the toxicology report, see the clear signs of the heart attack, along with the traces of illicit cocaine, and not dig any deeper. Considering the overweight man's health and the activity he was involved in at the time of his death, it would be an open-and-shut autopsy.

As she opened the hotel room door, she looked back at the lifeless body with a piercing, deriding glance. Men like him disgusted her, and even the scalding hot shower she would soon take would not eradicate his body oils or the smell of his skin fast enough.

Another mark etched into the hardened wall of an already tattered soul.

⸺◆○◆⸺

Merci climbed into the car beside her boyfriend and handler, Marcus Rollings.

"Well, hello, honey. How was your day?" Marcus said sarcastically as he reached over and patted her toned thigh.

Merci rolled her eyes and pushed his hand off her. "Dude, not in the mood. I need a hot shower. I can still feel him on me."

"You know you just killed the husband of a Supreme Court justice, right?"

She shrugged but didn't reply.

"How did it feel?" Marcus asked.

With a deep sigh, Merci pursed her lips. "About like the rest of them. He got what he deserved. There's one less asshole out there who will cheat on his wife."

"Sounds like a win-win," Marcus said with a toothy grin.

"Just get me to the hotel so I can cleanse his smell from my body."

The blond-haired man sat in the driver's seat of the metallic gray sedan, his back stiff, and nerves frayed. He watched as the woman with raven colored hair in the black cocktail dress left the Grove Park Inn via the side exit. The grand stone façade and deep red colored roof of the structure reflected the nearly full moon from above. The woman walked with a confident stride and gave no hint that she had just committed a murder.

He tracked her movements as she continued past the parking lot and crossed over to a side street. When she was out of sight, he started the car and moved forward, careful not to give away the tail.

Sure to stay a safe distance back, he observed the woman climb into the passenger seat of a white Aston Martin V8 Vantage three blocks from the hotel. Once she climbed inside, the car sped away.

The man reached into the center console, picked up his cell phone, and placed a call.

"Yes?" the voice asked after the second ring.

"She left the Grove Park Inn," the blond-haired man said.

"It's done?" the voice asked.

"Presumably. She left alone."

"Let me know when the staff finds the body. You might want to prod them along so we don't have to wait till morning."

"She's with Marcus in his Aston Martin. What do you want me to do?"

"Tail them," the voice stated.

"I'm on it."

"Just make sure you don't lose her. We've got too much on the line."

He audibly sighed. "I might be young, but this isn't my first rodeo."

"Good. Be smart. Make sure it isn't your last. Did you put the tracker on his car yet?"

"No, not yet. Marcus stayed in the vehicle while Merci was in the hotel."

"Just get it done tonight."

The line disconnected, and the blond-haired man watched as the vehicles taillights faded into the darkness of Innsbrook Road.

He carefully followed far behind Marcus and Merci as they navigated the streets of Asheville, headed towards Interstate 40.

CHAPTER TWO

WASHINGTON, D.C.

THE SUPREME COURT

Associate Justice Mary Brown entered the ornate Supreme Court courtroom through the east side entrance. Her eyes swept the expansive room containing twenty-four Old Convent Quarry Siena marble columns imported from Liguria, Italy. Other styles of Italian, Spanish, and even Algerian marble adorned the eighty-two by ninety-one-foot chamber, which had forty-four-foot tall ceilings that enhanced the awe factor of the imposing structure. The raised curved bench where the justices sat, along with most of the furniture within the room, was constructed from mahogany.

As the wooden gavel cracked, the distinct thud of the mallet on the wooden block disturbed the early morning silence of the packed courtroom. The gavel sound announced the entrance of the nine judges at ten a.m. sharp, and the Marshal's introduction heralding her and the other justices' entrance elicited a buzz throughout the room.

Until the one p.m. break, Justice Brown listened to oral arguments as they droned on as she reviewed the briefs stacked neatly in front of her by her staff. Three briefs covered her workspace, and the case currently being argued involved a bake shop owner in Oregon versus the state. Even though she kept an open mind, Justice Brown felt certain about which side the Constitution protected, with little need to hear the oral arguments.

One justice, two down from her, appeared to nod off ten minutes into the oral arguments. Mary learned quickly that after her appointment, he had a proclivity to sleep while on the bench. In fact, he appeared to doze off more than he stayed awake. Yet, his mind was sharp. Undoubtedly, the justice with the thick glasses and bad comb-over was a brilliant, walking, talking law scholar. Apparently, power naps did him well since he could still regurgitate oral arguments months later, even ones Mary swore he slept through.

Justice Brown was the lone exception from the other eight, a common thread that weaved through many aspects of her life. The only current justice who did not graduate from either Harvard or Yale, Mary graduated from Stanford. For everywhere else, except maybe in the current make-up of the Supreme Court, a Stanford law degree revealed one's brilliance. However, the other justices quietly derided her for her background. It was generally done playfully, but still, she got the general impression they looked down on her.

As the morning session ended, the justice two seats to her right awoke. Justice Brown followed the others as they made their way single-file out of the courtroom.

Once outside, Frank Halter, the Marshal of the Supreme Court, approached her. Nobody called him Frank, not even his wife and kids. They all called him the *Marshal*. Some of the older justices who had worked with him for years likely could not remember his real name if they tried.

"Madam Justice," the Marshal said in his deep, guttural voice, the one used to announce the justices as they entered the courtroom for the past eighteen years.

Mary turned and saw Frank's piercing brown eyes as they bore down on her twenty feet away.

"Yes, Marshal?" she asked.

"I need to speak with you, Madam Justice."

"Of course," she said.

His face contorted, and his normal warm grin faded into the abyss as if a shroud suddenly covered his head. "In private, please, ma'am. Your chamber is preferable."

Mary's throat tightened as an invisible grip exerted pressure on her chest. She nodded, turned away from him, and walked on, taking the left, right, then another right until she entered her inner sanctum. The footfalls of the Marshal were directly behind her the entire time.

Once inside her chamber, she sat behind her desk and motioned to the Kittinger chair across from her.

"Please take a seat, Marshal."

"I'd rather stand."

"You're making me nervous, Frank." She pointed directly at the ornate cherry colored chair. "Sit," she said, followed by the word, "Please."

Realizing this wasn't a suggestion, the Marshal sat. "As you wish."

Going straight after the elephant in the room, Justice Brown asked, "Who's dead?"

The Marshal swallowed hard. "Your husband, ma'am."

Mary knew this day would come. She suspected it would occur years before now. Even so, hearing the hollow words still struck her in a profound way. A sense of overwhelming sadness welled up from deep within.

The Marshal started to speak, but she raised her hand and spun around in her high-backed chair so he could no longer see her face.

Mary took several large breaths to control herself. She breathed in from her nose and out slowly from her mouth. The sound of her exhaling filled the room.

During the next three minutes, the Marshal said nothing.

Finally, Justice Brown turned back around and faced him. Her face was devoid of emotion, and her voice took on a monotone sound.

Her cross-exam began.

The Marshal was no lawyer, but as the head of the Supreme Court Police, he was a bright and intuitive man. The best option would be to simply answer her questions.

"How did he die?" Mary asked.

"Preliminary coroner's report believes it was a heart attack."

"Shocker." Sarcasm dripped from her tongue. "Where was he?"

"Asheville, North Carolina."

"The Grove Park Inn?" She asked.

"Yes, Madam Justice."

"We're in my chamber. Mary will do, not Madam Justice."

"As you wish, Mary."

Mary let out a deep sigh. "And I take it he wasn't alone?"

"No, according to hotel staff, he wasn't."

"Was the whore with him when he died?" The anger within her voice got stronger as the words spewed out.

He shook his head. "The staff said he was the only person in the room when they found the body, but several staff members saw him enter the hotel with a young woman in a form-fitting black dress."

Her expression softened ever so slightly as she tapped her long, slender fingers against the dark wood of her desk. "At least the fat fuck died alone."

"Mary!" The Marshal knew this would be a hard conversation, but he had no idea it would go this way.

Mary shook her head back and forth. "I'm sorry for my tone and harsh words, Frank. Your job is to protect us, not dive into the occasional soap opera that are the lives of Supreme Court justices."

"Well, I can confirm you're not the first justice to have a conflict with their spouse. Nor will you be the last."

She ignored the comment. "He didn't have any security with him, correct?"

The Marshal shook his head. "No, Mr. Brown mainly travels alone, unless he is with you and the Marshals Service on one of your trips."

She nodded and appeared to think as her eyes darted back and forth, then looked up toward the ceiling. "I always knew this day would come, and I suspected he'd be with a whore when the day arrived."

"I'm sorry, Mary. Even if your relationship was in turmoil, losing one's spouse suddenly must be devastating."

She pursed her lips and slowly shook her head. "I grew up with nothing, Frank. Less than nothing, in fact. I was the first person in my family to even graduate from high school. My parents were alcoholics. My father cheated on my mother incessantly. I told them both on graduation day, which they didn't attend by the way, that I was going to college. Explained that I would one day attend law school and be a judge. Instead of congratulating me, they both mocked me. My mother told me to get a home economics degree, find a decent man, and start popping out babies. My father said that women shouldn't be lawyers and I should forget about being a judge." Mary paused and shook her head. "I believe his direct quote was *only dyke's would want to become judges.*"

The Marshal listened, frowned, unsure of what to say.

"Nice father, huh? Not only a cheater but also a bigot."

He didn't say anything in response.

Mary continued. "I packed up what I could, left the house, and never went back home. Not ever. My parents didn't attend my college graduation, and never acknowledged anything I did in my career. I busted my ass and earned everything in life I received. There was no way I would take a handout from anyone or ..." She stopped, looked back from the ceiling where her eyes were affixed, and stared at the marshal. "I'm sorry for rambling. I guess I'm just at a loss."

"No apologies necessary. You're going through a traumatic event. Everyone responds to loss in different ways. No judgment on my end."

"Next steps? What about Chuck's body?"

"Two deputy marshals are already in Asheville. They will speak with the coroner and interview the hotel staff. Initial findings are that he died of natural causes. Like I said, it's believed he had a heart attack. Once the investigation concludes, they'll accompany the body back home."

"And the girl?"

"Not found yet. The Grove Park Inn has several security camera images of her, but no clue who she is. We could run the pictures through our federal database."

Mary shook her head. "Don't bother. He's hired so many whores over the years. She'll be high-end, hopefully discreet, and will keep her mouth shut. Working girls turn tricks to make money, not get drawn into national news like Stormy whatever her name."

"We can find her if you want, Mary."

"No. I don't want this to get out, Marshal. The fact that he propositioned hookers will not just sully my name, but the court's reputation as well. I want the Supreme Court's honor to remain at the forefront."

"We'll do our best to keep it quiet, Mary."

A horrible thought struck her. Something she couldn't shake.

The Marshal saw the visible change in her body language.

Before he could say anything, she responded. "I need to be alone."

"There's more for us to go over," the Marshal said.

"Later. Give me some alone time."

"Of course, Mary. As you wish."

The Marshal left, making sure to close the door after he exited her chamber.

Mary rose and went to the safe built into the wall, hidden behind a scenic picture of the Golden Gate Bridge. She spun the dial on the safe to the right, stopping at seven, then to the left until she settled on the number eleven, finally, once to the right, coming to rest on fifteen. The safe opened, and she removed the black folder from the middle shelf.

She brought the file to her desk and slowly opened it, flipping through the pages and pictures.

"I wonder ..." she muttered out loud, but in a slow, drawn-out tone.

Chapter Three

Hendersonville, North Carolina

Merci popped up in bed like a jack-in-the-box released from its restrictions. Beads of sweat rolled down her brow toward her delicate jawline. Perspiration covered her exposed, heaving chest as the sheet slid down to her waist.

She frantically looked around the tastefully decorated room. Her eyes darted from the white radiator under the window to the lavender-colored chair across from the canopy bed. To her right side lay Marcus, who slept soundly. Her sudden movements hadn't woken him.

Good. I must not have screamed out.

For a moment, she didn't know where she was as the fog of night muddied her memory. She leaned over and clicked on the brass lamp on the nightstand beside her. A place card on the table said, *The Henderson*. It all came back to her like a wave crashing against jagged volcanic rocks. Recollections of The Grove Park Inn, and Chuck Brown's thrashing about on the bed.

Merci slid out of the bed, used the bathroom, and paced about the room for almost thirty minutes. The only sound besides Marcus's gentle snore was an occasional creak of the hardwood floor as she moved around the perimeter of the suite. Finally, she decided to lie back down, but the peace she desired didn't come. Instead, her mind slipped back to the reason she woke in the first place.

As Merci's eyes closed, she saw only blood as the darkness morphed into light. She floated above the scene as if she were in a trance. In the center of the room, a crimson colored liquid flowed across the floor in a thick stream. It was a collection of her father's blood, both sisters, as well as the blood of the man responsible for all of their deaths. The man with the hollowed-out blackened eyes, the one who took everything from her. Merci's gaze locked onto the deceased person slumped in the room's corner, who bore the responsibility for the path she found herself on.

From above, Merci saw herself standing in front of the man who took everything, including her innocence. Her hand still gripped the hilt of the blade. The man's blood dripped from the tip of the steel and mixed with her family's spilled blood. Even at thirteen, she recognized the face of evil as her nostrils flared and her cheeks puffed. She spat on his face. Although her side hurt from the attack, she kicked his corpse until her foot ached and one of her toes fractured.

She wanted to bury her family. But not the piece of shit who took them from her. No, not him. Instead, she dragged his body by the ankles through the stream of blood and out to the middle of the dirt street. The hollow sound of his head thumped on each of the twenty-three steps as she pulled him through her family compound.

A rage overtook her. She searched the house and found what she wanted. With the accelerant spread throughout the complex, she stood near the front gate and lit the match. As she tossed it, she saw her past dissolve in flames and thick blackened smoke.

The blaze in Sierra Leone along the coast outside Freetown on Peninsular Road was visible for miles.

Merci left her attacker's battered body in the middle of the street and hoped the wild dogs would find it and tear it to shreds before the authorities arrived on the scene.

With her house engulfed in fire, she swiftly walked in the opposite direction.

Merci never looked back.

And like that, Merci de Atta found herself reborn.

Merci's eyes remained closed as she lay in bed, but sleep didn't greet her. Only her distant past played like a looped track within her mind for what seemed like several hours. After Marcus awoke, they showered and went for brunch. The front desk attendant called out to her as she breezed by.

"Here's that newspaper you asked for, Mrs. Twining," the lanky woman said as she handed Merci the local Asheville paper.

Merci smiled and thanked the woman. The name Twining was an alias. She varied them in most hotels, but for her visit to Hendersonville, she settled on the last name of one of her favorite authors, Lori Twining, from Owen Sound, Ontario, Canada.

Back in the room with a full belly, she looked over the paper. Nothing showed up about Chuck Brown's death. The internet was noticeably silent as well. The Supreme Court, or more likely the U.S. Marshals Service, kept things quiet, at least for now.

Good.

After they changed, she and Marcus headed a block over to explore downtown Hendersonville.

After they left, Marcus complained about the chill in the air. Since he forgot his beanie back home, he insisted on a replacement. On Fourth Ave, as they passed Sir Tom's Cigar and Tobacco Emporium, Merci pointed at the air conditioning unit above the store's sign, which teetered precariously, looking like it could fall out of the window at any moment.

They took a left and walked a block to the Mast General Store on Main Street. Merci continued to give him a hard time about his tendencies to be borderline OCD about his clothes.

"Whatever will you do if they don't have a Patagonia beanie?" Merci asked as she poked his side with her extended fingers.

Marcus didn't flinch. "You'll kill them all, babe."

She shook her head. "Pffft, you're the one who has to have the damn beanie. You can't afford my assassination services."

The store had quite a selection of goodies, and they shopped for over forty-five minutes. Luckily, Marcus found his gray beanie upstairs in the outdoor section. While he paid, Merci stood near the rail, looking down into the narrow space below. Most people scurried about the store, as most shoppers do, but one person caught her eye. The man had blond hair, and his movements struck her as someone who tried a little too hard to not draw attention to himself. He left the store before she and Marcus departed the second floor and made their way to the main level, but his occasional glances upstairs before he left unnerved her.

Merci shook it off and decided against bringing it up to Marcus.

All the shopping made her hungry, so they walked a block up the road to Umi, a Japanese restaurant she had read rave reviews about on Yelp and other online foodie sites. "They say this is the best sushi in western North Carolina," Merci said as they approached the wooden front door.

"Sure," he replied. "Everyone thinks their sushi spot is the best. My money is on Shimbashi Izakaya in Del Mar."

"Yeah, whatever," Merci said as they stepped inside.

An hour later, they exited Umi. "For my money, that was the best I've had in a long time," Merci said. "That spicy yellowtail roll was fabulous."

"Surprisingly, you won't get any argument from me. That was top-notch stuff. Not what you expect in some mountain town in Apply County, USA."

"Oh, Mr. Shimbashi Izakaya is the best, isn't gonna bash Umi now?"

"Nope, I'd like to get lucky later. You win."

"Coward." Merci rolled her eyes and smacked Marcus's ass hard enough to elicit a wince.

After they left Umi, Marcus pointed to the Casablanca Cigar Bar as they approached Fourth Ave. "We may need to come by here later for a nightcap and smoke, babe."

Merci rolled her eyes. "You and your Drew Estate habit."

He shrugged and said, "Who me?"

As they made their way hand in hand down Main Street, Merci saw a bakery close to Third Ave. "Oooh, sweets. I need a treat," she said as they approached the entrance.

"Girl, we just ate sushi. What gives?"

"I could use a little sugar to offset the salt. Plus, sweets kick my libido into a higher gear. So, there's that ..."

The words were hardly out of her mouth before Marcus grabbed her arm and pulled her into the McFarlan Bakery. "By all means, let's get you some sweet stuff," Marcus said as he led her further into the store. The etching on the glass near the door proclaimed it was a made-from-scratch bakery that opened in 1930.

As they stood in front of the glass display cases filled with pastries and goods, the overpowering smells of the old-fashioned bakery enveloped their senses. Row after row of tasty desserts beckoned as their eyes jumped from one item to another.

Marcus nudged her as they walked to the end of the large glass case. The petite worker behind the counter asked what he wanted. He pointed at one of the donuts on the lower shelf. "Well, that sounds good. I'll take an orange twist."

The girl nodded and grabbed one from the rack of donuts. They picked out several more decadent treats, and carried them out in a white box wrapped in twine as they exited the bakery.

Once outside, Merci's eyes narrowed as she glanced down Main Street, seeing the same blond-haired man a half a block down the sidewalk. He looked like he was staring at a glass storefront, but Merci knew better. She headed toward the man as two police officers caught her attention. They approached from the direction of the blond-haired man. Merci pivoted and turned the other way. A minute later, the officers passed her without incident, but when Merci looked back down the sidewalk, the blond-haired man had disappeared.

Marcus suggested a hike to work off the meals, and they spent the afternoon just down the road in Flat Rock at the Carl Sandburg Home National Historic Site. Merci adored poetry but wasn't familiar with Sandburg. She bought a collection of his poems at the gift shop and looked forward to reading about the "Poet of the People" when she returned to their hotel. The two hours on the walking trails, to the top of Glassy Mountain, and especially spending time with the famous goats on the property, helped Merci unwind.

Later, while back at the hotel, Marcus said he wanted to grab a beer. "There's a brewery within walking distance called Dry Falls, babe."

"A beer joint? Really?"

Marcus got close and gave her a quick peck on the cheek. "What? You like beer. I like beer. Let's go toss back a few beers."

"You win. Let's go grab a few cold ones," she said.

Chapter Four

— • —

Washington, D.C.

Eisenhower Executive Office Building

Nick Jordan, who currently holds the role of The Body Man, walked around the oval shaped room and periodically paused at one of the large whiteboards encircling the space. Each time he stopped, he would focus on the lists of names, classified intel papers taped to the board, and various photos sprinkled around the room. His mind would try to connect the dots to form a complete picture, but with far too many outstanding variables still unknown, the big picture proved elusive.

On a whiteboard by itself, behind the plain desk, a piece of yellow satin the size of a sheet of paper was affixed. Written in dried crimson colored blood at the top of the satin were four words centered and in bold:

KEEPER OF THE SECRETS

Under the cryptic words, a list of twelve last names was included, and those names gave Nick constant stress and internal turmoil. The names kept him up each night and kept the fire burning to crack the code and figure out how to prevent an untold calamity from occurring.

Nick's regular office was in the West Wing of the White House, only one door down from the most important office on planet Earth, the Oval Office. Nick's job was, in some ways, simple on paper, yet in practical application, one of the most complex and convoluted roles within the United States government.

As The Body Man, Nick's responsibilities focused on protecting the Office of the Presidency from internal and external threats. Unlike the Secret Service, which is tasked with physically protecting the current and former presidents, the role of The Body Man safeguards the office. Not the physical space, but the reputation of the role known worldwide as the President of the United States. The threats to the office often come from external forces, but sometimes the current inhabitant of the role does something so egregious that it threatens the position they swore to uphold.

When or if the reputation is threatened, it is the job of The Body Man to step in and either make the problem go away, prevent it from damaging the office, or clean up the mess if it has already occurred. There's no blueprint or instructional manual on how to perform the job, and since the president cannot be watched by one person twenty-four hours a day, it's a two-person operation. There's always one Body Man and an apprentice who will one day take over and continue the role. At that time, a new apprentice is chosen, and the cycle continues.

The current president, whom the Secret Service refers to as *Preacher* for his code name, proved to be one of the easier presidents The Body Man has dealt with. This is especially true after the previous president, code-named *Mogul*, became one of the more difficult ones in modern times. The threats to the office under *Preacher* came from outside sources.

⸻◆⸻

Nick paced the room as he had many times in the past several weeks.

Next door to the White House, the Eisenhower Executive Building was originally built for the War and Navy Department, but in 1949, it became the executive offices of the Office of the President.

Few knew that, because of major renovations in and under the west wing of the White House, while POTUS #43 was in the office, craftsmen created a full-scale replica of the Oval Office within room 11-7 of the Eisenhower Executive Building.

The replica's furnishings were gone, but the room remained oval, and the presidential seal still adorned the tray ceiling.

Nick looked up at the eagle with a scroll in its beak, an olive branch in one claw, while the other held thirteen arrows. He took his vow to protect the office more seriously than many take their marriage vows, and he would do anything, including giving up his own life, to protect the reputation of the office the seal represented.

His cell phone on top of the cherry-colored desk buzzed and shimmied around the desktop, which brought his thoughts back to the present.

With three long strides, Nick approached the desk, reached down, and answered the call.

"Jordan," he answered in a gruff tone.

"Stop pacing around that damn office, Nick. It's not going to reveal hidden truths."

The caller could not see it, but Nick rolled his eyes. "You call just to bust my balls, Furey? Or do you have meaningful intel to pass along?"

Luke Furey made a *tsk-tsk-tsk* sound. "Testy today, aren't we?"

"Not in the mood for it, dude. What do you have for me?" Nick asked.

"You said to reach out when I landed in Jakarta. So, I'm doing as I was told."

"Any leads?"

"Man, I literally just landed. But thanks for the use of the Bombardier. Last time I flew here, I was in the middle row of the economy seat on a commercial flight, stuck between an overweight woman and a priest. That's twenty-three hellish hours I never got back. I can get used to flying private around the world."

"Don't thank me, Furey. The United States taxpayers are the ones who foot the bills for the items that fall under these black budgets where we operate. If I paid, you'd be in the cargo hold locked in a crate with a pit bull."

"That sounds about right," Luke said.

"You have leads to run down?"

"I do. Spent the flight time going over everything we've been provided. The last monthly wire transfer ended up in a Bank Mandiri on Jl. Kebon Sirih near central Jakarta. According to the digital trail, funds were withdrawn in person at that location."

"Well, that's a start."

"He's here, Nick. And I'll find him and bring him in." Luke paused. "Alive."

Nick cleared his throat. "Good, be safe over there. And if you need anything, reach out immediately. No cowboy shit, okay? Do this by the book. We can't scare him off."

"We might have studied different books, Jordan."

"I'm sure. Check back in every eight hours, and if you need anything, call me anytime."

"Will do. You hear from Talia?"

"Not yet. She's supposed to call within the hour."

"Copy that."

Nick let out an elongated breath. "And Luke ..."

"Yeah?"

"Find him fast. I feel like time is working against us."

"I gotcha, and time is always working against all of us, Jordan."

The line went dead, and Nick looked back toward the ceiling and the presidential seal. He closed his eyes and whispered a faint prayer, hoping it would go higher than the ceiling.

CHAPTER FIVE

HENDERSONVILLE

DRY FALLS BREWING CO.

Contrary to what Merci expected, the brewery turned out to be a pleasant distraction, allowing her to unwind from what took place at the Grove Park Inn. A food truck, Heidi Ho On The Go, served good pub classics, and her flight of beers was topped-off with well-crafted brews.

As Marcus downed his second pint of Paddle Faster Pale Ale, he started talking about a new project he planned to dive into when they returned home to Washington. As he spoke, Merci glanced out the garage door-style glass windows and across the street. The metallic gray sedan in the parking lot on the other side of Kanuga Road caught her eye—not the car itself, but the person who sat behind the wheel. Merci felt her pulse quicken.

"Babe," she cut Marcus off mid-word. "I need to visit the little girl's room and freshen up."

Marcus nodded and looked up at the flat-screen television on the wall above the elongated bar as Merci walked toward the restrooms in the corner. The hallway included three doors, and Merci walked past the men's and women's bathrooms and instead opened the third door, which led outside.

Inside the gray sedan, the blond-haired man watched Merci disappear down the hall. He glanced at his watch several times while awaiting her return to the table with Marcus.

Chicks, he muttered.

Earlier that night, after he was sure Merci and Marcus had settled into their room, he made his way to the parking lot of The Henderson and installed the small hidden tracking device in the undercarriage of the Aston Martin. Unlike an AirTag or similar tracking device, the one the blond-haired man installed did not give off a constant signal. It remained dormant and could not be tracked via any device when not active. Every day at 3:33 a.m., an intentionally vague time in the middle of the night, it activated and sent out a signal via satellite to relay its location. The tracker then returned to a dormant state and would not repeat the process again for twenty-four hours. The only way for the device to be tracked was to be searching for its signal with a specialized device at precisely 3:33 a.m.

While waiting for Merci to return to her seat, he looked down at his phone several times.

⎯⎯◆⎯⎯

Without warning, the driver's side window exploded inward as chunks of glass bounced off the blond-haired man's blue button-down shirt. He had no time to react when he felt the razor-sharp knife blade pressed against his neck.

His eyes darted left as he focused on Merci. A snarled expression covered her face. Her piercing eyes looked almost red, as if on fire.

"Why the hell are you following me?"

He tried to answer, but the blade pressed further into his pale skin. Instinct kicked in, and his right hand reached for the side of the steering wheel. His fingers wrapped around the gear shift.

Merci's free hand thrust down into the man's crotch, and her fingers engulfed his balls. She squeezed with enough pressure to shoot pain through his scrotum and up into the pit of his stomach.

"Look fuckstick. If you put the car into gear, you'll lose your balls a second after I slice up your pathetic neck." The pressure on his neck increased as a bead of blood worked its way down the blade and dripped onto his Polo shirt.

The threat worked. He removed his hand from the gear shift.

"I'm not going to ask again," Merci said.

"I was hired to follow you."

"No shit, Sherlock. By whom?"

"Your employer."

"I'm an independent contractor. Try again." She pushed the blade harder, eliciting more drops of blood while at the same time squeezing the man's sac with renewed strength.

His voice rose an octave. "The people who hired you for the Grove Park Inn job are the ones who paid me to follow you."

"Why?"

He shook his head. "They didn't tell me that. They told me to watch you and not get caught."

"Well, you screwed that up, didn't you? I can assure you, the people who hired both of us don't tolerate failure."

"Look, I'm no threat to you," he pleaded as the pain riddled his body.

"Anyone who follows me is a threat."

He gulped hard. "The only thing they said was follow you, report back on your location, and don't get caught. That was the job."

"How did they hire you?"

"Internet." The pain overwhelmed his ability to think straight. "I got my job from the internet. It's how I get all my assignments."

Merci asked several more questions, but none of them proved helpful. "Last thing." She used a harsh tone.

He nodded but didn't reply.

Merci continued. "If I so much as think for a second you're following me again, the last thing you'll feel is me ripping off your underwhelming balls before I jab this blade through your temple. We clear?"

"Crystal," the blond-haired man said.

Merci let go of his balls and reached over to remove his cell phone from the center console.

"Password," she said.

He protested, but more blood droplets from the blade made him change his mind.

"It's 1-2-0-3-8-8," he said.

She punched the numbers in and the screen came alive. Next, she stuffed it in the back pocket of her skintight jeans. "Find your way back home, and don't let me ever see you again. Or else."

He watched as she collapsed the knife and put it back in her pocket as she walked away from his broken window.

Merci crossed back over Kanuga Road and took her seat next to Marcus at the brewery a minute later. The blond-haired man didn't wait for a repeat visit. As he drove away, he noticed the eyes of both Merci and Marcus glaring at him from inside the brewery.

CHAPTER SIX

MANHATTAN, NEW YORK CITY

ONE WORLD TRADE CENTER

The elevator doors opened on the seventy-sixth floor of One World Trade Center, leading to an ornate, modern-designed lobby with a Far East motif. Out of the elevator stepped a muscular man in a black Brooks Brothers suit, with a red tie, and shiny wing-tipped shoes. The tailored suit hung on his body in such a way as to accentuate his physique. He strutted through the expansive area and received more than one glance from the professionally dressed ladies who scurried around the office space.

The man walked through the lobby to an attractive woman seated behind an all-glass desk. Thanks to her ethnicity—born to a Filipino mother and Greek father—she had an exotic look about her. The young woman was certainly beautiful but not the sharpest bulb in the box. An older woman did the real administrative work from a small office, kept out of sight behind the beautiful woman.

The eye candy smiled as the man approached. "Mr. Joshua," she said in a sultry voice. "I'm so very happy to have you back."

"Miss Topintzis." He stopped in front of her. "Always a pleasure." He tapped his index finger on the smooth surface of her desk. "How have you been?"

"Lonely," she replied.

"Well, that's a shame."

She blushed as he stared at her with a gaze that pierced deep. "He's expecting you." She leaned down closer to the desktop, her ample cleavage pushing toward the top of her V-neck blouse. "Any chance you have some free time later?"

He nodded. "Ooh. I think I'll have a few hours available." Turning away, he walked from her desk, exiting the lobby, he took a left.

Mr. Joshua pushed the heavy wooden door inward. The strut in his step was more defined as he walked inside.

<hr>

With ash flooring, dim overhead lighting, and wood panels on the walls, the office felt more like it belonged in Big Sky country than lower Manhattan, especially considering the lobby's modern style. A large stuffed bison head adorned one wall, while the other wall across from it contained a floor-to-ceiling mural of the Rough Riders with Roosevelt leading the charge. A third wall had more of an oriental flair, which matched the lobby but not the office.

The man behind the desk grunted and pointed to the chair in front of his executive-style desk.

Mr. Joshua sat down and stared at the obese man. Their appearances could not have been more opposite. While Mr. Joshua prided himself on being physically fit and eating clean, the man across from him looked like he might be one Big Mac away from being flayed open on the operating room table while an emergency quadruple bypass took place to save his life.

There were no formalities or pleasantries. "Updates from North Carolina?" The obese man asked in a perturbed tone.

Mr. Joshua cleared his throat. "Two Deputy Marshals are onsite. They've spoken with the coroner of Buncombe County and the hotel staff."

"And?"

"My sources assure me the cause of death will be ruled a heart attack. And the Grove Park Inn staff have little to report besides seeing Mr. Brown arrive with a woman of ill repute and leaving hours later in a body bag."

"They have any images of her entering or exiting the hotel?"

"Yes, but they have no way of knowing who the supposed prostitute may be. Anyway, the U.S. Marshals have quietly told those involved to keep a wrap on what occurred."

The obese man grunted his approval. "Good. Anything else?"

"We may have a complication with Merci."

"How so?"

"We had her tailed as requested by the client."

"And?" The obese man appeared agitated. He picked up a gold colored pen and started to spin it around on the smooth surface of his desk.

"She discovered she was being followed while in Hendersonville. It's a quaint town about thirty minutes south of Asheville."

"Shit." The obese man turned in his chair away from Mr. Joshua. Without turning back, he asked, "What happened?"

"Merci confronted our man."

"Is he dead?"

"No, but she scared the piss out of him. Literally grabbed him by the balls, put a knife against his throat, and threatened him. Of course, after the experience, he's afraid to come in. Plus, she took his phone after having him unlock it."

He turned back around in the chair. "Is there anything on there that can trace back to us?"

"No. He was hired in a similar fashion to Merci. He knew why he was there, but almost nothing else. Said he told her they had the same employer for the job, but that's it."

"And you trust him?"

Mr. Joshua's eyes narrowed. "What do you think?"

The obese man grew quiet. He moved his neck from side to side, eliciting a large popping sound. "This could be problematic."

"What would you like me to do?" Mr. Joshua asked.

"Eliminate him. We can't have any loose ends on this contract. He's a nobody and won't be missed. However, he could place Merci at the scene. Do it yourself."

Mr. Joshua nodded. "Of course, and with pleasure."

"Do we need to be concerned about Merci?"

Mr. Joshua shrugged. "She was paid to do a job, and she did it. Sure, she might be pissed she was followed, but she'll get over it. Besides, we have another target for her. The amount goes up with this one. She'll play ball. Always does."

"And if not?"

Mr. Joshua frowned. "She will."

"But if she doesn't?"

"We have others who will take the contract."

The obese man turned his chair to face the Roosevelt painting. He rubbed his chin, seemingly lost in thought. "When will you approach Justice Brown again?"

"In a few days, I'll wait until after the funeral."

"And the case?"

"It won't be heard for at least three weeks, maybe four."

The obese man removed a leather planner from his top drawer and flipped it open, using his finger to go down the page. "We're running low on time."

"I disagree. Plus, she'll see things our way."

The obese man turned his chair back to Mr. Joshua. His gaze lowered to the planner and then slowly focused back on him. "I don't need to remind you how powerful our clients are, do I?"

"Of course not."

He pointed his fat, sausage shaped finger at Mr. Joshua. "They have a vested interest in the case before the Supreme Court. And they trust we will deliver on what they are paying us to orchestrate."

"We have all the leverage we need."

"If we don't succeed, it will reflect poorly on my firm. There will be consequences for any failure, and those consequences flow downhill. The same direction shit flows."

Mr. Joshua didn't flinch. Veiled threats, or even direct ones, didn't faze him. He nodded. "Trust me, I know what I'm doing."

The obese man struggled to get to his feet and then waddled around, leaning against the front of the desk. His girth made it difficult to squeeze between the piece of furniture and Mr. Joshua. The large bulge between his groin and navel revolted the younger, fit man.

"Where do we stand on the missing file?" The obese man wheezed slightly after walking around the desk.

"I've narrowed it down to less than twenty people who had access to the conference room where the file disappeared," Mr. Joshua said.

"That doesn't give me the warm and fuzzies."

"We will find the person who took the file."

The obese man tapped his pudgy finger on the desktop. "Our client does not know the document is missing."

Mr. Joshua nodded. "Yes, I'm aware of that fact."

"And it needs to stay that way."

"Understood."

"Losing the case will damage my client and prove very costly. However, if the content of that file sees the light of day, we're talking a doomsday scenario. Their business and others in the industry will be decimated. The public trust will be lost, and it's game over for all the major players."

"I'm aware of what is at stake." He paused and looked directly at the obese man. "I'm not the one who left the file in an unsecured conference room."

The pigmentation on the obese man's face turned beet red. "Excuse me?" Spittle formed on the corner of his mouth.

Mr. Joshua did not back down. "You heard me. I didn't misplace the file. You pay me to make problems go away and fix mistakes. Well, losing that file was not my mistake. It was yours."

A strange look overcame the obese man. He took several elongated breaths and slowly nodded. "You're right. I screwed up. Now you have to clean up my mess. Yet, here you sit, and the file is still missing. Accusations won't find the file. Now will it?"

Arguing would be pointless, so he took his cue and stood. As he walked toward the door, he spun back on his heel. "Like I said, I'm on it. We will recover the file."

"Don't fail me, Mr. Joshua, or we both might end up at the bottom of the East River."

A sinister smirk formed at the corner of Mr. Joshua's lips. "I can swim, boss. Can you?"

With his pudgy finger pointed at Mr. Joshua. "It doesn't matter if you can swim if they grind you into chum before they toss you into the river." The obese man let the words sink in. "I know you're a tough man, Mr. Joshua, but our client has much to lose if we fail."

Mr. Joshua nodded, but didn't reply to the overt threat. "Is there anything else?"

The obese man pointed to the Rolex on his wrist. "Tick-tock, Mr. Joshua, tick-tock."

Chapter Seven

— · —

Georgetown, Washington, D.C.

Mary Brown used her curled toes to pull the smooth brass lever toward her. Hot water flowed from the spout as it warmed up the oversized garden tub. She rarely used the custom-made bath, even though she insisted on installing it when she and Chuck bought and gutted the townhouse six years previously. But today, after everything that occurred, she needed to decompress, and a bubble bath allowed her to focus without distractions.

She spent most of her morning consumed by the funeral arrangements. Her two grown kids lived nearby in Northern Virginia, and she included them in the planning.

Chuck had been dead for less than thirty-six hours, which she found hard to get her head around. It still felt surreal.

Sure, at one point, becoming a widow seemed likely. After all, because of Chuck's weight and various health issues, including diabetes and high blood pressure, they all knew his ticker was a walking time bomb. Based on the initial coroner's report, it appeared his heart finally went out while with another one of his whores. Mary ground her teeth as she thought about the embarrassment it would cause if his last moments on earth ever made it into the media.

Chuck visited Asheville frequently and stayed at the Grove Park Inn most of the time while in town. The golf course was one of his favorites, and Chuck swore he had more than one run-in over the years with The Pink Lady, a resident and much-adored phantom said to roam the halls of the storied hotel.

Part of her thought she should feel a release now that he was finally gone. But in fact, the opposite occurred. Now more than ever, she wondered if the truth about their relationship would ever come out.

Reporters in the news vans maintained a constant vigil outside her townhouse on Dumbarton Street. It came with the territory. Not only was she a Supreme Court justice, but as a woman, the press seemed to hound her more than her male counterparts. The #MeToo movement might have given women a voice, but the old guard in the media still seemed to take pleasure in knocking women down a peg from time to time compared to their male counterparts.

After an hour in the tub and with some much-needed time to think, she drained the water and climbed out. Mary showered before getting dressed and going downstairs. Her two kids, their spouses, and the combined six grandkids occupied most of the first floor and basement. They were adamant to stay with her once they learned their father had died. It felt good to have the voices in the house, especially those of her grandchildren. She worked long hours, and Chuck frequently traveled. Most of the time she spent at home, nobody was there, so having her family present helped immensely.

Two uniformed Supreme Court officers stood by the front door, almost like sentries watching one of their justices. Two sedans parked alongside Dumbarton contained four U.S. Marshals. Even though Chuck's death was ruled a natural death by the coroner in Buncombe County, the Marshal of the Supreme Court insisted she have a round-the-clock increased security presence, more than the typical two U.S. Marshals who guarded her.

As she entered her open, brightly lit kitchen, she found her son and his wife cooking dinner.

Her son hugged her. "Did the soak do you any good, Mom?"

Mary smiled and gave him a motherly kiss on the cheek. "Yes, dear, it was very calming."

Just then, one of her granddaughters bounded into the room, almost like Tigger, excited to see Winnie the Pooh. "Me-Maw, the mailman came while you were upstairs. Can I go check your mail?"

Mary smiled. "Of course, my love. Come right back inside after you get it."

Her son said, "She's been wanting to ask you for an hour. I was starting to pull my hair out."

"Watch out or you'll be prematurely bald," Mary said with a crooked smile.

Her son rolled his eyes, and Mary followed her youngest granddaughter as she ran out the front steps, past the two officers.

The little blond angel jumped two steps at a time down the staircase leading to the sidewalk and skipped all the way to the mailbox at the end of the walkway.

A minute later, she was back and handed her Me-Maw a thick stack of mail.

Mary rubbed her thick, matted blond hair and thanked her for checking the mail.

As the commotion inside started up again, she sat in the front living room and flipped through the two-inch-thick stack of letters, fliers, and bills. About a third of the way through the stack, she paused. A handwritten envelope was tucked between a cable and a phone bill. Without a stamp or return address, someone must have placed it in the mailbox without sending it via the post office.

How could anyone do that with the constant presence of uniformed officers in front of the house? Mary wondered.

She tore open the envelope, half expecting a white substance to spill out. Her mind went back to the ricin attack a few years ago. Instead of finding a white powder, she pulled a folded cream-colored card. Her heart raced as she flipped it open.

Inside, it said: *We need to talk. I'll be in touch.*

A lump formed in her throat. It didn't need a signature. She knew who it was from as she recognized the penmanship from the previous letter she received.

It was him.

Mr. Joshua.

CHAPTER EIGHT

WASHINGTON, D.C.

Marcus entered the bedroom with a glass of Chardonnay and a bowl of plump strawberries. Merci lay on the bedspread close to the footboard of his king-sized sleigh bed. With her eyes closed, she appeared asleep as her arm rested at a slight angle, her hand close to her face. She wore hot pink mesh running shorts and a matching top that exposed much of her navel.

He slowed his approach and sat on the edge of the thick wooden bedframe, laying the glass of wine and bowl of strawberries on the nightstand beside the bed.

With her shirt scrunched up close to the bottom of her breasts, her ribcage was exposed as she lay on her right side.

Marcus ran his index and middle finger along her left side. Starting near her hips, his fingers slowly followed the contour of her figure along her ribs. Her light, bronzed skin reacted with goosebumps to his gentle touch. He stopped as he caressed the spot where she had the black widow tattoo. Oversized, the spider image roughly looked to be the size of a plum. His fingers rubbed against the center of the tattoo, and the raised skin colored red in the shape of an hourglass. The distinct marking was placed in that exact spot to hide the scar from a knife wound she received years prior.

Merci never wanted to forget the moment. A constant reminder of the second she went from an innocent girl in Sierra Leone to a woman with a burden most would find unbearable. The events that day altered her in ways few could fathom. For most victims of physical violence at a young age, it crushes them, but that was not the case for Merci de Atta. What she endured that day transformed her and made her into many things, including the persona of a black widow.

Her arm snapped down, as her hand caught his wrist, startling him. Using all her body weight, she tugged hard and spun toward the bed's footboard, pulling Marcus with her. She came to a stop with him on top of her.

Merci planted a tender kiss on his lips. "Were you trying to wake me?" she asked in a playful tone.

He shook his head. "I'm no fool. Never wake a sleeping lioness."

Merci smiled, then shoved him off. "Smart man."

"Sometimes," he replied. "Power nap help?" he asked.

"Not really, you know, sleep and I don't see eye to eye."

Marcus nodded.

She touched the raised red portion of her tattoo. "Are you in the habit of feeling up girls when they sleep?"

Marcus let out a guttural laugh. "I wouldn't describe touching your side as feeling you up. I mean, I can show you what feeling up really is if you'd like." He leaned in close as he said the last few words, placing his strong hands on her exposed hips.

"Meat hooks off." She pushed him away, totally screwing with him.

He fell backward, landing on the plush mattress.

Merci rolled over, coming to rest against his side.

"So what do you want to do the rest of the day?" he asked.

"I need to look for work."

He recoiled slightly. "Work? You said you would lay low for a while after the Chuck Brown contract."

Merci pursed her lips. "Yeah, I know, but for some reason, I feel restless. Maybe what I need to do is jump back into the saddle."

"Or maybe you should lay low like you said you would." He inched back closer to her. "Maybe take a trip?"

"Are you telling me what to do?"

Marcus shook his head. "Don't start that nonsense with me. You know I don't tell you jack shit. Never have, never will. I knew from the moment we met you were a free spirit. And what was it I told you?"

She let out a bit of air in a slow breath. "That you'd never hold me back. I was free to make my own choices. Come and go as I please. Blah, blah, blah … you look smokin' hot!"

"And all of that still stands true." He touched her jawbone, and his thumb slowly caressed her cheek. "I knew who you were when we met, and I accepted you then as I do now."

A tear trickled down her cheek. A rare sign of emotion from someone who hid her true feelings from almost everybody. But not from Marcus. "You saved me that night in Paris. If it wasn't for you." She grew quiet for several seconds. "I would have been dead in a ditch a long time ago."

Marcus shook his head. "No, you're alive because what's in here." He removed his hand from her cheek and pointed his index finger against her temple. "And also here." His hand left her head and he placed his finger on a spot between her breasts.

"You'll always be my savior." She slid on top of him and slowly, patiently kissed him.

Marcus ran his hands along her ribcage and moved his long fingers toward her lower back, not stopping as he reached her running shorts, which he slipped off in one quick motion.

CHAPTER NINE

MANHATTAN

BRYANT PARK

The blond-haired man walked down W. 40th Street toward Fifth Ave, his heart pounding like a blacksmith working over a piece of steel.

Why did I come? He asked himself in a whisper.

A nagging feeling of doubt grew stronger with each step as he moved past a sea of humanity oblivious to the inner struggle raging within. He stopped near a hot dog cart parked along the street and paused. The guy running the cart gave him a passing glance and sneer before a customer diverted the vendor's gaze.

With his car parked only two blocks away, turning around and leaving was still an option. Sure, they owed him money, but his life wasn't worth the money coming his way.

He ignored the doubts and ran across the street in front of a yellow cab that lay on the horn.

As instructed, he took a seat in a green chair next to a round table. Twenty feet away, children's laughter from the Le Carrousel filled the plaza.

The man with the blond hair didn't have to wait long as a sharp-dressed man took the seat across from him.

"Mr. Joshua?" the blond-haired man asked with a startled inflection.

The man nodded. "Thanks for coming, I realize you had some trepidations about meeting me in person."

"I did, especially since I screwed up."

Mr. Joshua shrugged. "Nonsense. It's water under the bridge. Merci is one of the best assassins in the world. It's not surprising she made you."

"But I was told not to get caught."

Mr. Joshua tossed his head back. "Ahh, don't worry about it. Let's go over everything that occurred one more time now that we are face-to-face. Then I can get you your money, and you can be on your way."

The blond-haired man felt the dread subside as he discussed the events in Asheville and Hendersonville. He spoke for several more minutes before Mr. Joshua thanked him and pulled out his cell phone from his pants pocket. Thirty seconds later, he said, "Check your account. The money should be there."

His eyes bulged slightly as he stared at his checking account balance. "That's more than we agreed to."

"Consider it a down payment on the next time I need your services."

He gulped. "Jeez, I thought you would be mad."

"Nope. In fact, I have something else for you to do here in the city."

"Really?"

"Yes, let's discuss it as we return to your car."

The two men walked down 40th toward Sixth Ave past the Bryant Park Hotel.

Mr. Joshua stood to his right, the blond-haired man less than an arm's length from the storefronts. They walked by an electrician's van with its hazard lights on.

Just past the van, Mr. Joshua pointed to an empty space with brown paper covering the floor-to-ceiling windows, concealing the inside of the former store. "This used to be a great mom-and-pop deli. Too bad the damn pandemic killed the business."

The blond-haired man looked to his left just as the door to the abandoned space opened. Mr. Joshua stiff-armed him, and the force of the strike thrust him into the darkened void. He stumbled to the ground, and as he rose, the sound of the door closing made a loud thud. Two men stood in front of him as he got to his feet.

"What the ..."

He never got the next words out as the blade dug into his spinal cord, severing the nerve at the C7 vertebra. Instantly, darkness overtook him as his legs gave out, and he crumpled to the floor.

The two men looked at Mr. Joshua. Both men displayed a look of respect at his precise strike.

"Load him up." Mr. Joshua removed the blade from the back of the blond-haired man's neck. With a back-and-forth motion, he wiped the blood on the man's shirt.

As instructed, the men hauled the lifeless body into a fifty-gallon drum a few feet from the door and sealed the lid. It took less than three minutes from the moment Mr. Joshua shoved him into the empty space until his body vanished inside the cylinder-shaped container.

Mr. Joshua handed each man a thick white envelope. "Good job. Of course, make sure this container is never found."

One man nodded. "Already have a spot picked out for this little prick's ultimate resting place."

"Yeah, right next to ole James Riddle Hoffa." The other man muttered in a thick New York accent.

The two men left first, loading the container on a hand truck as they wheeled it out the front door. They took a hard right and rolled it into the electrician van, which was idling in front of the storefront.

A few minutes later, Mr. Joshua stepped out, closed the door behind him, and turned left. Before he reached Sixth Ave, he placed a call.

"Yes," he said to the person on the other end. "I'd like to pull back a wire transfer my assistant just placed in error."

Chapter Ten

The White House

Oval Office

Nick approached the open northeast door that led into the most famous office in modern history, the Oval Office. As he stood in the doorway, he glanced to his left and caught the gaze of the president's administrative assistant, Patricia May.

His look conveyed a simple question. *Is this good or bad?*

Patricia shrugged as she looked at the open door.

He mouthed the words, *Thanks for nothing.*

She replied with a wink and a smile.

With a large stride, he stepped into the historic office and approached the Resolute Desk where the President of the United States sat, a stack of papers in front of him, his readers balanced precariously on the end of his nose.

Nick cleared his throat. "You wanted to see me, sir?"

The only sound was the door closing behind him. Patricia gave the president and his guest privacy.

President Thomas Collins peered up from the paper he held in his hand. "Ah, yes, Nicholas. Take a seat." He gestured to the rosewood chair beside the desk.

Nick pursed his lips. "Why do I get the feeling I'm in trouble?"

With an audible chuckle, the president replied, "Nonsense. Besides, since you don't work for me, you can't really get into any trouble. Now can you?"

"Everyone can always be in trouble, sir. You don't have to be my boss to find fault with something I've done or failed to do."

"It's not that, Nick."

Nick unbuttoned his suit jacket as he sat. "What do you need, sir?"

The president took off his readers and placed them on the desktop. "You saw my schedule for today?"

Nick smiled. "Mr. President, I saw your schedule hours before you were even up. It comes with the job description, I'm afraid."

"No doubt. So, you are aware I will not be attending the funeral for Chuck Brown?"

"Mr. President, I would be quite surprised if you attended Mr. Brown's funeral."

"Well, I did appoint his wife as a justice for the Supreme Court."

"That is correct, sir. But according to the reports I've read he was with a prostitute in Asheville at the time of his untimely death. That's not a great visual for the Commander-In-Chief with the Secret Service code name, Preacher, to be seen at the man's funeral."

"The press doesn't know he was with a woman of ill repute when he had the heart attack."

"They will, sir. Somebody will leak it to the media at some point. And if you're at the funeral, you will get blowback because of your attendance."

"You're saying in your role as The Body Man, you would advise me not to attend Chuck's funeral."

"No, sir. In my role as The Body Man, I have no opinion on whether you attend his funeral or not. But as a citizen who greatly respects the office you hold, I think it would be best if you skipped this one."

"I see."

"It's my understanding you and Chuck were not even acquaintances, sir. I believe you only met him once when you hosted Mary Brown at the Oval Office before she was sworn in to the court. Isn't that correct?"

"Yes."

Nick's gaze narrowed. "Then why would you feel the obligation to attend his funeral?"

The president cleared his throat. "Like I mentioned, I appointed her to the Supreme Court. And as I had breakfast this morning, I wondered if Mary might be offended if I did not attend the funeral. Or maybe even slightly pissed at what could be construed as a snub."

"I think if Justice Brown is pissed at anyone, it would be at her cheating husband for not only the adultery, but also the microscope his behavior might put her and the Supreme Court under."

President Collins nodded. "Valid point."

"Stick to the schedule today, Mr. President. If you feel terrible about it, send the vice president in your place. After all, that's one of the VP's job duties, right?"

The president nodded. "That and waiting for me to croak or get impeached."

Nick let out an elongated breath. "Politics is a funny business model, sir."

"Be glad you never entered it, Nicholas."

"Grateful for that every day of my life, sir." Nick Jordan stood and looked down at the president. "Anything else you need from me at the moment?"

With a shake of the head, the president replied, "No."

Nick moved toward the closed door he had entered a few minutes earlier.

"Oh, Nick. One more thing."

Nick pivoted and turned back. "Yes, Mr. President?"

"Any word from either Luke or Talia?"

"No updates yet, sir. They are both overseas, tracking down leads. As soon as I have more to report, I'll be sure to give you the pertinent details."

"As I'm sure you will. You and the rest of the team are doing a great job as usual."

"Not sure about that, Mr. President. We are way behind the eight ball at the moment and still not close to figuring out why this is happening."

"Have faith, Nicholas. Trust the team you have assembled and let the process work."

"I'm trying, sir." He turned around and opened the northeast door.

As he exited the Oval Office, he walked past Patricia and turned left. It was only a handful of steps before he reached his office door. Once inside, he opened the top right drawer of his desk and pulled out the thick folder. With the folder in hand, he headed to his workspace in the Eisenhower Executive Office Building.

Back to work, he muttered to himself as he turned right and made his way to the staircase at the end of the hallway.

Chapter Eleven

Washington, D.C.

Holy Trinity Catholic Church

Mary Brown sat in the front row of the Holy Trinity Catholic Church; the black veil shrouded her face and hid the scowl as she glared at the closed casket containing Chuck's remains. Her daughter sat on one side, while her son sat on the other. Their spouses and her grandchildren filled the remaining seats in the white painted wooden pew.

She expected the rage to subside on the day she put him in the ground, but the opposite occurred. As Father Fraser elaborated on the journey of life and the value of faith and family, Mary dwelled on the photos the man who called himself "Mr. Joshua" presented to her.

Naked pictures flipped through her memory, one after another, both Chuck and the whores appeared inter-tangled. The images burned into her subconscious revolted her. Chuck disgusted her. A part of her, a large portion, took glee knowing she had finally rid herself of him. She just had to get him six feet under to have closure.

Father Fraser asked one of Chuck's friends, Stu Rogers, to come forward for the eulogy. Mary stared at the floor and counted the minutes until the hellish ordeal would end.

Three rows from the back of the church, a sharply dressed man slipped into the pew on the far left of the sanctuary and melted into the crowd of mourners.

Merci de Atta sat in the church's last row, toward the building's right side. She wore a modest yet form-fitting Nicole Miller dress. The black dress struck her as cliché at funerals. While she did not want the outfit to draw attention, there was no way she'd show up looking like a nun, either.

She had not been to church in a while, avoiding it as often as possible. In fact, the last time was a visit to Westminster Abbey where Marcus dragged her to the first night of advent a few years prior. Oh, she believed in God, even prayed to the Almighty regularly. Yes, even a woman who makes her living killing scum of the earth can have a belief in a higher power. But churches creeped her out. It wasn't so much the church building per se as it was the organized religion. Merci felt religion had become the antithesis of what God truly stood for. She loathed religion—take that back, she resented religion. Over her lively thirty-two years, she saw much to give her pause. Having spent time in Rome, she felt certain the Catholic church was one of the wealthiest corporations in the world. Merci believed men, and of course women as well, used God as an excuse to deliver all sorts of pain upon others. It never ceased to amaze her when a mark called out to God the moment before she took their life as if God could really care less if the men she was sent to kill were saved from the wrath she delivered.

As the priest carried on up front, an uneasy feeling overtook her. She looked around, trying to find the source of the building unease. Her eyes homed in on the man in the dark pinstriped designer suit who snuck in the back. Most would have thought nothing of it, but very few were like her, and nothing about Merci was average. His gait and the way he handled himself stood out. Most men walk. This man strutted with a distinct confidence, even as he tried to blend in at the same time.

A predator senses a predator.

Something set this man apart from the others in the congregation. With her eyes forward as the funeral progressed, she watched the man out of her peripheral vision. Trying to be subtle, Merci texted Marcus. He had no desire to attend the funeral and thought her attending, since she ushered the man into the afterlife, seemed brazen at best. She told him her reason for going, but he didn't buy it.

Does the church have CCTV? she asked via text.

Marcus responded within thirty seconds. *It does, why?*

Can you hack into the feed? she asked.

Of course. Again, why? Marcus asked.

Someone just entered. He's out of place. Might be a triggerman.

Hold tight.

A minute later, he replied. *I'm in. Who am I looking for? I see you by the way. You look smoking hot.*

Merci ignored his tease. *Left side, third row from the back. Pinstripe…*

Got him. Pinstripe suit. If he's not in the business, he certainly fancies himself as a player. Uploading his image to my server.

How long till you get an ID?

I've got a backdoor to F.A.C.E. and other federal image repositories. It might take some time, though. There are literally billions of photos in the system. This one I captured is not the highest quality since it's from a low-end webcam. I'll probably have lots of false positives to sift through.

Minutes? Merci asked.

No. Hours. Maybe even a day.

Ok. Thanks.

I still think it's weird you're attending his funeral.

Just paying my final respects.

Yeah right. To the man you put in that casket.

He got what he deserved. Do you see her on the webcam?

It took Marcus a minute to adjust the screen to zoom out. *First row. I see her. Be careful.*

I'm always careful. Don't worry, I'll be back shortly.

What's for dinner?

You want me to stop on the way home?

Yes, please.

And get what?

Thai.

Of course. Merci put her phone away.

Thai, he always wants Thai. With that type of food being an aphrodisiac for him, she wasn't surprised. Although truth be told, it acted like one for her as well.

———◆———

Mr. Joshua felt someone's eyes on him. He studied the gathered crowd of mourners with small, subtle movements. Nobody stood out, but he couldn't shake the feeling that someone was watching him.

As he looked toward the casket, he saw Justice Brown. She would probably be pissed if she knew he attended her husband's funeral. But frankly, he didn't give a shit. Part of him wanted to go up at the end of the ceremony and confront her. Tell her he was the one who lined up her husband's death, and inform her it wasn't a natural death.

But he knew better.

With a heavy presence from the Supreme Court police and many U.S. Marshals on site, he wouldn't get close to her without setting off alarm bells in the eyes of law enforcement.

As the funeral ended, he followed the others, and they started the slow processional exiting the building. Mr. Joshua turned to his right, overhearing the conversation between an elderly couple who knew Chuck Brown.

When he turned back, he caught the glance of a woman in the back row. Her head turned so fast that he barely saw the side of her face and mainly caught the back of her head. Something about her felt familiar, but he couldn't place how or why. Her dress hugged her athletic frame, and he couldn't help but stare at her curves.

She hurried for the exit, and several extra rows of attendees blocked his ability to get out fast. Politely, he pushed his way through the crowd and stepped outdoors. Standing on the top of the eighth step near the large support column of the church, he looked down 36th Street in time to see the mysterious woman climb into an Uber and close the door.

He had no idea who the woman might be, but he suspected their paths would cross again.

Chapter Twelve

Eisenhower Executive Office Building

Nick felt like he was looking for a needle in a haystack. He knew the people on the list, or at least knew a lot about them. Trying to acquire their precise location was virtually impossible in several instances. Based on their training, he shouldn't be surprised.

His cell phone rang, and he perked up as he looked at the caller ID.

"Speak to me, Abby," Nick said excitedly.

"You might owe me dinner for this one," Abby said.

Abby Wright was a senior intelligence analyst with the NSA in the Special Collection Service, better known as F6. She was currently on loan to the president and worked directly with Nick on several top-secret projects. In her mid-thirties, Abby had jet black hair that she liked to wear in pigtails and a crimson colored tattoo of a winged animal on her chest. She had an uncanny resemblance to the character with the same name and likeness who used to play on the network television show NCIS. The comparison came up so often that Abby told people the writers at CBS based the character on her. It was a lie, but almost everybody fell for it when the words came out of her mouth.

"I'll pay up if it's good," Nick said. "Tell me what you found."

"You ever heard of SPBGMA?" Abby asked.

"Um, no. Is that Morse code or some cryptic TikTok video lingo?"

"No, Mr. Music Illiterate. It stands for Society for the Preservation of Bluegrass Music of America." Abby rolled her eyes, although Nick would have no way of knowing that since it wasn't a video call.

"Jeez, that's a mouthful. No wonder they call it SPBGMA. Why are you asking if I ever heard of this bluegrass thing?" Nick asked.

"Because Sean Howard apparently donates money to them regularly."

"Howie is into bluegrass? Jeez, these guys get into some weird stuff after they move on ... I had no clue."

"Well, I don't know what he thinks about the music, but at the very least, he supports the organization monetarily for one reason or another. And it's a hefty amount as well."

Nick frowned. "And this all matters, why?"

"I believe it is important because their national convention is coming up in a few weeks, and based on some of the electronic breadcrumbs I uncovered this week, there's a good chance he might come out of whatever rock he's normally under and attend the conference."

"You have my undivided attention," Nick said. "Where does it meet?"

"Sheraton Music City Hotel in Nashville, Tennessee."

Nick tapped his fingers on the desk. "Very interesting. And for the record, I happen to know a decent amount about all kinds of music, even bluegrass. I saw Billy Strings play in Asheville with friends a few years back. I don't make it to Nashville often, but I'm familiar with the area."

"The Sheraton is near the airport," Abby said.

"I might have stayed there. I've got a Marriott Bonvoy credit card and stay at their properties often on official and unofficial trips."

"Nice, well, I have a request."

"Lay it on me." Nick was unsure what type of inquiry she might have.

"I know with everything going on, the team is spread thin, so I was hoping I could go to Nashville and track Sean down if he attends. Sure, I don't have field training, but I'd like to prove myself."

"Well, if Howie actually attends, I don't see him being any kind of threat." Nick considered her proposal and rubbed his chin. "Although don't take this the wrong way, but a goth chick like you may stand out at a bluegrass type of convention."

"Is that bad?"

"I mean, I guess not."

"We need to find Sean, right?"

"We do," Nick said. "Whether Howie knows it or not, he is likely in danger."

"And I can still do my job remotely, I'll just be doing it from Nashville for a few days." Abby paused. "Pretty please?"

Nick chuckled. "Under that red lipstick, black hair, and tattoos, are you really a closet bluegrass groupie?"

"Would I tell you if I was?" Abby asked.

"Valid point. Marilyn Manson is gonna be let down, if it's true."

"Manson? You're two decades behind musically, buddy."

"But sure, you can go. Unless, of course, you track him down before the convention."

"I'm trying my best, unfortunately, like the rest of you guys, he's quite good at disappearing."

"You wanna fly commercial or private?"

"Do I get a choice?" Abby asked.

"You can use my jet. If something changes and I need it, Section Seven has a fleet at their disposal. We will get you down there one way or the other. Does the Sheraton have rooms available? I know conferences typically sell out of rooms."

"It has a few as of today."

"Okay, book a room, expense whatever you need."

"Appreciate it, Nick, thanks. I normally feel like the tech dork who never gets to leave her cubicle or conference room often."

"Traveling is surely not glamorous most of the time, but I agree, sometimes a change of scenery is helpful. Make sure to come to my office a few days before you leave, and I'll go over a few things with you."

"Will do."

Chapter Thirteen

—·—

Washington, D.C.

Marcus entered his living room and put the keys in the ceramic bowl closest to the entertainment center. The lights were out, and it seemed quiet—too quiet—not how he had left the place hours earlier.

He swiftly moved to the coffee table, bent down, and reached under the thick wood, but his hand only found an empty plastic holster.

Shit.

The distinct click of a hammer pulling back and locking in place made him stiffen. Someone had his .45 Kimber and was about to use it on him. He turned around slowly as he raised his hands.

"Bam!" Merci yelled as she let out a perverse laugh.

His mouth felt dry. "Jesus, Mary, and Joseph, you almost gave me a heart attack."

"Where the hell have you been?" She lowered the hammer and tossed him the heavy handgun.

"Radio Shack boinking my other girlfriend in the back storage room. You know, the one who doesn't draw a loaded gun on me as a joke."

"Whatever. You couldn't handle me and another woman at the same time. Besides, I think you're losing the edge in your old age. I had the drop on you."

Marcus shook his head. He looked at her skin-tight outfit, which appeared drenched. "You fell in the bathtub while I was out?"

"No smartass. It's called going for a run. Try it sometime." She walked over, kissed him on the cheek, then playfully tapped his stomach. "You could use some PT."

"Whatever, I have a six pack," Marcus said as he patted his midsection.

"You mean drank one."

He rolled his eyes. "So did the run help?"

Merci nodded. "Yeah, I needed to clear my head. How did the calls go earlier?"

Marcus put the gun back in the holster under the coffee table and sat on the plush leather couch. "Good. I took the metro downtown. It took me four stops and six burner phones, but I think I filled in a lot of gaps."

"So who is he?" She came over and curled up next to him on the couch.

"You gonna sit on my couch in your sweaty workout clothes?" Marcus asked.

Merci bit her lower lip. "Would you rather I take them off?"

"Why, yes, actually, I would."

Merci stuck out her tongue. "Too bad, you get to smell my stank. If you play your cards right, I may be down for a game of strip poker later."

"Deal, I'm all-in." Marcus patted her thigh.

"Please continue."

"According to my sources, his real name is Prescott Avery. He's the son of an investment banker who grew up in Connecticut. Parents sent him off to some rich kid boarding school in upstate New York when he turned eleven, and he graduated from Columbia University near the top of his class with a degree in economics. He doesn't go by his real name, though. Everyone refers to him as Mr. Joshua."

"Prescott? Really? His name makes him sound like a douche. His background isn't helping either. And he calls himself Mr. Joshua? What is with that?"

"Oh, I haven't got to the good stuff yet."

"Please, pray tell. Continue."

"So, Mr. Joshua, or Mr. Douche as you may want to call him, has a legit side and a not-so-legit side."

"Boring, legit side, first, please."

"He's an investment banker like his daddy. Works for the same investment firm his dad founded in the seventies."

"Great, he was born with a silver spoon up his ass." Merci sighed. "And the not-so-legit side?"

"Where do you want to start? The guy's into drugs, guns, young girls, and has been known to employ mules to smuggle people in from Mexico."

"So forget being a douche. He's an asshole who needs a bullet between his eyes."

"You know how the game works, babe. You smoke this asshat and another one will take his place before the body gets cold."

"Then we smoke the fucker that takes his place as well."

"I hear you, but let me get to the really good stuff."

"There's more?"

"Want to venture a guess who he hired recently?"

Merci's eyes narrowed, but her shoulders went in an upward motion. "No clue."

"The guy who was following you in Hendersonville."

"Wait ... you mean?"

"Yeah, babe. He hired him, which means he hired you to kill Chuck Brown as well."

"Damn, I didn't see that coming." Merci got up off the couch and paced around the living room. Her path was in the shape of a circle around the coffee table, like Scrooge McDuck around his worry room.

"Neither did I," Marcus said.

"So why was he at the funeral?"

"Still trying to work that out. But there's more."

Merci sighed. "Splendid. What?"

"He has close ties with a lobbyist/consulting firm based in New York."

"Which one?"

With a slight smirk, Marcus replied, "The Fulbright Group."

"Now them I've heard of."

He nodded. "Yup, they hired you through indirect channels many times over your illustrious career."

"What's going on here? Why did they want a Supreme Court justice's husband dead?"

Marcus shrugged. "Not sure. I'm still trying to piece together parts of the jigsaw puzzle."

"You think he knows what I look like? Maybe he was there at the funeral for me?"

Marcus shook his head. "I doubt it. You said he didn't make eye contact with you, right?"

"I don't believe so, plus I was disguised."

"Maybe it wasn't a good idea to go pay your last respects after all."

Merci frowned. "Or maybe it was serendipitous luck. Think about it. We wouldn't know about Mr. Joshua if I didn't go with my gut."

"That is true," Marcus said.

"Trust me. A woman's intuition is more powerful than a man's hunch."

Chapter Fourteen

Manhattan

Sheryl Hopping held the manila folder. Her hands trembled as she slowly shook her head. *What the hell have I gotten myself involved with?*

She unclasped and opened the envelope only once, the day she found it mixed in with the stack of papers she picked up from the conference room table. After the meeting adjourned, she gathered what the attendees left, placed them on the bottom of her stack of folders, tucked them under her arm, and left the room. An hour later, she sorted through the discarded papers at her desk. At the bottom of the stack was the oversized manila envelope. As she pulled apart the metal clasp, she paused and kept the envelope closed. She recognized the markings on the outside and knew whatever it contained must be important.

Sheryl closed the envelope and walked toward her boss's office. However, something inside her told her to hold up, so she turned around and returned to her desk.

She told herself she *had* to open it. After all, everyone who knew her would attest she had always been on the nosy side. Yet she fought the urge and decided to leave the envelope closed, at least for the moment. Butterflies formed in her stomach, and she wondered if not bringing the papers directly to her boss was a mistake.

The afternoon passed in a blur, and before she knew it, her boss left early, which was not normal for him. Since he left, she placed the closed envelope in her laptop bag, thinking she would give it to him first thing the next morning.

The next day, she awoke with a serious sinus headache and called out sick. Tucked away in the laptop bag, she forgot all about the envelope.

On the day she returned to work, the tension inside the office was palpable. She forgot her laptop bag at home, which was not how she wanted to start the day back in the office. Two hours later, she heard the screaming from her morbidly obese boss's office. A wall of her office butted up against his and she could hear what he was yelling about.

His raised voice ranted about a missing file, and not just any file, the one she clearly found.

Sheryl got scared, almost afraid enough to tell him the file was home in her laptop bag. But then she overheard some things that gave her pause and made her rethink revealing that she had the envelope. Later that afternoon, Mr. Joshua approached her desk. He looked frustrated, and even though the conversation started pleasantly, it soon turned ugly as he asked her about a file missing from the main conference room.

He pointedly asked her if she had found the manila envelope. With her best poker face, she lied and told him she had not. Surprisingly, he believed her, asked her who might have access to the conference room, and left a few minutes later after Sheryl provided him with a list of employees who used the space during the day in question.

A day passed, and she watched as person after person she listed as having access to the conference room entered her boss's office. Minutes later, when they left, each employee looked like they had aged because of the tongue-lashing the obese man gave them.

———◆○◆———

Sheryl decided to no longer let her fears control her. She opened the envelope to see why the missing file had gotten her boss so worked up. As Sheryl pulled out the stack of papers, she counted the pages quickly. There were six. She laid them on the table as her kettle whistled from the kitchen. A few minutes later, with a cup of hot tea in her hands, she sat down. Placing the cup to the side of the papers, she flipped back the cover page and read every word.

Each paragraph she read tightened the knot in her stomach, and each page made the bile churn and move higher up her throat.

Nausea overcame her as she finished reading the last few words. The upset feeling in her stomach turned to a dizzy feeling swirling in her head. She had to lie down for a minute to comprehend the full scope of what she read. The brief rest on the couch turned into an hour. Every moment she lay there, her mind grappled with what to do with the info contained on those six pages.

Who can I tell?

There was no way Sheryl could keep this to herself. And she sure as hell could not return the papers inside the envelope. Once the genie came out of the lamp, there was no way to put him back.

She pushed the cup of tea away from her and considered grabbing something stronger from the cabinet under the kitchen counter.

After another hour of contemplation, she knew without question to make copies of the six pages. Her ongoing dilemma was who she would send them to or what she would do with them.

Should I go to the police?

No answer seemed like the right decision, but one thing was for sure. Her life was in danger if anyone found out she had the contents of the envelope.

The question she wrestled with and needed to answer was how could she protect herself and those closest to her while at the same time making sure the info she now possessed saw the light of day?

By four a.m., she had devised a game plan. It wasn't bulletproof, but she thought she could protect herself if she followed it—at least, she prayed she could.

Chapter Fifteen

One World Trade Center

Ambrogino "Geno" Romano intimidated many people during his life, but rarely did anyone return the favor. However, the way Mr. Joshua looked at him inside the small, nondescript office made his skin crawl. They sat across from each other for almost a minute before either man uttered a word.

For the last forty-eight hours and in painstaking detail, Geno and two of his technicians went through hundreds of hours of video surveillance footage shot inside the seventy-sixth floor of the One World Trade Center building. As the head of security for The Fulbright Group (TFG), Geno oversaw all aspects of the leadership team's safety while also ensuring the data contained within the organization remained protected. Geno spent twenty years in the military and joined TFG several months after he retired.

Twenty employees—well, at this point, they were officially POIs or people of interest—were under his direct watch. They were POIs who, at some point during the day in question, entered the executive conference room. Their movements inside and after they left were analyzed and scrutinized until Geno's eyes wanted to bleed.

Unfortunately, no smoking gun existed. From what Geno and his men could tell, none of the twenty employees left the conference room with the folder in question.

"So you're sure the video feeds show us nothing?" Mr. Joshua asked once again.

"No, it shows us lots of things. Most of it is mundane, but it doesn't reveal if anyone left with the file."

Mr. Joshua didn't try to hide his displeasure. "So it what? Up and disappeared like a fart in the wind?"

"I like the Shawshank reference, but I have no clue what happened to the file, nor do I have any proof it was even in the conference room."

"That's not something our boss will want to hear."

"Is there any chance he is mistaken, and the file is somewhere in his office or at his penthouse? Maybe he didn't bring it to the office that day."

Mr. Joshua shook his head. "Not possible. He and I reviewed the file in his office before the meeting that morning. He had it on him when we left to go to the conference room, I'm sure of it."

"And the material inside the folder is consequential?"

Mr. Joshua frowned at the question. "Look, we're talking earth shattering shit here, Geno. If this file falls into the wrong hands. Well ..." He became quiet.

Geno nodded. "Okay, I get it."

"What about the one-on-one interviews you conducted? What exactly did you tell them?"

"Only that a file was misplaced," Geno replied sternly. "And it had sensitive personnel information inside it."

Mr. Joshua pursed his lips. "And nobody owned up to finding it?"

"Copy that," Geno said.

"You believe them?"

"A few of them were slightly suspicious regarding their body language," Geno said. "But I think it was mainly because they were nervous. I've been told I can be frightening."

"And here I thought I was the only person who intimidated people." Mr. Joshua raised one eyebrow, imitating the look the Rock made famous.

Geno ignored the comment and facial expression.

Mr. Joshua continued. "And your guys searched everyone's desks thoroughly?"

Geno nodded. "Yes, we went in after hours and gave their offices the white glove treatment. Nada. Of course, whoever removed the file from the conference room could have taken it with them when they left the office that afternoon."

"Next steps?" Mr. Joshua asked as he thumped his fingers on the desktop. "Time is running short, and the boss won't take the excuse that it simply disappeared. We've got to find it."

"We have cameras outside the conference room. Twelve people in question walked out of the conference room with nothing in their hands and weren't carrying any bags or cases. There's no digital evidence they took anything. So, unless they ate it or stuffed it down their pants, I don't think they took the missing file."

"And the other eight?"

"Based on the video footage, they had either folders and papers in their hands or were carrying bags big enough to hold files. We searched their office space and interviewed all of them. Which one took it? I simply can't be sure."

"And?" Mr. Joshua asked. "What's your course of action?"

"I would suggest the next step is to search their vehicles and places of residence."

He stroked his chin before he replied. "Is that something you can facilitate?" Mr. Joshua asked.

Geno's face contorted into a full-on scowl. "The boss didn't hire me because of my charming personality."

"Yeah, me neither." Mr. Joshua paused. "The boss told me you kicked down a few doors in your former occupation."

"More than a few."

Mr. Joshua just stared at him. The look is best described as an icy glare. "Well, this type of operation won't work that way. This can't cause any blowback. If you send people into the homes of these employees, they can't leave a trace."

"Relax, the guys I work with know what they are doing. They all know how to be ghosts, get in, do what is required, and get out without leaving any evidence of their presence."

"Good," Mr. Joshua replied.

"But their services ain't cheap."

Mr. Joshua shrugged. "Cost is not a concern. Just get the missing file."

"Copy that."

An awkward moment occurred as Mr. Joshua stared at the wall behind Geno with a quizzical look. "I can't believe we have nothing in place to track sensitive files?"

The comment struck Geno. "Say what?"

"Isn't there something we could do to track files?"

"Shit, why didn't I think of it?"

"Think of what?"

"This missing file. Did the boss use the new folders I gave out last month?"

"Of course, the ones with the redesigned logo?"

"Correct." Geno snapped his fingers.

"He did. Why?"

"I can't believe I forgot."

"Forgot what?"

"We started putting RFID tags on every sensitive folder."

"What's an RFID tag?" Mr. Joshua asked.

"A radio frequency identification sticker."

"You mean we've been spinning our wheels when we could have been tracking this file all along?"

"Well, not necessary, at least not yet."

"You're not making any sense." The frustration and anger showed clearly on Mr. Joshua's face.

"RFIDs can be complicated. We can activate tracking capability on them, but it's not configured that way, at least not yet. It's our first go at the technology, so initially all we are using are tags that can be located with a handheld reader device."

"Then how does that help us?"

"Well, when we enter the employees' houses or cars, we can fairly quickly use the handheld reader to see if any RFID tags are present. I can also check their office space here after hours."

"So the device can track these tags from far away?"

"No, we've got to be within several feet, but if they are not in anyone's car and we need to check where they live, at least we would not need to go in and toss the houses. We should be able to go room by room and find any file with an RFID tag quickly.

"How long will it take to search the eight homes?"

"Under ideal circumstances, I say we should plan on a week. Not all these people work the same hours, and they have family members in the house during the day. So, it'll take time to case out the joints and create an infiltration plan for all eight."

"You've got ninety-six hours."

Geno's mouth dropped open. "Are you kidding me? That's not enough time."

Mr. Joshua leaned in closer.

Geno could smell the stale coffee on his breath.

"Ninety-six hours. Find me the damn file, or you can tell the boss you failed and deal with the consequences."

Geno pulled back on the collar of his pressed white shirt but didn't respond to the obvious threat.

Mr. Joshua looked down at his watch and furrowed his brow.

"Am I keeping you?" Geno asked.

"I've got some things to tie up before I catch the Delta shuttle this evening."

"Meeting the judge again?"

"Yes, in the a.m. For coffee."

"She know about it?"

A wide smile formed on Mr. Joshua's face. "No, and I'm likely the last person she'll want to see."

"Good luck."

"Luck is for the unprepared." Mr. Joshua stood and left the drab office.

As he exited the space and without turning back, he uttered four words, "Ninety-six hours, Geno."

Chapter Sixteen

At Cruising Altitude

Merci stretched her legs along the plush Air France La Premiere class seat. Opulence is not a word typically used when describing air travel nowadays, but in Merci's opinion, Air France went above and beyond with the La Premiere flying experience on transcontinental flights.

Marcus sat next to her. Their seats, 1B and 1C, were in the center of the plane with aisles on either side of them. With the beige curtains drawn shut, it afforded the lovers an element of privacy not common on most commercial flights.

Twenty minutes after takeoff, he raised his thick tumbler, containing an old-fashioned, in the air toward her. She bumped her margarita glass against the tumbler, which he held firm.

"See, I told you it would be a good idea to get away," he said as their glasses clanked against each other. "Although I didn't know you would book the expensive seats."

"Well, I used your AmEx black card." Merci said the words with a devious smirk spread across her face.

"Figures." Marcus rolled his eyes.

"Seriously, we've done well for ourselves. It might be a little vain, but I don't think I can ever go back to coach seats. Once you have the finer things in life, your expectations don't want to be downgraded."

Marcus nodded. "Valid point. By the way, speaking of the finer things in life, I booked the Shangri-La for our brief stay in Paris."

"Oooh, my fave. You know how to win a gal over, don't you?"

He winked. "I try."

"Did you sign me up for a spa as well?"

He arched his eyebrows. "Maybe."

"I predict a happy ending for you in the cards," Merci said as her tongue slowly glided along the bottom of her upper lip.

They grew quiet for a few minutes as they sipped their drinks.

"Can I ask you something?" Merci's expression tightened.

Marcus nodded. "Of course, babe. What's up?"

"Do you think I'm running away from my problems?"

"What? By leaving D.C.? You finished a job, and you need to unwind. This trip is a good thing."

"No, I mean in general. By what I do for a living. Am I just ignoring what happened to me in the past?"

Marcus put his drink down and cupped her hands in his. The warmth of his skin and the feel of his touch sent pulses through her body. "My long answer and short answer are the same." He grew quiet, seemingly lost in thought.

"And that is?"

Marcus smiled. "No, my answer is no. You're doing what you were born to do. The past is not only gone, it's dead. Only the future matters. If this is what you need to do, then it's what you do. It's quite simple, actually. You're not running away from anything but moving toward what awaits."

Merci stared into his eyes. Her glance could be distant, even icy at times. But as she focused on Marcus's eyes, her look softened. She leaned over the partition and kissed him affectionately on the lips.

A single tear formed in the corner of her lashes as Marcus gently brushed it away with his thumb before it could slide down her light, bronzed skin.

She uttered two words, "Thank you."

Marcus said nothing but smiled in response.

For several moments, they simply stared at each other. The love that waned in the first several years of their highly unorthodox and extremely convoluted relationship reignited after the events in Hong Kong, and then solidified as time passed. Their relationship might be unconventional, but so was what they both did for a living. The bottom line is that it worked for them.

Eventually, a flight attendant interrupted their gazes to refill their drinks, and Marcus settled into a book, while Merci logged onto her Netflix account to binge a new series from her list.

Six and a half hours later, the jumbo jet touched down at Charles de Gaulle Airport northeast of Paris proper. One perk of the La Premier package was that a worker whisked them off the flight and brought them directly to passport control. Bypassing the main line, the immigration officer hardly gave them a passing glance as they cleared customs and found themselves in a chauffeured car within minutes.

"Veuillez nous emmener à Holybelly," Merci said to the driver.

The driver nodded, "Oui."

Marcus frowned. "Babe, we just ate breakfast on the flight. Holybelly? Really?"

"You know better than to come between this woman and her second breakfast."

"Great, I'm in love with a hobbit."

"A famished hobbit in search of her precious." Merci rubbed her belly.

"I didn't think there was any other," Marcus said. "Great book by the way, I love Tolkien."

"Movies are better. Especially that Strider. He's easy on the eyes."

Marcus rolled his eyes. "You'd leave me for Viggo, huh?"

"Leave? No. But everyone is entitled to one free pass. Besides, I know the girls who are on your list. If Salma Hayek were on our flight, you would have introduced yourself."

"Babe, she's married to a billionaire. She wouldn't be on our flight, even if we are in the pricey seats."

"I can't blame her, neither would I if you got me a G650."

"Whatever. Back to our discussion, books are always better. Hollywood sucks at adaptations."

"Nope. The debate is over. I refuse to argue in the City of Love." Merci snuggled in against his broad shoulder.

"Now, that we can agree on." Marcus wrapped his arm around her.

On the way into Paris, Merci had the driver quickly detour to the Gare du Nord train station. Merci got out and returned five minutes later with a black duffel bag.

"Thought we weren't working on this trip?" Marcus asked.

Merci raised her eyebrows. "Never know when something might come up."

"Always be prepared, huh?"

"As a former Boy Scout, I thought that was your mantra?"

"Actually, I was an Eagle Scout."

Merci smiled.

⁕

Two hours later, after a scrumptious breakfast, the driver dropped them off at the Shangri-La Hotel. After getting checked in and being shown to their room, the couple showered, broke in the bed, which seemed to have a predominant squeak on the left side closest to the headboard, and showered again.

After she got dressed, Merci took out the black duffel bag and reviewed its contents, transferring some of it to a much smaller dark gray Kavu rope sling bag she could wear as a purse or sling over her back. Confident it had everything she might need in a pinch, she zippered the duffel bag and slipped it under the bed.

Later, as they sat on their balcony overlooking the Eiffel Tower, she raised a glass of Kir to toast the weekend away in their favorite city.

"So, what do you want to do the rest of the day?" Marcus asked.

"Not a damn thing," Merci replied.

"Chillaxing it is then."

She cocked her head to the side, as her tongue moved along her upper lip slowly from one side to another. "Actually ..."

"Yes?"

"I'd like to catch something at the opera house if there's a performance tonight. For old times' sake."

"Ahh, reminiscing about our first date?" Marcus asked.

"Always," Merci said with a wide smile plastered over her face.

"Let me call the concierge and see what they can do."

Marcus got up from his seat on the balcony and stepped inside the room. He returned a few minutes later. "We're in luck. Got the last two tickets for a ballet tonight at the opera house."

Merci sank into her chair and let out an audible giggle. "We're gonna have one hell of a weekend."

Chapter Seventeen

Paris, France

The next morning, Merci walked hand-in-hand with Marcus over the Seine River across the Pont d'léna Bridge. Also called the Jena Bridge, Napoleon ordered the structure to be built overlooking the military school and named it after his victory in 1806 at the Battle of Jena.

A student of history, Marcus loved crossing the bridge each time they visited the City of Light, admiring the four sculptures, two on each end. Merci, for her part, wasn't as fascinated with history and simply wanted what stood at the corner of Pont d'léna and Quai Branly.

The food at Aux Delices Du Pont d'léna was nothing special according to Parisian standards. You could find the local fare on any street corner throughout Paris. However, this specific location held a special place in Merci's heart. It was the place where Merci laid eyes on Marcus for the first time. Truth be told, the moments leading up to their meeting served as dark memories in her recollections, but how their first interaction went and, more importantly, what occurred after that moment shaped her life and radically changed her future.

All these years later, every time they came to the city, she insisted they go to Aux Delices Du Pont d'léna, order two chocolate croissants, and each have a café crème. Marcus obliged, and after getting the food and drink, they crossed over Quai Branly to find a bench under the steel gaze of the Eiffel Tower.

"Thank you for this," Merci said as they sat practically on top of each other at one of the green park benches that lined the trails at the base of the tower.

Chain link fencing surrounded the tower, a sign of the times after the various terrorist attacks that punctuated the years following the turn of the century.

"Wouldn't want to be anywhere else," Marcus replied, his arm draped around her shoulders. "Although I'm surprised every time we come to the city, you insist on returning to this very spot."

"Well, it's where we met after all, dummy."

Marcus smirked at the insult. "I know, but considering how you were when our paths crossed. I just ..." He paused as he considered his words. "I thought it might bring back lots of bad memories."

Merci shook her head. "Quite the opposite. You saved me that day. Every moment from that point on has been a gift. It all began at this spot, and thanks to you. This is my place of salvation, and your selfless act created only beautiful memories."

He blushed. Unsure how to respond, he pointed to the top of the tower after a few moments of awkward silence. "Did I ever tell you about my first time up there?"

"Not that I recall."

"Wanna hear it?"

"A loss of virginity story from you?" She winked. "Of course."

"Well, it wasn't that exciting." Marcus threw his head back and let out a guttural laugh.

"But I bet it involved a pretty lady."

"Well, there were a few of those that night."

"No doubt, Mr. Casanova."

"So, I visited Paris when I was nineteen years old on a trip between my freshman and sophomore years at college."

"Ah, yes, the great Reformation history tour of Europe you've alluded to over the years. I still can't believe you attended a strict religious college. Boy, would they be disappointed to know you bedded me!" Merci let out a boisterous laugh. "You morphed into a godless heathen."

Marcus rolled his eyes. "As I was saying, we had a few free nights in Paris and decided to take a boat ride on the Seine River, followed by a late excursion up the Eiffel Tower, which resulted in a few bruises and scars."

"Is that how you got that mark on your ass?" Merci let out a short giggle.

"Actually, that was when you stabbed me the night in Bali when we got drunk after you took out that Saudi prince."

"Oooh, yeah, that was a good night. I had forgotten about the switch-blade incident, though."

"My ass doesn't, but as I was saying."

"Yes, please continue your story, Deuce Bigalow."

"So, it's midnight on top of the tower, and these somewhat hot chicks with foreign accents ask us if we want to lie in the grass and smoke some Mary Jane."

"I knew there'd be hotties in this story."

"Then this dick, I guess he was the security guard or something, shows up out of the blue with this massive chip on his shoulder and kicks us out. Tells us the tower is closed ..."

Merci's gaze left Marcus after the first few words as she visually tracked a flamboyantly dressed man a hundred feet beyond Marcus's left shoulder. The man in the bright canary yellow suit had two girls on either side of him. His hands firmly grasped both women at the elbows as he pulled and jerked them down the path past the tower. Both women were clearly in distress, yet nobody paid them any attention.

Except Merci.

She doubted herself. *Could it be him? I thought he was dead? I searched for him and found nothing.* Yet every fiber in her knew the man was exactly who she thought he was.

The swagger in which he walked, the short, although now graying, goatee perfectly styled, but most strikingly, the way he handled the two women with him. They were both prostitutes, and by the look of things, neither one of them was the bottom bitch based on how he manhandled them, treating them like day old meat you'd toss to a pack of wild dogs.

Marcus stopped mid-sentence, seeing the change in Merci's demeanor. He looked over his shoulder in the distance, trying to determine what or who caught her attention and transformed her within seconds. "What is it?"

"It's Jean-Luc."

"Who the hell is Jean-Luc?"

An unquenchable fire suddenly raged in Merci's eyes as she stood like a spark escaping a flame. With her eyes affixed on the man strutting down the path, she replied. "The pimp."

Some people are like roaches and don't know when or how to die. Jean-Luc was one of those individuals.

"Oh, shit!" Marcus grabbed her arm, catching her between the wrist and elbow.

"Fucking let me go, Marcus." Her reply came in a deep, enraged tone.

He knew better than to hold her back, but the look in her eyes concerned him. "Don't do something you'll regret."

"The only thing I'll regret is if I let that piece of shit live another minute." Merci pulled her arm and broke free from his grasp. She reached behind her back and placed her hand on the butt of the Sig she took from the black bag before they left the hotel.

Marcus opened his mouth to protest, but knew a caged beast must be allowed to hunt when finally set free.

CHAPTER EIGHTEEN

CATOCTIN MOUNTAIN PARK, MARYLAND

CAMP DAVID

Once a month, Preacher assembles select cabinet members to meet for an entire day at Camp David, known formally as the Naval Support Facility Thurmont. Located within Catoctin Mountain Park in Frederick County, Maryland, Camp David has served as a presidential retreat since the Roosevelt administration. Originally dubbed Shangri-La by President Roosevelt, he modeled the main lodge after his vacation home in Warm Springs, Georgia. President Eisenhower eventually renamed the facility after his grandson, David.

Every president since 1942 has used the presidential retreat as a respite from the fishbowl of the White House and Washington, D.C.

Besides an escape from Washington, Camp David hosted world leaders, including Winston Churchill and Nikita Khrushchev. The Egyptian president and Israeli prime minister signed the Camp David Accords there in 1978, making the camp a household name.

While some presidents rarely used the retreat, in favor of other properties, President Collins found solace in the camp and visits two or three times a month if his schedule allows. He made it a point early in his administration to have his cabinet meet at Camp David once a month. It was primarily a day trip, but many of the cabinet members would come in a night early and make it an overnight visit.

Nick Jordan stood on the front stoop of the Laurel Lodge under the canopy of tall trees as he waited for the final member of the president's cabinet to arrive. Several minutes later, the Attorney General pulled up in a forest green golf cart.

Without commenting that he was late, Nick nodded when the AG approached. "Mr. Attorney General," Nick said.

"Mr. Jordan," the AG replied. "Did they start already?"

Nick shook his head. "No, sir, they were waiting for you."

The Laurel Lodge, the largest cabin on the property, is where meals are normally served and meetings are held. Besides having three conference rooms, the lodge has a fairly accurate replica of the Oval Office for use by the president, as well as a large dining room and a living room. President Collins preferred to keep his meetings at Camp David with his cabinet informal, so they typically took place in the spacious living room. The president's full cabinet consists of twenty-five members, but only a dozen get invited to Camp David once a month.

Initially, alcohol was served at the afternoon session, until the Secretary of Energy, Jesús Martinez, had a few too many one day. Going through a divorce at the time, Jesús got pretty wasted and said things he never should have said in front of the president. It caused quite a scene, and he even offered his resignation letter the next day after he sobered up. The president did not accept his letter, but did ban alcohol for the next six months at their monthly meetings.

Six months later, the president changed his stance and allowed drinks, but each member was limited to only two. And just to prove he had a sense of humor, the president and everyone else, except the Secretary of Energy, called the first round *Jesús Juice* in honor of the secretary.

With the selected members of the cabinet finally in place, the president called the meeting to order.

Even though he was not part of the cabinet, The Body Man, Nick Jordan, also attended the meetings. Ninety-nine-point-five percent of the time, he said nothing and merely sat in the back of the living room, away from the circle of cabinet members. Like a fly on the wall, Nick heard all and absorbed what was necessary while discarding the things not needed to fulfill his role.

Most months, Preacher typically reviewed items in recent President's Daily Briefs (PDB) and asked direct yet thought-provoking questions to his trusted team. The cabinet meetings would normally last from after lunch until late afternoon, sometimes stretching into the early evening hours.

As the meeting wrapped up, the president's private chef, Drew Ward, entered the living room to inform the cabinet about the dinner menu he and his team had prepared.

After dinner, most of the cabinet members returned to Washington. Only a few stayed at Camp David for the evening. President Collins allowed them to bring their families, although only a few did so this month.

The president returned to his cabin, the Aspen Lodge, and the small office where he planned to get some work done that evening. His wife of forty-two years, Ali, didn't join him at Camp David this trip. She opted to stay back at the White House and had several grandchildren over to watch movies while snacking on delectable baked goods from the White House pastry chef.

A loud knock on the office door caused the president to look up over his readers as he placed the intel report on the desk. "Enter," he said.

Nick opened the door and stepped into the relatively small space. "It's so small in here, sir. Like a mouse in a shoebox."

The president chuckled at the comment. "I would think you would be right at home here then."

Nick looked sheepish in his facial expression. "Me? Yes, sir. But I would think you'd rather work in the other spacious office. It seems more your style."

"Nonsense. I spend enough time at the Oval while in Washington. It's more home-like when I come up here. It's cozy and reminds me of my office in Hendersonville."

"That makes sense, sir."

"Do you need something, Nicholas?"

"Just letting you know Sam arrived and I'm headed back to D.C. in a few minutes. Just need to grab my bag."

Samantha Tahlib, or Sam as she preferred to be called, worked under Nick as his apprentice for the role of The Body Man. The first female Secret Service officer to hold the role, she accepted the position after the untimely death of the previous apprentice, Danny Frazier.

"Hopefully, you're going home to sleep in your townhouse that you rarely see anymore."

"No, sir. I have a lead I'm following. Meeting up with an old friend to help shake a few trees."

"Jeez. Do you ever stop being The Body Man? Taking a night off to rest is okay, right?" Before Nick could reply, the president cut him off. "I know, I know. You will give me your standard line from that Bon Jovi song about sleeping when you're dead."

"Well, I was going to quote Metallica this time and say I sleep with one eye open. That is when I sleep, sir."

"Father Time will catch up with you eventually, son. You can't burn both ends of the candle forever."

"When that day comes, sir, Sam will be The Body Man and I'll be in a far-off land sipping Mai Tais while chasing pretty islanders around the beach every night."

"Sounds like a lonely existence if you ask me." The president's look showed disapproval.

Nick scrunched his lips. "Not all of us have an Ali, sir."

"Yours is out there, Nick. When you step down and step back from this crazy job, maybe you'll find her."

"Maybe, Mr. President. Maybe."

"Safe travels back to D.C. and hope the lead pans out."

"Me too."

Nick closed the door before he left and spoke with Sam for a few minutes before he returned to his cabin to retrieve his duffel bag.

An hour and twenty minutes later, the government-issued Suburban dropped him off at the corner of N Capitol St NW and F St NW at The Dubliner.

As Nick climbed out of the SUV, the driver said, "Have a Guinness for me, Jordan."

"That I can do," he replied before closing the door and entering the pub. He was greeted by the sounds of the house band playing The High Kings' rowdy tune, Irish Pub Song.

CHAPTER NINETEEN

PARIS

Merci turned and moved several steps away from Marcus, her gaze intently focused on Jean-Luc, who appeared unaware of what was stalking him.

"Lala," Marcus said in a forceful tone from behind her. He had one card to play and decided, for her sake, he had to throw it down.

Merci paused, her body tensing as Marcus used the one name that caused her rage to ebb, if only for the briefest moments. It was the name he only used at the most intimate of times, and never had he uttered it in public before or in such a harsh tone.

Her head snapped back, and she locked eyes with Marcus. "What?" Her eyes softened, and the fire subsided.

Marcus shook his head. "It's broad daylight, and there are witnesses everywhere. This isn't the way."

"He's alive and right here in plain sight."

"I know. We can do this together, another way."

A snarl formed at the corner of her lips. "This is something I have to do alone for me. Don't try to stop me."

"I'm asking you to be smart. We can follow him and do this in private. He'll pay, and you'll get the vengeance you crave."

Her eyes narrowed. "No. He dies right here, right now, at the pillars where he bartered with the dreams of innocent girls for decades. Blood has covered the streets of Paris in the past, as will his today."

The rage of fire returned to her eyes.

He had lost Lala over to the beast who dwelt within. He'd either help her complete her task or stay out of her way. When awakened, the devil within always prevailed.

Merci turned away and strode toward Jean Luc, who was now less than seventy feet away.

"And away we go," Marcus muttered as he gave chase.

———◆○◆———

Jean-Luc practically dragged Chloe and Adele along the path at the northwest corner of the steel tower. They both cost him money the night before, pleasuring the punter who skipped out on paying. Yes, he should have paid, but it was up to the girls to take the payment before they delivered the goods. And then, instead of owning up to what they did, they lied. A liar always knows when someone is trying to play them. That accounted for two strikes. Jean-Luc wasn't about to allow them a third. Now that he had caught them, he muttered constant curses and threats without a care for who heard him or observed his abusive actions.

Chloe pushed him with her free hand and tried to yank her arm away.

He doubled down on his grip, twisting the skin of the lowly prostitute, and in a sharp tone screamed, "Putain de chatte" as his gaze focused on a person in the distance.

With a rapid pace, a woman approached and caused Jean-Luc to pause his vile insults. It took his memory a second to process the image and register what his eyes relayed to his brain. Ten years had passed, but her face hadn't changed. And the fire within her eyes burned brighter than he had ever seen while she worked for him.

"Ça ne peut pas être!" Jean-Luc exclaimed in a panicked tone.

"Quoi?" Adele asked.

Jean-Luc's grip released both girls as his body shook. "La veuve noire!"

Chloe, who spoke fluent English, looked at Adele. "The Black Widow?"

Jean-Luc turned on his heels and sprinted toward Quai Branly. The two hookers no longer existed in his mind. The only thing that mattered was escape. He needed a way out.

Merci's pace accelerated as she put a distance between herself and Marcus. She moved like a lioness sprinting through the tall grass. The Sig in her right hand remained at her side, pointed to the ground. She saw the look Jean-Luc gave her. He clearly recognized her when she was still more than fifty feet away. He turned to run. She adapted, and the pace of a lioness turned to that of a cheetah as he made a run for the wide boulevard directly ahead. The small Kavu sling bag she wore on her back bounced back and forth as her strides grew longer and her feet smacked hard against the gravel path.

He moved faster than she expected. Clearly, time had not been as cruel to him as she would have hoped. The foot chase made her feel alive and renewed.

Luck appeared on Jean-Luc's side. He arrived at Quai Branly as two locals pulled up in matching red and white scooters. These weren't the touristy 50cc scooters that flooded the roads of Paris and maxed out at 30mph. They were owned by locals, and the 125cc models could go 60mph. Jean-Luc struck the driver of the closest scooter with a closed fist, knocking him off the bike, which fell to the ground and skidded along the pavement.

Less than twenty feet away and with the Sig raised to shoulder level, Merci resisted the urge to put two rounds into the back of his head. It would be quick death, but the piece of shit deserved something much slower, more painful.

She watched as Jean-Luc picked up the bike and threw his leg over the seat. He revved the engine. The scooter accelerated, and he headed west before hanging a right, turning north onto Pont de Bir-Hakeim across the river.

Merci arrived at the remaining scooter seconds after Jean-Luc raced away. The startled driver looked down at his friend, who lay prostrate on the ground, then over to Merci, who stood at his side. She put the barrel of the Sig against his cheek and pressed it into the soft flesh.

"Foutre le camp," she said. Translation, "Get the fuck off."

The driver didn't need to be told twice. He raised his hands off the handlebars and held them in the air as he slipped off the bike.

Merci tucked the Sig behind her back and climbed onto the scooter, giving chase to Jean-Luc.

Marcus arrived with no scooters left to steal, but he wasn't about to abandon his girl, who was playing a high-stakes game of cat and mouse on the streets of Paris. A cab sat idle on the side of Quai Branly. He jumped in the back, pointed to the red and white scooter currently turning into Pont de Bir-Hakeim, and in broken French said, "Suivez ce scooter." Meaning, "Follow that scooter."

Chapter Twenty

Washington, D.C.

Mary Brown climbed out of the black Suburban on the corner of Third Street and Pennsylvania Avenue, two blocks from the Supreme Court. A frequent patron, she visited the location most mornings when court was in session. Before she closed the thick, armored door, she addressed the two U.S. Marshals inside the government-plated SUV.

"I'll just be a few minutes, guys. No need to come in."

"Madame Justice, we were told by the marshal to stay with you no matter what." The Judicial Security Division officer in the passenger seat opened his door and climbed out of the vehicle.

"I got this, Phil. I am just grabbing a cup of java like I do every morning. Besides, you'll be able to see me from the windows."

Phil frowned and shook his head.

"You realize that up until this week, I came here most days on my own, right?"

"Yes, ma'am, but the Marshal said ..."

Mary's eyes narrowed. "I can handle Frank Halter. Trust me."

Phil protested, but after a tense few seconds, decided against pushing the issue. "We'll be watching you from the sidewalk, ma'am."

"I'm sure you will. You boys want something? It's on me."

Phil and the agent driving said, "No thanks," simultaneously.

"Suit yourself. I've never known a fed to turn down free coffee." She turned and walked the few steps to the front door.

As she did almost every day of the week, Justice Brown strode into the Starbucks without getting even a glance from anyone inside. Of course, she was dressed in regular clothes, like most workers stopping in on their way to the office. If she had walked in wearing her black robe, she would have turned a few heads.

She recognized two of the girls behind the counter. Caitlyn, who had a hearing impairment, stood behind the cash register. She had red hair, a round face, long eyelashes, an ever-present smile, and a small-town look about her. Caitlyn had a full ride at Gallaudet University, which paid for her education, but she worked at Starbucks for extra spending money. She reminded Mary of her own granddaughter, who was still in high school.

Maika stood behind the espresso machine, her thick black hair pulled tight into a bun. She attended Howard University, and Mary always thought she was the feisty one of the crew. Naturally, Mary took an immediate liking to her.

Two people stood in front of Justice Brown, waiting to place their orders. A few minutes later, her turn came.

"Well, hey, Mrs. B., you want your usual?" Caitlyn asked.

"You know it," Mary replied with a warm smile.

"You good? Not seen you in a few days." Although she could not hear much out of either ear, she excelled in reading lips and often could understand better than those with perfect hearing.

Even though the news of her husband's death made the front page of the Washington D.C. papers, clearly Caitlyn had no clue about his passing. Mary wasn't surprised unless it appeared on social media. These days, young people are oblivious to most news stories. She decided against saying anything. "Living life, my young friend," Mary said warmly.

"One flat white," Caitlyn called out.

"Make that two." The voice from behind spoke in an authoritative tone.

Mary felt a presence move next to her before seeing who copied her order and now stood at her side. Her throat tightened as her eyes locked onto the man's face. "Mr. Joshua, we bump into each other again."

"You know this guy?" Caitlyn's appearance changed as she took on a questioning look.

Mary kept an even tone in her voice. "He's an acquaintance."

"And I'm paying," Mr. Joshua said as he handed the barista a twenty.

Caitlyn shrugged. "Make that two flat whites."

Maika said, "Aah-ite. Good to see you Mrs. B."

"You too, Maika. You making those grades?" Mary asked.

"You know it."

"Good to hear. If you need anything else, let me know."

"Fo sho, Mrs. B."

Mary moved to the end of the counter to wait for her drink to be made. She turned slightly and gave Mr. Joshua a sharp look. "To what do I owe the privilege this time?"

"Just need a moment of your time, Madam Justice."

"Pretty sure I made it clear the last time we spoke, there was nothing else to discuss."

"Hear me out is all I ask."

With the coffees ready, Mary thanked the girls and started for the door.

"Two minutes. That's all I need." Mr. Joshua stood in front of her, blocking her way to the door.

Mary paused. Every fiber of her being wanted to tell him to go to hell. Even throwing the scalding coffee in his face felt like the right thing to do. But her calm side prevailed, the part of her firmly ensconced in the judicial ways.

She looked toward the empty table closest to the floor-to-ceiling window. "You've got two minutes, Mr. Joshua. Not a second more."

As they took their seats, she glanced out the window, seeing Phil move at a rapid pace her way. She waved him off, and he stopped at the door with a glaring look at the table where she and Mr. Joshua sat.

Mary looked away from the outside and back toward her unwelcome guest. Before he spoke, she looked at her watch.

"And your time starts now," she said.

CHAPTER TWENTY-ONE

PARIS

Merci followed about a hundred yards behind Jean-Luc. For a scooter, the motorized bike appeared nimble and handled the sudden jerks as she swerved between cars. She pressed the accelerator as hard as the engine would allow, yet she didn't gain on Jean-Luc.

"Come on you piece of shit, move," she yelled out in anger as the gap between them stayed the same.

Jean-Luc drove like a man possessed as his scooter hurled down the tree-lined Av. Kleber north toward the Arc de Triomphe. Merci needed to catch him before he reached the Arc, where taking one of the dozen avenues branching out like rays from the sun would be easy.

A half mile down the road, Jean-Luc narrowly missed a parked car. He swerved erratically to the left and clipped the side of an oncoming bus, causing the scooter to lay down hard on the road. He rolled off and stopped against the side of a tree trunk.

Stuck behind several slow-moving cars, Merci saw his crash ahead and knew she had to take advantage of his accident. With an oncoming car bearing down fast, she turned into its lane and revved the engine. Horns blared around her, and her normally steady heartbeat rapidly increased as the front fender of the oncoming car came closer and closer.

She narrowly got ahead of the slow cars and darted back into her lane a fraction of a second before plowing head-on into the oncoming vehicle. It would have been like a bug splattered on a windshield.

Jean-Luc was back on the scooter once more, but she closed the gap to less than thirty feet because of his accident and her death-defying pass.

Looming less than a quarter mile away, the top of the imposing Arc de Triomphe came into view. Pedestrians screamed as both scooters continued to weave in and out of traffic on the busy avenue.

As the Arc got closer Merci knew she wouldn't catch him before he reached the roundabout, not unless he screwed up and laid down the scooter again or ran into a vehicle.

Far in the distance, the sound of sirens wailed. No doubt they were zeroing in on the red and white scooters raising all kinds of hell down Av. Kleber.

Merci only had one play. She couldn't risk him reaching the Arc and disappearing in the sea of traffic around the iconic monument.

With her left hand on the handlebar, she reached behind her back and drew the Sig. She raised the weapon and aimed. Merci had a clear shot at Jean-Luc. They were approaching fifty miles an hour, and the cobblestone roadway made keeping control of the scooter challenging with two hands, let alone one. The problem was trying to keep the weapon steady, which proved impossible. She fired twice, with the first two shots going wide and striking the van in front of Jean-Luc's scooter, causing the rear window to explode. With the rear window blown out, the driver hit the brakes, causing Jean-Luc to decelerate, closing the gap between him and Merci.

She fired three more times in rapid succession.

Pop-pop-pop. The sound of the rounds reverberated between the narrow buildings lining the avenue.

The second round found its mark as it struck just below his left shoulder blade. Somehow Jean-Luc swerved around the now stopped van as the avenue ended, opening up to the chaotic intersection of the Arc de Triomphe. The force of the bullet caused him to slump forward as the scooter entered the myriads of cars circling the monument.

A black Peugeot struck his scooter with enough force to throw him headfirst over the handlebars. He landed on his back as his body skidded along the roundabout. Jean-Luc was bloodied and his body twisted into a grotesque shape. The vehicles circling the grand thoroughfare came to screeching halts as his body came to rest.

Merci could turn right and escape down the Avenue Des Champs-Élysées, but she couldn't run away. Merci had to know if he survived. And if he did, well, she knew what must be done.

With the traffic ground to a halt, Merci steered her scooter toward the body lying in the roadway halfway between the sidewalk and the monument. People got out of their vehicles as the sound of sirens grew closer.

A crowd of people approached the bloodied person sprawled out on the ground.

Merci's scooter skidded to a stop, and she jumped off. As she did so, she raised her Sig and put two rounds into the air. It had the desired effect as people scattered and ran away from the sound of gunfire.

She stood next to Jean-Luc, who lay there motionless except for his chest, which moved up and down as he gasped for breath. He opened his eyes as she stepped over him, putting his torso squarely between her two spread legs.

Blood formed at the corner of his lips, and as a blood bubble spilled out in broken English, he said. "Merci, please show me Mercy."

Sirens drew closer. They were less than half a block away.

Now or never.

She would have rather caught him and made him suffer, but at this point, the only option was to finish things.

Merci leveled the Sig at his broken body.

"Fuck you, Jean-Luc," she said as she put two rapid rounds in his chest puncturing his heart with both shots. Both rounds killed him, but it wasn't enough. Two more bullets entered his forehead as fragments of skull, brain matter, and blood sprayed over the stones of the cobblestone roadway.

Back on the scooter, Merci pushed the accelerator and darted down the Champs-Élysées seconds before the French police arrived on the grisly scene.

She drove like a bat out of hell for almost a mile. The distant sirens grew fainter as she gradually eased off the throttle, slowed down, and blended into the regular traffic pattern. When she reached the Pont Alexandre III bridge, which connects the Champs-Élysées quarter with the Invalides, she parked the scooter. At the base of one of the four gilt-bronze statues that adorn the bridge, she slipped the small gray sling bag off her back and pulled out a blond wig and a different color shirt. It wasn't a dramatic change, but it would be enough to fool the average person, although it would do squat for facial recognition cameras. Walking to the halfway point across the bridge, checking both ways first, she tossed the Sig into the Seine River. Next, she hailed a cab and made her way to where Marcus would know to find her.

They both knew if the shit hit the fan, they were to meet at the place where they shared their first kiss. It happened a decade earlier, overlooking Paris at night while sitting on the steps of the Sacre-Coeur. The Paris skyline glistened in the distance as they both sipped on a Coca-Cola.

Chapter Twenty-Two

Washington, D.C.

Associate Justice Brown looked out the window and made eye contact with the U.S. Marshals tasked with keeping her safe. She moved her head sharply toward her shoulder, letting him know he could move back closer to the Suburban and not stand so close to the window.

Mr. Joshua watched her intently, yet he said nothing.

She looked back at him. "I told you, the two minutes have already started."

"The clients I represent hope you've reconsidered their offer."

Mary shook her head. "My answer hasn't changed. It's still no."

"What would make you change your mind?"

"Look, Mr. Joshua. Like I told you last time. I'm an officer of the court. Cases are brought before me, and I hear them without prejudice. The case in question has not been heard. Until that time, I am a neutral party and completely unbiased. I won't render a judgment without hearing the case."

A slight smile formed on Mr. Joshua's lips. "But, Madame Justice ..."

She cut him off, and her eyes narrowed as her face took on a stern look. "Let me be perfectly clear, sir. If you think you can come in here and try to strong-arm me into voting one way or another, you've got another thing coming. I can't be bribed, intimidated, or swayed in any way, shape, or form. And trying to do so is a federal offense."

"Madame Justice, I've not done any of those things you've mentioned. I'm merely wanting to articulate the position of my client ..."

Once again, she cut him off. But this time, she pointed to her watch as she did so. "Your two minutes are up, Mr. Joshua. You can leave here and tell your client I'll vote based on the facts of the case and nothing more."

She stood, her gaze focused on the door.

"Sorry to hear about your husband. It must have been such a loss for you." Mr. Joshua spoke in a tone mixed with sarcasm and disdain.

Mary froze.

"Who knew Asheville could be so dangerous?" Mr. Joshua asked. "I've always had a wonderful time at The Grove Park Inn when I've brought my lady friends for visits."

"Excuse me?" Mary's tone rose several octaves as she spoke. "What the hell did you just say?"

"I mean, let's be honest with each other, Mary. When you're banging as many hookers as Chuck did eventually the old ticker just can't keep up with all that excitement. Am I right? Although having a heart attack while you're nailing a hot piece of ass. Well, that can't be too bad of a way to go for any man."

Her eyes opened wider. *How did he know? The papers said he died of natural causes, and the marshal insisted those who knew the truth would only be part of the inner circle.*

A crimson hue covered her face as the rage within her grew. "How dare you ..."

Mr. Joshua pointed to the chair. "Take a seat, Mary."

Her gut said to walk out the door without turning back, but her brain told her to stay. Mr. Joshua had something else besides photos to try to blackmail her with. She sat back down. "Do you really think having pictures of my husband with a bunch of prostitutes is going to what? Get me to rule in favor of your client?"

He smirked and tapped his temple a few times with his index finger. "Well, it crossed my mind, yes."

Mary scowled at him. "It won't. Go ahead and release the photos, I don't give a shit. Chuck is dead anyway. But if you think I can be blackmailed into ..."

Mr. Joshua shook his head. "I'm not trying to blackmail you, Mary."

"Then what are you doing? What game are you playing?"

"I'm simply encouraging you on which way to vote on this case, which is of extreme importance to my client, and to be completely honest, to the entire country."

"You're full of shit, Mr. Joshua."

He put his hands up in mock disgust. "Sheesh, did you really think this was a shakedown? Of course not. I just want to remind you that you are the deciding vote in a case that is imperative for the people I represent to win. And I'm asking you to join the other four justices who will rule in favor of my client. Please, of course."

Mary couldn't believe the gall of the sanctimonious asshole. "Let me be clear, young man. I'll vote against your client if this is the game you're going to play."

"Wow! What happened to you being unbiased? Now you'll vote a certain way just to spite me and my client?"

"Guess all that unbiased talk went out the window when you tried to blackmail me." She put her palms firmly on the tabletop and rose. "And I'll tell the two U.S. Marshals outside to come arrest you as soon as I step outside. You'll be charged with obstruction of justice."

Mr. Joshua laughed. It was a loud, obnoxious laugh.

The tone startled her. She sat back down.

He waved his finger back and forth as he shook his head. "You'll do no such thing, Mary."

A bemused look spread over Mary's face. "And why not?"

Mr. Joshua raised his arm and spoke into the left cuff of his pressed shirt as he gazed out the window. "Paint him."

Mary followed Mr. Joshua's head movement and looked toward the sidewalk, seeing a red bead suddenly appear on the forehead of the U.S. Marshals tasked with protecting her. Phil looked around, oblivious to the dot directly above his nose and moving ever so slightly back and forth.

Her heart beat fast, and she looked back at Mr. Joshua.

"Pop!" he said, following it up by clapping his hands together. "Just like that, Mary. If you say a word about this conversation to anyone, those two marshals who guard you will be dead before you can climb into that fancy vehicle the tax-payers provide you. No one can know about our conversation. I mean your kids, other members of the court, even your dog, and especially not Frank Halter."

Her eyes widened at the mention of Frank's name.

Mr. Joshua continued. "Yes, the one and only Marshal of the Supreme Court. We know about your life, family, friends, and even what deodorant and shampoo you like. Good choice, by the way. The Native brand is of very good quality and better for the environment."

"How do you know …?"

Mr. Joshua shook his head. "I know everything, Mary. Not only do I know *everything*, but I see and hear everything, so don't think for a second you can tell someone about this conversation without it coming to my attention. Even your office, the inner sanctum, has ears. What was it you called Chuck the day the marshal came into your office and said your husband was dead?" He paused for a moment. "Oh, that's right I believe your exact words were, '*at least the fat fuck died alone.*' You remember saying that, don't you, Mary?"

Her throat tightened. Sweat formed on her upper lip. She didn't know how to respond. A slight tremble appeared in her left hand.

Mr. Joshua stood and pulled an envelope from under his jacket. "This is for you, Mary. Don't open it yet. I'll be in touch to tell you when to take a looksie at what's inside. You might need a little while to let our conversation sink in. You know, reconsider my client's generous proposal. My client expects an affirmative response next time we speak. Or … well, we don't want to go there … not yet!"

Mary was in a stupor. Fear overcame her and paralyzed her body from moving.

"Have a wonderful day, Your Honor, and don't forget we see, hear, and know all." Mr. Joshua turned his back on her and walked out the door. As he stepped onto the sidewalk, he smiled at Phil and then went in the opposite direction from where the Suburban was parked.

Mary buried her head in her hands for a few seconds and took several deep breaths, in through her nose, out through her mouth. *What the hell do I do?*

CHAPTER TWENTY-THREE

THE WHITE HOUSE

Nick sucked in a gulp of brisk fresh air as he exited the east entrance and made his way out of the White House at a hurried pace. It had been a late night at The Dubliner, and he had too many drinks. However, he felt the meetup was necessary and would prove productive. As with countless other nights since he took the job, he slept in his office on the worn-out leather couch.

The president returned from Camp David very early in the morning, and Sam was back at the same time. Even though he technically should have been off work and home resting, Nick's life revolved around the role of The Body Man. Taking a day off wasn't in his wheelhouse.

As he stepped outside, a slight tremor ran down his right arm. The tingle began near his shoulder, and made its way to the top of his fingers. He used his left hand to apply pressure, easing the involuntary movements. Nick needed a few minutes to clear his head, something difficult to do inside the constrictive walls of the West Wing. As he approached the east security checkpoint, Willy Daley stood statuesque, blocking the exit primarily secured by an eight-foot-tall wrought-iron gate. Willy's six-foot-four, two-hundred-thirty-pound frame painted an imposing figure against the backdrop of the impressive fence.

Willy's formidable posture softened slightly as Nick approached his position.

"Mr. Jordan," Willy announced in his booming voice as he stuck out his arm.

Nick grabbed the extended hand and returned the firm shake from the senior officer of the United States Secret Service Uniformed Division. "Willy, it's been a minute. How has Dolores been during her recovery?"

Willy's wife of thirty-eight years was diagnosed with an aggressive form of cancer eight weeks prior. The doctors mitigated the risk of death with a newly developed combination of chemotherapy and radiation. Early prognosis appeared positive, but she wasn't in the clear. Willy took some much-needed FMLA time to be with his wife as she battled the horrific disease. He returned to work a week prior, and today was the first time Nick had seen Willy since he came back.

He made the sign of the cross. "She's doing much better, Mr. Jordan, thanks for asking. The good Lord has seen fit not to take her from me. I give him thanks and all the glory every day. By the way, the bouquet of flowers and chocolates you sent sure lifted her spirits. And I really enjoyed the *Band of Brothers* DVD set you sent for me to watch. It helped me stay positive during the whole hospitalization process. Very kind of you to think of us during this time."

Nick grabbed Willy's arm and gave it a gentle squeeze. "Nonsense, Willy. I might not wear the badge anymore, but we are still part of the same brotherhood. I'm happy to know what I sent seemed to help. It's the least I could do."

Willy smiled as he opened the heavy gate so Nick could exit the property. "Headed to your usual spot?"

Nick nodded. "Yes, I'm a creature of habit at times, I guess."

Both men turned toward the White House as a firm, yet feminine voice came from the direction of the building's east exit.

"Nick, hold up!" the woman yelled.

He patted Willy on the shoulder and moved toward the approaching figure. "Guess my chat with Abe will need to wait a little bit. Give Dolores my best."

"I will, Mr. Jordan."

Nick met Sam halfway between the guard shack and the White House. "Jeez, I needed some fresh air and time away from this place. What is it?"

"I've been trying to call you for the past five minutes, but your phone kept going to voicemail," Sam said in a matter-of-fact tone.

"Yes, because I silenced the phone, Sam. Like I said, I needed a few minutes."

"I know, and I'm sorry, Nick, but you're needed in the Situation Room. I wouldn't be tracking you down if it wasn't dire."

Nick followed Sam as she quickly made her way back to the east entrance of the White House.

Sam looked back over her shoulder once they were inside the east wing. "Before you ask, I don't know anything, Nick. I was just told to find you and bring you to the Situation Room ASAP. That's the extent of my knowledge."

"Great," he replied.

⚬

Seven minutes later, Nick and Sam entered the secured Situation Room complex on the west wing's ground floor. Made up of not one room but a series of rooms it houses three conference rooms. The Situation Room is an intelligence management center that is comprised of almost 5,000 square feet. Staffed by close to one hundred thirty members of the National Security Council staff, its directive is to monitor and help deal with foreign and domestic conflicts. Insiders refer to the series of rooms as "the Whizzer."

A duty officer led Nick and Sam to the primary conference room, known as the J.F.K. room in honor of the former president, where top officials usually meet for secure briefings.

Once inside, Nick saw the President of the United States sitting at the head of the conference room table. Of the twelve available chairs, six on each side, not including the president's seat at the head of the table, only four black leather chairs were currently occupied. Gathered in the room besides the president was the Director of National Intelligence (DNI), the National Security Advisor (NSA), the Director of the Secret Service, and the head of Section Seven, a secretive part of the government known by very few.

President Thomas Collins gestured to the empty seat to his right. "Take a seat, Nick. There's been a development you need to know about." The president looked at Sam. "Thanks for tracking him down."

Sam nodded, "My pleasure, sir."

The large digital screen on the wall opposite Nick showed a real-time satellite image with the bolded words, *Fundäo Island – Rio de Janeiro*, in the top right corner.

With the words on the screen alone, Nick had a pretty good idea what this was all about.

President Collins cleared his throat. "A body has washed ashore on an island in central Rio. Details are still sketchy, but a positive DNA just came back."

Nick didn't have to wait for the president to say anything else. He knew exactly which former Body Man had retired in that portion of South America. "How did they kill Jacob? And who found his body?"

Chapter Twenty-Four

Manhattan

The clock was ticking and the longer Geno took, the greater the chance he'd get his ass chewed out from the boss. He rented a white box van and had a friend print off two magnetic signs he affixed to either side of the van that read Brooklyn Electrical. His cover when he searched each of the eight houses was that they were electricians fixing some faulty wiring, in case anyone they ran into questioned them. They even wore gray jumpsuits with the fake insignia of the electrical company sewn onto the chest. As cover goes, he did a pretty good job with little notice.

He almost went with Brooklyn Plumbing, but he knew squat about what it took to be a plumber. He worked with an electrician during his summer breaks in high school before joining the military. The older guy, a friend of his fathers, wanted him to be his apprentice, but Geno was straight up with the guy and told him he needed a summer job only and wasn't interested in working a trade job as his career. Little did Geno know trade jobs would lead to the new class of millionaires in the coming years. But at least he could talk the talk if anyone questioned him and his guys when they searched the eight residences spread throughout the five boroughs of New York City.

Geno had four guys with him. Matteo, Leo, Gus, and Trey. They were men he trusted and worked with when discretion was needed.

Only five employees owned cars, and they could easily search those at the office. They hadn't found any files inside the vehicles.

First up, they drove to Brooklyn. Beverly Crumpton rented a one-bedroom apartment in a brownstone on Marlborough Street. She worked in the accounting department, and from what a few of the girls said, Beverly, with her raspy voice from years of smoking, appeared to be a busybody and loved to put her nose where it didn't belong. Geno had no reason to choose her over the other seven, but he had to start somewhere. Back at the office, he had one of his guys keep an eye on her in case she left for some strange reason and headed home. His guy could give them a heads up, so they didn't have an incident occur as they searched for the file.

Before they got out of the van, Geno set the guidelines. "Look, lads. This isn't a smash-and-grab job. Leave the place like you found it. We are here to find the file but not toss the place. I know none of you are campers, but if you were, this would be a *leave no trace* situation. Get in, try to find the file, and get out. These employees don't need to know we were here, or it'll be all of our asses!"

Geno looked back and forth between all four men: Matteo, Leo, Gus, and Trey, who all nodded when he asked, "Got it?"

Beverly lived on the second floor in apartment 2C. Leo had the snap gun, also known as a lock pick gun, and within fifteen seconds, the tumbler lock disengaged, and they entered her apartment. Immediately when they stepped inside, it was clear Beverly didn't keep the cleanest place. Discarded, half-eaten Chinese food cartons lined the kitchen counter. A large picture of her late husband Billy next to the meal remnants.

"Jeez, she's a slob," Gus said as they entered the apartment.

Each of the four men had an RFID hand scanner they could use to search for tags. The scanners had a maximum range of three feet, so they had to move slowly and make sure they searched each room thoroughly. Geno assigned each man a room, and they searched every nook and cranny for any RFID signal. They also visually looked around and even physically searched drawers, cabinets, and under furniture.

It took them about forty-five minutes to search the apartment and say with certainty that the file was not present.

Careful to leave the messy dwelling exactly as they found it, the men slipped out, re-engaged the lock, and climbed into the van.

Geno crossed off the first address from his list of eight residences. "One down, fellas, seven more to go."

"She might not have taken the file," Gus said, "but they need to fire that broad for how she keeps her apartment. What a dump. My college dorm was cleaner than that place, and trust me, that's saying something."

Geno nodded and started up the van. "One more stop in Brooklyn before we head to Queens. We'll probably only get into three places today, so we'll need to pick up our pace tomorrow. The third one today is quite large, and they have a dog, so that one may be tricky."

"How do we deal with the pooch?" Matteo asked.

Geno held up the tranquilizer gun. "Pew-pew. You get to take the shot, smart guy."

"Aww man, I don't want to shoot a dog."

Geno frowned. "Jeez. It's a tranquilizer dart. He'll just fall asleep."

"Even so," Matteo said. "It's a dog. I love dogs."

"Would you love the dog if it gnawed on your leg or maybe bit your sac?"

Matteo extended his hand. "What do you know. I'll take the gun."

"That's the spirit," Geno said.

Chapter Twenty-Five

Paris

Merci de Atta did not like being told no, but it wasn't leftover adolescent rebellion or any form of entitlement, where she felt her opinions mattered more than everyone else's. She just despised being caged and repressed, and after years of forced submission, she promised herself nobody, no man or woman, no figure of authority would ever control her again.

"I didn't fly to Paris to stay in a goddamn hotel room." The words came out of her mouth like a hiss from a serpent.

Marcus put his hands up. "Look, babe, I get it. But I think it's best we lay low for the time."

"Noooo ... I don't think you do, or you wouldn't be insisting I stay holed up in this room."

"And I don't think you fully grasp the ramifications of your actions."

"Yes, Marcus, I killed a pimp. The man who sold my body to the scum of the earth in and around Paris when I was still legally a child." Her mouth shape formed a snarl. "Oh, I get what I did."

Marcus shook his head. "No, babe, you don't. You killed a pimp in the middle of the Arc de Triomphe. There were dozens of witnesses, and traffic cameras were plastered all over the roundabout."

"And your point is what exactly?"

"They have your image. They have video of you shooting a man in broad daylight after a chase on scooters through the streets of Paris."

"A pimp. I killed a fuckin' pimp in broad daylight. And yup, they most certainly have video of me shooting a pimp. Get it right."

He stepped closer to her and put his hand on her shoulder.

Merci pulled away, her anger visible on her face. She walked toward the balcony and paused at the doorway, looking out over the Paris skyline. They had moved hotels to stay closer to the Sacre-Coeur, hoping to blend into the city.

"Is my face plastered all over the news or papers?" she asked.

Marcus frowned. "You know the answer is no. At least not at the moment."

"And I'm already wanted by Interpol. What President Collins did for me only applied to the United States."

"So what's another murder on the rap sheet?"

Merci rolled her eyes. "I know how to disappear, Marcus."

"I'm well aware of that. But I think you need to be smart, and going out in Paris is not a smart idea. The facial recognition system here is not as vibrant as, say, London, but it is still active. The last thing you need to do is kill a cop who spots you, or worse, you might get caught."

Merci bit on her lower lip. Deep down, she knew he was right. He normally was when it entailed logical matters. But she rarely admitted defeat, even to the man she loved. "And what do you suggest? We hole up in Paris indefinitely?"

"Actually, no, I think we need an exfil plan. Getting out of Paris sooner rather than later would be wise, and the less we use public transportation, the better."

She glared at him but said nothing at first. "Traveling on my passport, even one of the numerous fakes, isn't smart. We both know the cameras at the airport and passport control are getting better each year."

"I agree. You need to stay in the shadows. At least let things die down before you emerge."

He was right, but she hated to admit it. She paced around the small hotel room for several minutes. "Get a rental car. We can drive to Brussels."

Marcus pursed his lips, then nodded a moment later. "Actually, that sounds like a good start."

"I have a former business acquaintance who has a shop in Brussels."

"Freddy?"

"Yes, you remember meeting him in Antwerp that time?"

"How could I forget? Don't you remember Freddy and I had to bury two bodies that night?"

Merci shrugged. "I was up for over forty-eight hours on that contract, and some of the details are fuzzy."

"And after we meet Freddy, then what?"

"Well, he has a boat docked in Blankenberge used to smuggle all sorts of illegal contraband off the mainland. He'll be able to get us across the channel into England. I've got some markers I can call in. We need to get to Oxford."

"Why Oxford?"

"We can catch a flight back to the US. Off the record, of course."

"You sure, you want to go back so soon?"

"Like you said, I committed a very public murder in the streets of Paris. Party's over. Time to head home."

"What you did was completely impulsive and put you at tremendous risk. But I know why you did it, and I understand why you acted in the heat of the moment. I guess you can sleep better knowing he won't harm any more girls." Marcus put his arms out, and she walked over to him. The anger from a few minutes earlier dissipated with each step.

Merci embraced him. "If I had to do it all over again, I'd do it in a heartbeat. I'd shoot that fuck on the steps of the Paris Police Prefecture while he stood next to the French President if I had the chance."

Marcus's thick arms tightened around her as he drew her closer. "I know you would, babe. And somehow I'm sure you would get away with it."

Chapter Twenty-Six

One World Trade Center

Mr. Joshua watched as the obese man spun the pen around on the table counter-clockwise as he glanced out the floor-to-ceiling window. His gaze appeared fixated on a tugboat slowly churning its way along the Hudson River headed in the direction of Ellis Island. The large man stopped spinning the pen and touched his short, pudgy finger to his lips. "So, essentially, you threatened her."

Mr. Joshua nodded slowly. "More or less."

"And how did she take it?"

"She's a Supreme Court justice. The factory that creates them adds an extra pinch of stoic to every model."

The obese man pursed his lips, seemingly not thrilled with the analogy. "Did she seem scared?"

"I think so. Her body language changed dramatically after I stated that everything she said and did was being monitored."

"Good, maybe she'll finally play ball."

"That's what I think will happen," Mr Joshua stated.

"Move forward with Merci."

"Offer her the contract?"

The obese man grunted. "Yes. And double the amount."

"It was already going to be generous."

"Just do it. Don't be stingy when you're playing with house money. Haven't you been to Vegas before?"

"More times than I count. Even spent time in the Clark County lockup."

The obese man chuckled. "I hope she was worth it."

"They are all worth it, at least for a few hours. Until they are not, and eventually all of them are not."

A slight smirk formed in the corner of the overweight man's thick lips. "That's wisdom if I've ever heard any."

Mr. Joshua raised his eyebrows. "Learned that from years of experience chasing skirts."

"Missing file update?" The obese man's expression turned serious.

"Geno and his men started searching house by house. They've narrowed it down to eight employees."

His eyebrows narrowed. "And?"

"We'll find it," Mr. Joshua said confidently.

"You better."

"I let Geno know the seriousness of that file."

"Did you tell him what was inside?" The obese man's face turned to a snarl as he asked the question.

"Of course not. Only you, I, and the client knows what those pages reveal."

The obese man nodded. "Good. By the way, another one of our clients called early this morning."

"Which one?"

"The microchip manufacturer, Cyberdyne."

"And?"

"It appears a few of the scientists responsible for the creation of a new micro-processor might have loose lips."

"We all know what that does to ships."

"Our client asked if we could arrange their reassignment to another location."

"You mean terminated?" Mr. Joshua asked.

"No, their intent was clear. These scientists are brilliant, and what they created is cutting edge. Killing them would not be beneficial to Cyberdyne's bottom line."

"Where will we relocate them to?"

"The client wants them to be moved to the facility in Costa Rica near Cerro Chirripo."

"When?"

The obese man shrugged as much as he could with very little neck. "Yesterday."

Mr. Joshua stood. "We're a little thin at the moment, but I'll get right on it." As he turned and made his way to the office door, the loud, boisterous voice called out behind him.

"There are a lot of moving parts right now."

Mr. Joshua turned before he opened the door. "Yes, there is."

"You sure, based on the critical nature of each piece, you don't need some assistance?"

"I work best alone. You know that." Mr. Joshua didn't wait for a response. He opened the door and stepped toward the expansive lobby, making a beeline for the attractive administrative assistant. "Miss Topintzis," he said as he stopped in front of the exotic woman's desk.

Her face beamed as he approached. "Mr. Joshua. Are you free to get a drink later?"

"I think I can make time for another tryst, I mean, drink. How about we meet at The Dancer?" He looked down at his oversized Omega watch. "Say nine o'clock tonight?"

"I'll be there," she replied, giving a not-too-subtle wink.

CHAPTER TWENTY-SEVEN

MANHATTAN

UPPER EAST SIDE

Sheryl Hopping walked into the FedEx office at the corner of Seventy-Eighth Street and Lexington Avenue. Her pulse raced like a thoroughbred as it sprinted around an oval-shaped track.

As she approached the center of the store, she had to clear her throat twice before she could speak. The lanky girl, with hot pink hair, a hooped nose ring, and a large neck tattoo, who worked behind the counter gave her a blasé look as she approached. Sheryl removed the folder from her oversized teal purse and handed it to the girl whose nametag read Liza.

"Yeah, what do you need today?" Liza asked in a less than enthusiastic tone.

"Three copies of this." Sheryl handed the folder to the girl.

Liza looked at the contents of the file. "Yeah, that's easy enough. Anything else?"

"Three mailing envelopes also, so I can mail them out after you make the copies."

"Got it." Liza reached under the countertop and removed three white nine-by-eleven envelopes, plus an order form for each. "You can fill the addresses out on these sheets as I get those copies going."

Sheryl took out the sticky note with the three addresses and wrote the first one. Her hand visibly shook as she held the pen and copied the address. She took a deep breath to calm her nerves. A twinge of doubt crept up as she wondered if sending these three people a copy of the file might endanger them somehow.

Liza returned with the copies.

Sheryl took the three stacks of papers, which were still warm, and laid them side by side on the counter, removing three sheets of paper from another folder she had in her purse. She paper-clipped the personalized letters to each file and stuffed the three stacks into the mailing envelopes. Once she had it correct, she handed the three white FedEx envelopes back to Liza.

It took Liza a few minutes to enter the address provided into the system and print off mailing labels. "Tracking numbers for each package are on the bottom of the receipt." She handed the receipt to Sheryl. "You can track each one's progress by using this number." Liza circled the tracking numbers for each envelope on the receipt.

Sheryl thanked Liza and headed toward the door.

Outside, her pulse still raced. She headed three blocks west, deciding to take a stroll through Central Park to walk off her anxiety. When Sheryl reached the Met, she bought a soft, salted pretzel from a street vendor parked in front of the museum. Breaking off pieces of the pretzel, she sat on the steps and ate it as an endless stream of tourists and locals paraded by her, unaware of the angst inside her mind.

She considered the fallout from sending the files, but dismissed the guilt that crept into her mind. If her worst fear occurred and something happened to her, then she needed to ensure that the truth of what the pages contained saw the light of day.

As she chewed on the soft pretzel, she thought about what to do with the original file. Taking it back to the office was out of the question, but she wondered if she should bring it to her apartment on Eightieth Street. A safe deposit box seemed like a good idea, but she also thought needing to lock up the document might be slightly paranoid.

Her cell phone rang, and she pulled it from her purse. The caller's ID said *Ella Hamilton*, the elderly woman who lived directly across the hall from her apartment.

Ella didn't even wait for Sheryl to say hello. "Are you having electrical issues in your apartment, Miss Sheryl?"

The abruptness of the statement and the strange question confused her. "Umm, no. Why do you ask?"

"Well, I was trying to mind my own P's and Q's, but I saw some men enter your apartment. There's an electrical van parked out front."

"I didn't call anyone," Sheryl said. "And don't know of any issues."

"Maybe the super let them in?"

"I'm not far away. I'll come by and see what's going on. Thanks for the heads-up, Ella."

"Anytime, dearie."

The call disconnected, and Sheryl stood. She had no idea why electricians were in her apartment. As she made her way down Fifth Avenue, she tried calling the apartment supervisor, but his phone went to voicemail after the fourth ring.

What is going on? She quickened her pace and discarded the wrapper from the pretzel in a trash can a block from the Met.

Chapter Twenty-Eight

Georgetown

Mary Brown sat at her kitchen table with an agonized expression covering her normally joyful face. For the first time since the day Chuck died, she was all alone. In the past, solitude filled her with peace and comfort. Not this time. No calmness engulfed her alone in the house. Anger slowly pulsated throughout her body as she sat rigid in the high-back wooden chairs, and her eyes narrowed as she focused on the white envelope Mr. Joshua had given her at the coffee shop. Two fingers on her left hand rhythmically tapped against the table's polished surface.

As a judge, she mastered controlling her temper and not letting her emotions get the best of her. Erratic, passion-fueled judges rarely reached the top echelon of the judiciary.

Sure, over the years, various entities tried to sway her decisions in cases, but she never crossed any lines. Nobody had ever attempted to blatantly blackmail her into voting one way or the other. That is, until Mr. Joshua approached her and handed over the pictures of Chuck with his whores. The audacity of the intimidation shocked her, but because of the sensitive nature of the photos, she decided against sharing what occurred with anyone else.

She figured that after she turned him down, the matter would go away. Clearly, she was wrong.

Part of her wanted to open the white envelope to see what he would try to use now to sway her into voting the way his client wanted. As she picked up the envelope, a voice within told her to rip it up and throw it away. Whatever he included inside the envelope would only lead to more pain, and the bottom line was that she wouldn't let someone blackmail her.

She wasn't sure what game Mr. Joshua was trying to play, but she did know that no matter what, she couldn't let him win.

As she sat at the table, a thought occurred to her.

Was the house bugged?

He said her office at the Supreme Court was and this turned out to be a revelation she had difficulty believing. However, Mr. Joshua repeated verbatim what she said to the marshal, so she had to assume it was true. With her office compromised, it only made sense that her house would be as well. Her eyes darted around the room, looking for anything out of place. Could he have eyes on her right now, or heard everything she said in her home?

The fact that Mr. Joshua might have that much access paralyzed her with fear.

A deep-seated desire rose from within, telling her she must reach out to someone and share what was happening. But her inner circle hadn't changed in many years.

She left the table and headed upstairs to her study, next door to her master suite. Mary spent many hours in the study scrutinizing legal briefs and writing opinions. The desk and her leather chair acted like trusted friends when the house felt lonely and nobody else was home. She opened the bottom right drawer at her desk and removed the stack of yellow legal pads that filled the space. With the drawer empty, she carefully removed the false bottom, revealing a space three inches deep that covered the entire drawer area. Three burner phones lay at the bottom.

Mary removed one of the phones. The battery was fifty percent charged, so she went straight to the text icon at the bottom right of the screen.

She held the phone for several minutes and considered whether what she was about to do made sense. Would it do more harm or good?

Mary had a solid friendship with her chiropractor, Dr. David Richards. Her back gave her fits, and a dear friend recommended Dave when she moved to Georgetown. The relationship was purely platonic, after all Dave was happily married, but she valued his opinion and thought he might have some sage advice on how to move forward. He knew about Chuck's indiscretions with prostitutes, and at times she reached out to Dave discreetly for his counsel. The only question was how she could ditch her protective detail, and if the house was being watched, how could she sneak out without Mr. Joshua knowing?

Meeting with Dr. Dave was risky, but she felt so alone and lost that she needed to try. She agonized for almost an hour before she picked up her cell phone and sent several concise texts.

It's Mary.

There's something going on.

I need to talk with you.

It's important.

I can't let my security detail know I'm sneaking out of my house.

Will you meet me?

She didn't expect an immediate response. She wondered if the recipient would even reply, since even though she said who she was, the number would not be one Dave recognized. She wouldn't blame him if he ignored the texts.

As she stared at the phone, it vibrated, letting her know a new message had arrived.

It said:

Of course, Mary. Where do you want to meet?

She considered her reply.

Before she could respond, she heard the text notification ding on her primary cell phone, an iPhone, which sat on her desk. She focused on the iPhone as she picked it up and clicked the messages app.

The message had no number. It said *UNKNOWN* where the phone number should be.

Mary swallowed hard as she opened the message.

There were four messages, and the icon showed that a fifth one was being typed. They were all direct.

You need to text Dr Richards back, NOW!

Tell him everything is ok.

False alarm.

You're struggling after the loss of Chuck.

She never felt her heart beat so fast, and she had experienced labor twice as a younger woman. The fifth message popped up and caused her to panic.

Let me be clear, Mary. If you try to leave this house and meet with David Richards, he'll be dead before you make it out the front door. Are we clear? If you try that shit ever again, someone close to you will pay the ultimate price for your reckless ideas. Like I told you. We see all, hear all, and know all.

Mary had no choice. She texted Dave back and said exactly what she was told.

She had her answer. Not only was her office bugged, but so was her house and even her lines of communication. A deep sense of dread permeated her as she poured herself a drink and retreated to her living room couch. The thought of someone watching her as she sat in her home caused shivers to run throughout her body.

CHAPTER TWENTY-NINE

THE WHITE HOUSE

THE WEST WING

After the meeting in the Situation Room and learning about Jacob's death, the rest of the morning became a blur for Nick. Sam met him at the Navy Mess, a small dining facility next to the Situation Room in the basement of the West Wing. In a perfect world, The Body Man and his apprentice would work opposite shifts and rest up when each was not "on the clock." Sam worked a tremendous number of hours but maintained a somewhat stable schedule.

Nick did no such thing.

After meeting with Sam, he swung by his office to find Abby Wright standing outside the door. A large, wrapped item leaned against the wall near where she stood.

Nick pointed at the item. "Hey, Abby, whatcha got?"

Abby smiled. "A gift for you."

Nick motioned at the door. "Come on in. I don't like surprises normally, but it must be pretty good if it's from you."

Abby carried the mysterious gift inside and handed it to Nick as they stood beside his desk.

Nick could tell by the size that it was some sort of framed item. As he tore open the wrapping paper, his eyes grew wide, and he recognized the item immediately.

The gift was a framed movie poster from his favorite movie growing up, *Back To The Future*. And as a special bonus, it appeared to be signed by all the actors who played key roles in the filming: Marty, Doc, Lorraine, and Biff.

"No way! Abby, this is awesome. How did you get it signed?"

Abby chuckled. "You know me, Nick. I'm kinda a nerd. I went to the Los Angeles Comic Con last month. And as you can see, I happened upon the cast. They were signing memorabilia, and I immediately thought of you."

"Can I give you a hug without getting sued for harassment?" Nick asked with a wide grin plastered over his face.

"I mean, I better get a hug!" Abby exclaimed.

They exchanged a warm embrace as friends do.

"Thank you for this. I'll treasure it forever." Nick placed a hand on his heart.

"I know you are a minimalist, but I thought you may have a spot for some retro eighties item."

"Hell yeah, it will be displayed with pride. I might even put it up on the wall next to the framed Farrah Fawcett poster in my mancave." Nick winked as he said the last part.

"You boys and blondes in red bathing suits."

Nick pursed his lips and shrugged. "No matter what these woke weirdos might try and say, you can't take the boy outside of the dudes who grew up in the seventies, eighties or nineties."

Abby laughed. "Thank goodness for that."

They talked for another ten minutes before Abby left, and Nick sat on the worn leather couch. He stared at the poster and could not wipe the grin off his face for a while.

⸻ ❧ ⸻

The role of The Body Man was pretty much Nick's entire existence. After the chain of events surrounding Mogul, the previous president, Nick, changed in untold ways. There was the physical alteration. Those closest to him noticed the subtle changes, but the events also affected him in other areas. He owned a townhouse in Vienna, Virginia, about sixteen miles from the White House. Prior to his kidnapping and torture at the hands of The Sanctum, he often stayed at his townhouse while not working. It served as his safe space, his castle, you might say. But not anymore. The home still contained most of his belongings, but it no longer acted as a refuge. He considered selling it on more than one occasion, but with his elderly neighbor Rose Lewis across the street, he felt obligated to hold on to the place. Even though Rose was rarely home anymore. She stayed with her son in Colorado most of the time after the incident that took place in her home because of Nick's occupation. The altercation spared Rose, but it cost the FBI Agent Wes Russell his life.

Already a private person to begin with, Nick withdrew even more after what occurred. Most nights, he slept on the worn leather couch in his West Wing office. Sometimes he would stay at the Hay-Adams Hotel two blocks from the White House. Unknown to most people, the government always maintains four opulent suites and six deluxe rooms on the seventh floor of the luxurious hotel. The rooms are set aside for foreign dignitaries and guests of the White House or other agencies. Some notable guests included Amelia Earhart, Charles Lindbergh, Sinclair Lewis, and Frank Underwood. Even POTUS #44 stayed there with his family before taking the oath of office because the Blair House was occupied the night before his inauguration. Marilyn Monroe visited the hotel occasionally, but that tale is for another time. A secret passageway accessed via the lowest level leads to a tunnel that runs under Lafayette Square and connects to the basement in the White House. This is the route Nick would take anytime the president forced him to call it a night and stay in one of the government rooms at the Hay-Adams. He kept the room key 7124 in his pocket at all times. There was also an entrance point to the same tunnel leading into the White House basement via the St. Regis Hotel, a block from the Hay-Adams. Both hotels were utilized discreetly over the years to usher VIPs into the White House without the press or prying eyes knowing about the visits.

⸺◆⸺

After lunch with Sam, Nick headed back to the office in the Eisenhower Executive Office Building. He checked in with Luke, who had nothing of substance to report from Jakarta, and made multiple phone calls to operatives who were trying to track down the names he had given them.

Nick knew enough about investigations to realize that you must temper expectations and can't force a resolution, especially when there are so many unknown variables still in play. However, the lack of progress bothered him to his core.

A knock at the door caused him to look up from the file he was currently poring over.

The person who banged on the door didn't wait for an invitation. Hank Norris strutted inside the office and approached the chair across from Nick's desk. He sat down with a wide grin plastered across his face.

Nick stared at him but didn't say anything. His eyes narrowed on the man he replaced. The former Body Man himself.

"What is it?" Hank asked. "My fly down or something. You're looking at me weirdly."

"I'm just surprised."

"At what?"

"To see you back in the White House complex. First, it was Café du Monde that warned me about the danger I faced. Then here in D.C., you gave me the intel on Senator Goldstein making inquiries about me. And now we've come full circle, and you're back on White House property. Never thought I would see that day."

"Yeah, well, the events surrounding The Sanctum changed the paradigm for all of us. Now, didn't it?"

"It appears that way. But, it's good to see you back here anyway," Nick spoke sincerely. He gestured to the cabinet on the far wall. "Can I offer you a spirit?"

"POTUS lets you have a liquor cabinet in the office?"

Nick smiled. "Preacher never comes over here, but if he did, I would be surprised if he would say anything." Nick pointed at one bottle in particular, lined up on top of the cabinet. "Have a nip of Four Branches Bourbon. It has your name on it."

"Ah, I see Mr. Trott was either here or sent you a goodie box."

"Actually, I had dinner with Mike and Cheryl in Budapest a few months back while on a trip with POTUS. He sent a few Founders Blend bottles back with me."

"Nice. Well, I'll be honored to have a sip to remember."

Nick got up, moved to the cabinet, and poured two glasses of amber liquid into thick tumblers. He handed one to the former Body Man. "Good to see you, Hank. This is a rare treat."

"Same to you, my friend. And this is one of the few places I can go now without a security detail."

Nick frowned. "It's for your personal protection, Hank. You know the threats The Body Man role faces right now."

"I get it, but I'm not used to being protected. I'm used to doing the protecting."

"You don't need to tell me twice. I know this is very unorthodox. But until we figure out what is going on, it's necessary. You got my text about Jacob, right?"

Hank nodded. "A damn fine agent, even if he did mess up big time. The role of The Body Man was better for having him back in the day."

"I know being back here is not ideal, but would you be willing to go to Rio and run point for me? See what you can dig up?"

Hank stood like his pants had suddenly burst into flames. "You don't have to ask me twice. Rio has hookers and blow, right?"

Nick let out a hearty laugh. "I'm sending you to Rio, not Colombia."

"Oh, that's right, I knew some agents had some fun in one of those South American countries a few years back."

"Yeah, they were naughty boys. And I'm sure you know exactly where they were. Nothing gets past you, Hank."

"In all seriousness, hookers and blow aside." Hank winked and had a wide grin plastered across his face. "I told you I would help anyway, anytime, and getting out of D.C. is a bonus."

Nick tossed back his Four Branches and extended his hand. Hank grabbed it and gave a firm shake.

"I never thought we would work together again," Nick said. "And I wish the circumstances were different, but I'm glad to have you on board."

Hank smiled. "Nick, you were a tremendous apprentice, and to be honest, I think you've been a much more astute Body Man than I ever was or ever could be. Like I told you before, I'll go to hell and back for you. Just point me in the direction of where the devil is and what you want me to do to him."

"You were a superb teacher, Hank, and I don't deserve such high praise. Sit down for a few minutes, and I'll show you what we have on Rio and Jacob's death. We'll figure out a game plan and get you down to South America quickly."

"Can I ask you a question?" Hank asked.

Nick nodded. "Yes, of course. What's up?"

"It's about the list of names you found attached to the chief's body." Hank pointed to the list that hung behind Nick's desk.

"Sure, what do you want to know?"

"I know the investigation is continuing, and you have raised more questions than you have answered. But what does your gut tell you?" Hank pointed to his midsection. "What does your insides say is going on?"

Nick looked around the room. His eyes lingered upward at the presidential seal atop the ceiling, then settled back on Hank.

The two men locked eyes.

"I think it's a takedown, plain and simple."

Hank's eyes squinted. "A takedown of the role itself or something bigger?"

"Bigger, Hank. And it will be quite the *Downfall* if my worst fears are realized. Let's just hope my suspicions aren't correct."

Chapter Thirty

Kidlington, England

London Oxford Airport

Merci and Marcus approached the light blue hangar, the structure farthest away from the main terminal at the London Oxford Airport. A sharply dressed man greeted them at the side door and led them inside the expansive metal structure.

Once inside, an all-black Gulfstream G650ER with a yellow tail glistened under the bright overhead fluorescent lights. The sharply dressed man walked Merci and Marcus toward the staircase leading to the plane. A woman dressed in a form-fitting teal dress met them at the base of the stairs.

"Miss de Atta, a pleasure to see you again." The woman extended her hand and lowered her head as she spoke.

Merci received her hand and noticed the firm grip as they shook. "Nice to see you again, Jasmine. Is your boss here?"

Before the woman could answer, a man exited the plane and descended the steps. The man wore gray silk pants and a white shirt unbuttoned far enough down to display his rug-like salt and pepper chest hair. Thick gold necklaces hung around his neck, completing his ensemble, while gold rimmed aviator glasses covered his eyes. He raised his arms above his head as he saw the two guests. In a loud booming voice, which was heavily accented, he said, "Merci, Marcus, welcome to Con Air!"

Marcus smiled at the obvious reference to the Nick Cage movie, which he fancied.

While Merci let out an audible laugh. "Laszlo," she said.

Laszlo stepped onto the polished concrete floor and embraced Merci like long-lost friends.

"My God, you look good." Laszlo stepped away and took in her figure from head to toe. "Like always. Somehow your figure only enhances as you get older. How is that possible?"

"A woman never gives away her secrets," Merci said. "At least not for free."

Marcus stood just off to the side but said nothing. He was quite used to men making comments about her body, and it didn't bother him since he knew whose bed her fancy shoes would be under later that night.

Laszlo Tolvaj, a Hungarian-born opportunist, turned to Marcus. "Mr. Rollings, it's good to see you again. I trust you are keeping our African princess safe in this extremely dangerous world."

Marcus grunted and rolled his eyes in an exaggerated fashion. "You and I both know she marches to her own drum, Laszlo. If anyone keeps someone safe, it is her doing so for us."

"Valid point, my friend." Laszlo patted Marcus's upper arm in a firm manner several times.

"Thanks for making room for us," Merci replied. "Especially on such short notice."

"Of course. I heard about that nasty business that took place in Paris."

"Jean-Luc had it coming. He's lucky I didn't have more time to make him suffer. I would have liked to feed his balls to whatever creatures troll the murky waters of the Seine."

"Without a doubt, my princess. I was glad to hear you could finally exact your revenge."

"You're sure we won't have to go through passport control in Washington?" Merci asked.

Laszlo frowned. It appeared the question might have insulted him. "My dear, if that were to occur, I'd have a handful of unhappy passengers on my jet. People using my services are doing so to ensure they enter the United States away from the prying eyes of the all-seeing alphabet agencies."

"Just double-checking. I can normally enter without incident, but after what happened in Paris, I don't want to push my luck."

"Absolutely. You were smart to call me."

Merci pointed to the jet. "She's good-looking."

"Ah, yes. Do you like the color scheme?"

"Yes, looks like a mangrove snake. Beautiful and slightly deadly."

Laszlo smiled broadly. "Like yourself, my princess."

"Touché," Merci replied.

He gestured to the stairs. "Enough small talk. Let's get you in and ensure you are comfortable for your flight." Laszlo led them up the Gulfstream stairs as he continued talking. "The cabin is equipped with Wi-Fi, and the stewardesses can get you just about anything you need, comfort, food, or drink-wise."

He led them inside the cabin with the exuberance of a father showing off his newborn for the first time.

Inside the plane, the color scheme was all white. Twelve plush leather captain chairs lined the plane, six on each side, with ornate glass tables shared by the two chairs facing each other.

Laszlo showed them to the only two open seats.

Merci surveyed the cabin the moment she stepped onto the plane. Besides the three young and extremely attractive flight attendants, she sized up the ten other passengers on the Gulfstream. Purely by glancing at facial features and dress, she surmised that four appeared Middle Eastern, two Asian, two Eastern European, and the final two looked South American. A regular smorgasbord of international criminals who could not risk entering the United States through proper channels.

"If you require anything at all on the flight, let one of my girls know." Laszlo kissed Merci on both cheeks and patted Marcus on the back of the shoulder.

"You're not joining us on the flight across the pond?" Merci asked.

"No, my dear, my business interests keep me in the UK these days."

"Another time, then," she said.

"I can't wait," he responded. "Let me know next time you are in London, and I will take you and Marcus to The Berkeley. Marcus Wareing is a dear friend, and you are guaranteed to have a delectable meal."

"Sounds like a plan," Merci replied.

Laszlo kissed her hand, left the cabin, and descended the airstairs.

Three minutes later, the aircraft's forward door was closed, and one of the attendants took their initial drink and food order. They both decided on a stiff drink, for obvious reasons.

At cruising altitude, Merci fired up her laptop and got online. The icon at the bottom of her screen indicated she had a new email.

Merci opened the email. Her eyes widened as she recognized who sent the cryptic message.

Marcus watched her expression change from curiosity to shock. "What is it, babe?"

"Son of a bitch," she replied.

CHAPTER THIRTY-ONE

MANHATTAN

Geno looked both ways down the hall and confirmed the coast was clear. The building did not employ security cameras, so he didn't have to contend with the hassle of disabling them or wiping the data clean.

He tapped Leo on the shoulder, indicating it was safe to proceed. Leo crouched in front of the door, almost like he stopped to tie his shoes, and used the lock pick gun to disengage the lock in seconds.

Deadbolts are such a false assurance, Geno thought. He had no way of knowing that a set of eyes belonging to an elderly African American woman who lived across the hall followed their movements from her peephole.

Ella Hamilton watched intently as Geno and his team entered Sheryl's apartment. As soon as they entered she placed the call to Sheryl.

As the men breached the doorframe, Geno activated the stopwatch function on the Timex Ironman Triathlon watch he wore since his military days.

They were officially on the clock.

Inside the apartment, the team got to work. This being their third break-in of the day, the guys found a flow and went from room to room with confidence and exceptional speed. Each of the four men moved their RFID hand scanners in a left-to-right pattern as they passed through the rooms. When faced with taller items like bookshelves, dressers, and closets, they pivoted to an up-and-down motion.

Like many renters in Manhattan, Sheryl's apartment was modest, and by modest, it meant small. TFG paid Sheryl well, but not that well. Comprising a galley-style kitchen, bathroom, living room, three closets, and a single bedroom, the apartment measured less than five hundred square feet. For some who live in the heart of NYC, the square footage would be seen as reasonable, while those with extreme wealth have walk-in closets in their brownstone and penthouses bigger than Cheryl's entire place.

Geno figured it should take them less than fifteen minutes to search the apartment.

Matteo, Leo, Gus, and Trey assembled back in the kitchen. Geno looked down at the stopwatch. Thirteen minutes and forty-five seconds showed on the face of the watch. "Anything?" he asked.

The four men shook their heads in unison.

"I found Molly," Gus said.

Molly was Sheryl's cat. Geno warned the men that there would be a cat somewhere in the apartment, and above all, they had to make sure they didn't let her out.

"Where was she?" Geno asked.

"Under the bed," Gus said. "She hissed at me, but besides that, she seemed to be, well, a cat."

"Cat's are assholes," Matteo muttered.

Geno shrugged. "You're one to talk."

Matteo winked, "Game respects game."

"Anything else?" Geno asked.

"Nothing," Trey, the youngest guy on his crew, said. He was the one with dirty blond hair. "The place appears clean, boss."

"Shit." Geno glanced down at the paper he removed from his pants pocket. "I would have bet good money on Sheryl being the one who had the file. That only leaves us a couple more to search. We've gotta find that damn document."

"If it's not here, it's not here, boss," Matteo replied.

"I know." Geno spoke in a resigned tone as he turned and headed for the door. He looked out the peephole, which showed the hallway clear, and turned the doorknob.

Sheryl reached the entrance to her apartment building at Eightieth Street and Lexington out of breath. She panted hard and placed her hands on her knees as she took in a large gasp of air. The jog for five city blocks from the Met to her apartment physically drained her. As she looked around, she noticed the white van parked on the side of the street with the name Brooklyn Electrical on the side of the vehicle.

Maybe they were just electricians? Sheryl thought.

She lived on the third floor and took the stairs since her building had an elevator that performed like Elisha Otis created it himself back in 1853. As she reached the landing on the third floor and turned right into the hallway, she saw five men standing just outside her apartment door, thirty feet away. As she started down the hallway, they moved toward her.

Sheryl froze as she locked eyes with the man in the front of the group—Geno Romano.

She instantly knew why he was there. Sheryl turned to run back down the staircase knowing the mere act of running would likely implicate her.

As she descended the stairs, Sheryl clutched her handbag tightly taking the stairs two at a time. She heard her name called out behind her in a boisterous tone, but she didn't stop. When she reached the bottom floor, she heard the sound of heavy footfalls as the pack of men closed in on her.

She felt like a ship without a rudder as she burst out the door onto the sidewalk. Sheryl turned left, and headed for the corner of Eightieth and Lexington. The imposing features of the Unitarian Church of All Saints stood before her on the other side of Eightieth Street.

The smart play was to hail a cab and pray they could disappear into the sea of vehicles before Geno and the men with him could catch her.

Distracted as she reached the curb, she heard the smack of feet on concrete directly behind her before a thunderous voice called out again.

"Sheryl!" Geno bellowed with an inflection of concern and anger in his voice.

She turned as her foot stepped off the curb and looked over her shoulder to see Geno and four men less than ten feet away.

Her mind screamed, *Run.*

Distracted by the sound of her name being called out, Sheryl continued to move backwards into the roadway and never saw the coach bus that carried a full load of Japanese tourists. The Prevost bus barreled down Eightieth and crossed over Lexington at a slightly jarring speed on account of there being a green light.

She took three strides onto the road, which turned out to be two strides too many.

⸺◆⸺

Geno watched in horror as the bus struck Sheryl.

The impact of the high-speed collision between flesh and metal hurled her body through the air and contorted it in a grotesque shape as her flailing figure moved like a piece of fabric caught up in a strong wind. The force of the collision knocked her out of her shoes, ripped her oversized teal bag from her grip and to the ground.

Sheryl's bag landed near the filthy curb at Geno's feet. At the same time, her body flew about twenty feet down Eightieth Street and smashed into the rear window of a yellow taxi which pulled to the side of the street to let people out. Her head and torso passed through the window while her lower extremities dangled outside the vehicle like a rag doll.

With all eyes on the body protruding from the back window of the cab, Geno reached down and opened the teal bag. There, in plain view, he spotted the company folder. He recognized the insignia on the outside of the folder since he had designed it and given it to senior management.

Geno scooped out the folder and left the teal bag on the ground next to the curb. He didn't open the folder, but it felt like papers were inside it.

He walked with his four men at a moderate pace over to the van. Geno climbed into the passenger seat and stuffed the file into a brown leather over-the-shoulder style bag on the floorboard. Under no circumstances did Geno want to draw any unwanted attention to himself or his men. Sticking around the scene of the accident would not benefit him. After all, he got what he came for, and getting it back to the office ASAP was the only thing that mattered.

⚬

Three blocks from the intersection, Geno placed a call.

"Yes?" Mr. Joshua asked as he answered on the second ring.

"I've got the file," Geno said.

"Who had it?"

"Sheryl Hopping."

"No shit? Guess I shouldn't be surprised. Any issues retrieving it?"

"Yes."

"What happened?" Mr. Joshua asked.

"Sheryl is dead."

"*What?*"

"Relax, we didn't do it. It was an accident. Bottom line is we have the file."

"I want a full debrief in my office."

"I'm on my way with the file." Geno hung up and let out a long breath.

"We good, boss?" Trey asked as he pushed his dirty blond hair out of his eyes.

Geno frowned as he clutched the brown leather bag in one hand and steered the van with the other. "We are now," he said.

He looked into his rearview mirror, towards the direction where the incident happened, placed the bag on the floorboard, and quickly made a sign of the cross. Next, he whispered a silent prayer for Sheryl. He may not be a practicing Catholic, but nobody deserved to depart this life that way.

Chapter Thirty-Two

Washington, D.C.

The private jet landed at Dulles International Airport and taxied to the Dulles Jet Center. With the hangar doors open, the jet pulled into the expansive space as the outside doors were quickly closed. Two US Customs and Border Patrol officers met the plane and climbed the airstairs once lowered. The man and woman boarded the plane with stern expressions on their faces.

Inside the main cabin, neither officer glanced toward the passengers.

Merci watched with interest as the man and woman spoke with the petite, blond attendant near the front galley. The worker reached into her pocket and handed a small cream colored envelope to one of the customs officers. The man's expression changed as he opened it and looked at the contents. He looked to his left, and his female partner nodded. The envelope went into his front pocket, and both officers left the plane without a glance down the aisle at any of the passengers. No passports were presented. No questions asked. Corruption in D.C. was not exclusive to Capitol Hill or 1600 Pennsylvania Avenue.

Merci and Marcus had their luggage within five minutes and headed to the parking spaces outside the jet center. Four spaces from the main entrance sat Marcus's Aston Martin. While cruising across the Atlantic, he called a friend and had the vehicle dropped off.

The drive back to his apartment remained relatively quiet, as had most of the flight from Oxford. Marcus learned over the years when to speak and when to shut up. He knew when Merci needed time to think. With the roads practically empty, they encountered few other vehicles on the drive home.

"You want to get married?" Marcus asked from the sofa across from the plush leather seat where Merci sat. They had been back home at his apartment for about an hour. He spoke the words with no hint of humor, an expression that sounded dead serious.

"What the hell did you just say?" Merci's head snapped up from the laptop screen. Her eyes bulged, and a puzzled expression contorted her face.

"I think you heard me. Do you want to get married?"

Merci shook her head back and forth. "Have you lost your ever-loving mind?"

"No. I think it's the sanest idea I've had in ages."

Merci didn't know what to say as an awkward silence filled the air.

Marcus remained quiet. He waited for her to respond.

After a solid minute, Merci finally opened her mouth. "Marriage police, hold up." She put her hands out from her body. "Don't you remember what Cosmo Kramer said about marriage?"

Marcus chuckled. "Yeah, he said it's prison."

Merci sighed. "Well, he's right."

Marcus's expression switched to that of puzzlement. "You've never been married. How would you know?"

"Duh, I've never smoked crack either, but I know I don't want to start."

"Whatever." Marcus wasn't able to hide the frustration in his voice.

Merci raised her voice an octave. "Can you even name one couple who's had a solid marriage? You know your parents were a burning train wreck that only stayed on the tracks for the sake of you kids. They went their separate ways once you and your sister were out of college."

"Ray and Barb Tanguay," Marcus replied.

"The friends of your mom who babysat you for years? The ones who were like second parents?"

"Correct. They didn't have a perfect relationship. But it worked well."

"Yeah, I remember you telling me about them."

"Plus, my friend Brian from college and his wife Jennifer. They have it figured out."

"Okay, so two people you know have marriages that work. But they are the exception. Most marriages fail. The divorce rate in this country is over fifty percent. And a lot of those who stay together, it's only because of the kids or religious guilt. Statistics prove that only about fifteen percent of people who get married are actually happy."

"Goddamn, babe, you're jaded!"

"I'm a realist. I see things as they are, not as I hope they might be."

"So, you're completely against marriage?" Marcus stared into her eyes.

"Marcus, I love you, and I think we have a good thing going here. Let's not screw it up by getting a piece of paper that legally and financially ties us together. Besides, marriage is a horrible contract for a man to sign; the woman has all the leverage. You should be thanking me for trying to talk sense into you."

"That's a load of shit, Merci. It's not the marriage contract that matters. It's the connection."

"And can't we have that without going to a justice of the peace, or hiring some pastor?"

Marcus let out a deep breath. "Not sure this conversation is going to get us anywhere."

"I mean, honey, did you think I was going to melt, scream, and be all into this idea? You know me better than that, don't you?"

He bit his lower lip and rubbed his palms against his legs. "I just thought we had progressed, and the next step would be a smart idea."

Merci got up from the chair and sat on his lap. "I don't just like you, I love you." She took his hand and tucked it through the top of her T-shirt, placing it between her breasts. "You are here. And you'll always have a spot there. I don't need some legal agreement to make you closer. I'd die for you, Marcus Rollins!"

He kissed her gently on the lips.

The moisture of their skin aroused both of them.

"And I for you, Merci de Atta. Getting to call you my bride would mean something to me, though."

Merci sighed and buried her head into his broad shoulder.

Chapter Thirty-Three

Washington, D.C.

The marriage conversation faded away and was not brought back up. Marcus went out for a run. He returned an hour later, covered in sweat, with his T-shirt drenched.

Merci sat in the oversized plush chair the entire time he was gone. As he entered the living room, she had a questioning look. "You went out in that shirt?"

Marcus looked at her, then down to the large image of an eagle that covered his chest. "Um, yeah, I love this shirt."

"It's a good round-the-house T-shirt, but not an out-in-public one."

"I was out getting exercise, not trying to catch some tail."

Merci raised her eyebrows. "And you wouldn't catch said tail in that shirt."

"What? You don't like the eagle?"

"Ehh, it's okay, but the shirt just looks old and worn out."

"That's because it is one of my favorites, and yes, it is old and worn out. I love my eagle shirt. It's classic Van Halen apparel."

Merci shrugged. "We can agree to disagree. Would you like me to buy you better-looking running shirts?"

"Nah, I'm good. I don't tell you what to do, you don't tell me what to wear. Isn't that part of our deal?"

"Suit yourself."

"I will." He moved closer to her.

"Subject change." She gripped the laptop with one hand and passed it to Marcus. "You gotta take a look at the document I just got."

"Do I want to see this?" The expression painted over her face caused him to hesitate as he gripped the device. "Is it about what happened in Paris?"

"Nope."

Marcus flipped the MacBook around so he could see the monitor. His analytical skills kicked in the second his eyes focused on the screen, and he started with the email before he clicked on the attached document. As he got to the part about the *payment for services rendered*, he blew a long whistle. "That's a lot of fucking money. I guess we know now what that cryptic email you got on the flight back stateside was all about."

"I know. Besides, who is making the request? Did you see what's inconspicuously missing?"

Marcus nodded. "Umm, yeah, the target."

"Exactly. That's a shit load of money to offer upfront and leave the mark out of the offer sheet."

Marcus rubbed his chin. "Maybe Mary Brown is the target this time?"

Based on her facial expressions, especially how her eyebrows dipped toward her nose, Merci clearly did not agree. "No, I don't think so. I researched Mary's court cases before the hit on Chuck. She's a swing vote on many high-profile legal battles. My gut says they need her vote either in favor or against something coming up."

"Well, it says once you accept, they will deposit half the money in your offshore account and provide the dead drop location for the intel on the target. After you get the intel sheet at the drop site, they will transfer the rest of the money. That's a lot of bucks to pay before you actually do the deed."

"That's another thing." Merci frowned. "What is this, the Cold War? Everything is electronic these days. Why would they want to set up a physical dead drop location? That makes absolutely no sense."

"Makes me think the target is sensitive and they want to mitigate the chance it's intercepted via electronic delivery," Marcus said. "Again, I think that points to Mary being the target. I bet it's gonna be some *Mission Impossible* type shit, and after you read the intel sheet it disintegrates or something." He smirked as he said the last part.

"You watch too many spy movies. That's not how it works, Jason Bourne."

Marcus put his hands out. "Whoa, you don't want me to be Jason Bourne."

Merci pursed her lips. "And why is that? He's pretty hot."

"Because all his lady friends die in the movies. And you are my lady friend. I want you to live."

"True, but maybe Jason should choose better, and they would actually make it to the next flick?"

"Possibly."

"What concerns me is that a client has never demanded that I be there for an in-person dead drop. It's always electronic." Merci huffed. "I don't know. Something doesn't add up."

"Girl, you know I never tell you what jobs to take or turn down, but the amount of money they are offering is disappear type money. It's five times what they paid for Chuck Brown."

"Again, why? I almost wonder if an offer like this is a way to draw me out of the shadows."

Marcus flung his hand in the air. "Guess I hadn't thought about it like that."

"They had me tailed in Western North Carolina. Maybe I'm the one being targeted."

"You sound paranoid. You did the job at the Grove Park Inn and left no trace. Why would they want to take you out?"

"Why does CVS ask for your phone number when you buy a pack of gum?"

Marcus nodded, "Good point."

Merci shifted in the chair as he handed her back the laptop. "Besides, a sense of paranoia is what's kept me alive this long."

Marcus nodded, "True, but still."

"An offer that large, yet no target is listed, and requires a drop location, makes me wonder."

"Then is it a hard no?"

Merci gave him a devilish smirk. "Well, I didn't say that."

"See, I told you the money is enticing."

"Of course it is. I'm not in the habit of being a non-profit. I just want to live long enough to enjoy the fruits of all my labor. I mean, we don't need the money. Those diamonds we scored from Charles Steele set us up for life. We've got FU money at this point. It's all about the hunt for me. And taking a piece of shit off planet Earth drives me."

"Agree. This line of work is like a real-life chess match at times."

"So what's my next move?"

"This isn't a timed chess match, so take whatever time you need, and consider all the ramifications before you slide your next piece on the board."

"Above all, I must avoid a move that takes out the queen."

Marcus's eyes narrowed. "You mean, it's imperative to make a move that protects the king?"

She laughed. "Nah, the king can take care of himself. It's my ass I'm hard wired to protect."

Chapter Thirty-Four

One World Trade Center

Geno rarely experienced anxiety, however, as he stepped off the elevator and walked toward the executive office suites, his heart rate increased with each heavy footfall from his Salomon boots. By the time he reached the attractive admin assistant who sat behind the glass desk, beads of perspiration formed on his forehead.

"He's waiting for you, Mr. Romano," the exotic-looking woman said. She noticed the perspiration. "Everything okay, Geno?"

He half smirked, half grimaced as he stared at the attractive woman. "Just peachy. Another day in paradise. Thank you for asking, Miss Topintzis."

Geno walked into the office, closed the door behind him, and paused as it appeared his boss was still on a phone call.

The obese man looked up, holding the phone in his right hand. With his left hand, he waved Geno over to his desk and indicated he should sit in the chair directly across from it.

Geno took a seat, placed the brown leather bag at his feet, and glanced around the expansive office.

The call lasted several minutes, and his boss became more irritated by the second.

"I don't want excuses, I want answers." The obese man slammed the receiver in the cradle and released an elongated breath of air.

Geno smelled the foul stench of cigarettes and pickles from the other side of the table. *Jeez, what a slob.*

"People are so fucking incompetent." The obese man shook his head and banged his knuckles on the desktop.

Geno said nothing.

His boss spun a pen in a clockwise motion. "I hear you have something for me?"

"Yes, I do." Geno reached down into the bag and pulled out the folder. He handed it over to the obese man with the care of Indiana Jones passing the chalice of Christ over to his father.

The obese man opened the clasped folder, removed, and scanned the contents comprising the file. "Did you look at the pages?"

"No, sir. I felt the envelope to make sure it wasn't empty, but was told not to open it. I followed the instructions you gave me."

"Good, smart man." The obese man rubbed his round chin with his pudgy fingers. "The fewer eyes that see this, the better. It's toxic info to even have in our possession."

Geno glanced around the room. "Where's Mr. Joshua?"

"He had to leave. There was an urgent matter that required his attention. He should be back within a few hours."

"Understood."

"So, you confirmed Sheryl died in the accident?"

The question surprised him. Geno shook his head. "Umm, well. Not exactly."

"What the hell do you mean, not exactly?" A snarl formed on the lips of the obese man.

"I mean, I watched her get hit. She got creamed by a tour bus. Nobody survives a crash of that intensity. We watched as she careened through the air, and last I saw, half her body was dangling from the rear window of a yellow cab. I didn't wait around since I didn't want to get questioned, so I grabbed the folder from her purse, and we fled the scene, careful to not draw any attention to ourselves."

"That means you assume she's dead but have not confirmed it to be the case."

Geno swallowed hard. "Umm, yeah, that's correct, sir."

The obese man pointed his grotesquely proportioned finger toward his office door. "Then you'd best get out there and make sure she's dead. No living witnesses. You got that?"

Geno stood, grabbing his leather bag before he rose. He slung the strap over his shoulder. "Of course, sir. I'll contact the hospital."

"Corpses tell no tales, yet the living can always indict."

"Yes, I understand." Geno headed for the door.

"And I want a visible confirmation that Sheryl Hopping is no more." The obese man flipped through the pages of the file as he spoke.

"And how do I go about doing that?"

"How the hell do I know? Go to the city morgue, claim to be her brother from Jersey. Just get me confirmation she's dead. Got it?"

"I'm on it." Geno reached for the doorknob.

"One more thing," his boss said before he could open the door.

Geno turned. "Yes?"

The obese man held up the file. "How do you know she didn't make a copy or tell someone about the content in this folder? After all, it was in her possession for multiple days."

Geno shrugged. "I don't know what she did with the folder when it was in her possession. How would we know that?"

"She's not married, right? No boyfriend?"

"None that I am aware of, sir. But I have no way of knowing who she may have spoken with between when the file went missing and I retrieved it."

The displeasure in his boss's puffy face was clear. "Well, not only do you have to get me proof of her death, but I now need you to find out if she made any copies and confirm if she spoke with anyone."

"How do you expect me to find out if she made copies or discover if she talked with anyone?"

"Check her cell phone, for starters."

Geno shook his head. "It wasn't in her purse, so we don't have it."

"Well, that means it was probably on her when the accident happened. Which means it's part of her personal possessions at the hospital or morgue."

"Likely."

"Then I guess you know where you are going next, don't you?"

Geno sighed. "No doubt, sir." He didn't wait for more back-and-forth. He turned the doorknob and rushed past Miss Topintzis without a word.

CHAPTER THIRTY-FIVE

WASHINGTON, D.C.

"Grab a drink. I'll be back in a few." Merci stood up, left the living room, and headed to the bedroom. Only a fool would not comprehend what the devilish smirk displayed on her face implied.

Marcus was certainly no fool and did not have to be told anything twice. A cold one normally hit the spot after a run, anyway. As he popped off the bottle top, he leaned against the granite counter and took several long chugs from the ice-cold imported German brew.

Two minutes later, and like a whirlwind, Merci stepped into the living room fully naked. He never tired of seeing her pert breasts or the curvature of her perfectly proportioned backside. But even though Merci was a ravenous beauty in his eyes, much more attracted him to her. It's the inside that drew him in and held him tight. Some assassins might be heartless, but not Merci. Within her was a complex maze of retribution mixed in with passion, kindness, and a zest for life.

Merci craved the lust in his eyes like a junkie craves their next score. As she turned and left the room, she muttered two words. "Join me."

Marcus downed the rest of the cold brew and tossed the empty bottle in the pull-out garbage drawer.

Showers were therapeutic for Merci. The steam cleansed away the memories of the lives she had taken, and the scalding water blotted out the marks left on her soul.

She climbed in the shower first, but Marcus was only a few steps behind her as he stripped off his clothes. Frequently, she told him the greatest perk of his apartment was the walk-in tiled shower.

The space quickly filled with steam as she turned the regulator to full hot.

As the nearly scalding water beat down on her naked body, she turned and pressed herself into him. For his part, Marcus scrubbed her back in smooth circular motions with the exfoliating scrubber.

"Why do you put up with my craziness?" Merci pouted her lips.

Marcus chuckled. "Because I love you."

"Yeah, well, don't my nonsensical antics sometimes bother you?"

"Like killing someone in Paris in broad daylight?"

Merci smiled. "Yeah, something like that."

He shrugged. "Can I be honest?"

"Please, do."

"All chicks are crazy to some degree."

Merci smiled. "No truer statement has a man ever uttered."

"It's the degree of crazy that holds a man or pushes him away."

"Makes sense. So how crazy am I?"

Marcus's eyes rounded. "Babe, I've seen you kill men with a bottle opener, a nail file and even an empty wine bottle once. So my answer is you are hardly crazy at all. I like my balls attached where they are. Plus, I enjoy the thought of breathing."

Merci's smile widened. "Now that's a really smart answer."

"I mean, everyone is a little crazy, as long as you can find the crazy that keeps you on your toes and helps accentuate your joy. Hold on to them as hard and as long as you can."

"How did I end up with such a smart man?"

"You clearly won the population Powerball, babe."

Merci grew quiet for a moment as the hot water beat down on both their naked bodies. She turned away for a second, then back to him. "I'm going to take the job."

His head turned at a slight angle. "Are you sure? Even without knowing the target?"

"It's enticing, and I feel like I need to hunt. Maybe I need to let a little of the crazy out."

"If that's what you want." Marcus rarely questioned her decisions, and the incident in Paris was a rare exception to the rule. He knew better. "I got your six, babe, now and always."

"Yeah, yeah, yeah, that's what every man says when he's naked in a shower with a beautiful woman. It's only so they can get a little action."

He wrapped his powerful hands around her hips and pulled her toward him. Their flesh intertwined as water struck their bodies from the multiple shower heads. "I'm not every man."

"I know." She gently kissed his lips. She turned the shower flow to a pulse setting and put her head against his broad shoulder. As she let the water beat down her upper back, she said, "Yes, taking this job is what I want."

They stood there for several minutes in silence. His hands held her at the waist and he drifted his fingers toward her butt. With slow yet strong strokes he massaged her lower back at the two indentations just above the crease of her curved ass. The pressure of his strokes grew by the second. His fingers moved from the curvature of her backside and up her spine with the precision of a masseuse. She let out an audible moan more than once.

He knew what she liked and how to please her.

As the water pulsated down her back, Merci's hands cupped him as she lifted her head off his shoulder and kissed him sensually.

Chapter Thirty-Six

One World Trade Center

Mr. Joshua stepped into the obese man's office like a stiff breeze forcing open a screened door.

"Geno retrieved the file earlier today," the obese man said as he looked up from his cellphone.

"Yes, I know," Mr. Joshua said. "He called me earlier. One less problem on our plate."

"True. But we don't know yet if she made copies or told anybody. She ran when she saw Geno and his men, which implies Sheryl looked in the file."

Mr. Joshua nodded. "No doubt. If she had the file in her possession, it's virtually guaranteed she looked at it. Plus, innocent people rarely run. Since Sheryl took off when she saw Geno, she must have known she was in some sort of danger based on what she read."

The obese man spun a pen on the smooth surface of the table. "Your text said you had some news. Is it about the client in mid-town you visited this afternoon?"

"No, it is not. It's much better news than that."

"I'm listening."

"Merci agreed to the job."

The obese man stopped spinning the pen. "Really? Without you specifying the target or asking any questions?"

Mr. Joshua tilted his head. "Correct. The response was simple and direct. It merely said, *Accepted*, that's all."

"I'm legitimately surprised. I expected her to at least ask some questions or push back on the fact that no target was listed in the offer sheet."

Mr. Joshua nodded. "As did I."

"And are you sure an in-person dead drop is a smart move? After all, she will see you."

"I think she already knows who I am."

"How could that be?" The obese man raised his eyebrows.

"She was at the funeral for Chuck Brown. I had Geno pull the security footage. I didn't see her at the time, but I felt someone staring at me. When I reviewed the tapes, sure enough, she looked directly at me."

"But how could she know who you are?"

"Marcus is very adept at technology. I suspect he somehow found out about me. Don't know that for a fact, but I have to assume she knows who I am."

The obese man touched his pudgy finger to his lips. "More reason for you not to be present at the dead drop."

"I disagree. I think me being there is a smart move. Since she likely knows who I am. I want her to know I'm hiring her for this next contract."

"But she can be deadly."

Mr. Joshua let out an audible *hmm* sound. "So the hell can I."

A wide grin formed over the round face of the obese man. "You're taken with her, aren't you?"

"She's attractive, that is for sure. And she is quite intelligent. As well as being highly skilled in the art of murder. But no, I'm not interested in her as you may think. I prefer my woman to be much less capable of lethal acts, and to be honest, not as bright. I want them to have certain skills, but Merci has too many skills at her disposal. That's not what I pursue."

"Then why be there?"

"Call it professional courtesy, or say I want to size her up. Either way, I'll be at the dead drop site."

"What if she confronts you about what happened in Hendersonville?"

"Then I'll remind her she's an independent contractor who is paid an exorbitant fee, and sometimes there are strings that come with these types of contracts."

The obese man frowned. "Just be careful. I don't need you dead."

"Careful is something you tell your naïve kids to be. I'll be prepared and ready. I never walk into a situation without a plan to get out in one piece." Mr. Joshua walked towards the door. "Plus, I'm not going there alone."

Chapter Thirty-Seven

Georgetown

Mary Brown was trapped inside her own home. Based on the overt threat from Mr. Joshua, not only was her house bugged, but so was her phones plus her chamber inside the Supreme Court. Her skin crawled as she wondered if it was audio only or did he had video surveillance as well.

Is he watching me now?

Does he see me everywhere I go in the house?

Even in the bathroom or shower?

Her body shuddered as she considered how invasive it was to have someone watching your every move.

She wanted to reach out to the Marshal and warn him of what happened. But that would only risk Frank's life and who knows how many other personnel at the court or on her security detail.

Mary grabbed a bottle of spring water from the fridge and returned to her office. The envelope Mr. Joshua gave her sat on the desk. Part of her wanted to rip it open and see what he gave her this time. Another part of her wanted to throw the thing in the fireplace and burn it. She knew either action would likely have consequences, and for now, she needed to stay calm and not do anything rash.

A knock on the front door startled her and caused her to jump slightly in her chair. At the same time, the wall-mounted speaker to her right came alive with the sound of Dennis, one of the U.S. Marshals on duty at her house. "Ma'am. There's a clerk at the front door from the court for you." Mary walked over and pressed the intercom button. "I'm upstairs, Dennis, tell the clerk I'll be down in a minute."

Mary grabbed a sweater that hung loosely from the back of the chair and threw it over her head as she proceeded to the steps that led downstairs.

A minute later, she opened the front door to find Kim Daub, one of the law clerks for the Chief Justice of the Supreme Court, standing on her doorstep.

"Sorry to bother you, Madam Justice." Kim blew a tuft of hair out of her face.

Mary smiled. "Looks like the chief justice is working you to the max."

With a deep exhale, Kim replied, "Does he know any other way?" She immediately regretted the choice of words. With a slight stammer, she said, "I mean, he ... well ..."

Mary touched her shoulder. "It's okay, Kim. The chief justice works all his clerks hard. You're not the first to have it beat you down, and you certainly won't be the last. But trust me when I tell you that if you're tough enough to stay on top of his workload, you can pretty much work at any law office in D.C. in a heartbeat once your time at the court concludes."

The words appeared to mitigate the concerned look spread across Kim's face. "Thank you, Madam Justice. I'm certainly grateful for the opportunity and know plenty of others would give a lung to have the chance ..."

Mary cut her off, but in an extremely kind manner. "Kim, you're just getting your feet wet, but trust an old bird who has flown around a lot of skies in her days. Comparisons don't get you far. There are always others who are more successful and much further up the ladder. Just be the best darn version of yourself. Work hard and try to keep your nose clean. Impress the chief justice, and you can punch your card anywhere you choose to go next."

"Thank you, Ma'am. It's difficult to keep things in perspective sometimes."

Mary let out a slight chuckle. "Girl, I'm in my sixties and still struggle with doing that just about every day."

"I thought with age came wisdom?"

"Oh sure, the older you get, the wiser you get about some things. But you also realize there's more you don't know than you'll ever have time to learn. It's a balance, and not always an easy one. But you'll find your footing and discover your path." Mary paused and pointed at the satchel hanging on Kim's arm. "I assume you didn't come to my house to get lectured about life and what you need to learn."

"I'm certainly grateful for the advice and wisdom, and I'll take it to heart. However, no, I came bearing gifts from the chief justice."

Mary rolled her eyes. "Yay, more light reading, huh?"

"Briefs and such for the upcoming case. He asked me to deliver copies to all the justices." Kim pulled the packet from her over-the-shoulder bag and handed the sealed manila folder over.

As she held the thick packet slightly upright, Mary said, "Guess I have my homework for the night. And to think I was hoping to binge the latest episode of *Tulsa Kings*."

Kim looked upward. "I won't tell the chief justice you skipped reading the briefs if you won't, Madam Justice. My advice would be watch Stallone, the briefs will still be there in the morning."

CHAPTER THIRTY-EIGHT

WASHINGTON, D.C.

J. EDGAR HOOVER BUILDING

Nick walked through the revolving doors into the uniquely designed building located on Pennsylvania Avenue. It was the first time he had set foot in the J. Edgar Hoover Building in several years. Instead of taking a car for the short drive from the White House, he opted for some fresh air and walked the eighth of a mile. Two Secret Service agents joined him on his stroll. He still wasn't accustomed to having them around, but the president insisted, given the danger he currently faced. After initially protesting against the protective detail with great reluctance, he realized it was a fight he could not win. Nick, more than anyone, appreciated the irony that the one who protected the Office of the Presidency now had his own layer of protection when he left the White House grounds.

He instructed the two agents to wait for him in the lobby, assuring them he wouldn't be terribly long.

With the two men standing back, he approached the security checkpoint on the main floor. Nick flashed his White House ID, granting him access to the FBI headquarters. Even with his clearance, he had to wear a visitor's badge attached to his belt. The large red letter "V" superimposed over the FBI seal with the word VISITOR made him feel like a tourist. When he moved around the White House, he needed no badge or identification.

As Nick stepped off the elevator on the seventh floor and turned right, he glanced around at the furnishings. Not much had changed since his last visit. Walking past the door that led to the director's suite, he turned left and proceeded down the hallway to the last door on the right. The brass sign beside the door read, Office of Parabellum Projects. Nick shook his head as he stared at the placard.

Without knocking, he turned the doorknob and stepped inside the office. The room was modest and tastefully decorated. FBI Senior Special Agent Eli Payne sat behind the large mahogany desk closest to the door, while FBI Special Agent Kat Stone sat at an identical-looking desk at the far side of the room. They both looked up as Nick stepped inside the office.

"Well, lookie what the cat dragged in." Eli glanced up from the file spread over his desk.

Kat put her cell phone down, and a wide grin formed as she saw Nick, but she said nothing at first.

Nick whistled quickly as he stopped a few feet into the office. He pointed at Eli's desk. "Has TLC contacted you about starting your own reality television series? Look at that damn desk. How do you not get lost?"

Kat nodded. "Preach it, Nick!"

Eli flipped Nick the bird.

"I still can't believe the two of you have a nook on the seventh floor, only a few doors from the director's office."

"What can I say." Eli scowled. "The president and the director of the FBI both took a liking to us after the events that took place under the last administration."

With an audible *hmpf* sound, Nick said, "Give them a little bit more time, and they will realize the error of their ways." He looked at Kat. "Not you, Kat. The director promoting you up to the seventh floor was a brilliant idea." He turned and pointed at Eli. "But bumping Payne up here. Well, that was an ill-conceived move."

"You come all the way up here just to crush my nuts? I already have Mila to do that at night, plus Stone during the day. Did you at least bring us some Crumbl cookies?"

Nick looked at Eli, and then he turned his attention to Kat. He scrunched his face. "Did he just ask for Crumbl cookies?"

"Yup. Mila started having bad cravings last month, and now he has to bring her a three-pack of cookies once or twice a week. Based on his expanding mid-section, I think he buys six and eats half on the way home."

Eli mouthed several derogatory words in both of their directions before he patted his stomach. "I'll have you know, unlike most men who put on weight when their partners get pregnant, I've actually lost seven pounds. Thank you very much."

Nick looked at Kat. She rolled her eyes and mouthed the letters *b-u-l-l-s-h-i-t*.

With a finger at the front door, Nick turned back to Eli. "So the Office of Parabellum Projects. O-P-P really?"

Eli looked sheepish. "Yeah, you know me."

Kat rolled her eyes. "See what I have to put up with each day, Nick. I work with a man-child who will soon be the father of an actual child."

"I can get you a job at the White House in eight seconds flat. Just give me the word."

"Oh no!" Eli exclaimed. "You're not stealing my partner."

"But seriously, back to the sign on the door." Nick cocked his head backward. "The director actually let you name the new department that?"

"Hell, no," Kat said with a deep sigh. "That sign was Mr. Doo Doo for brains here, his idea of a funny joke. I think he bought that sign at Things Remembered or some cheesy mall store that will personalize and engrave just about anything you're willing to pay for besides your johnson."

Nick and Eli looked at each other and made an *eeek-type* face at the thought of getting their junk engraved.

"Dare I ask what your division is actually called?" Nick asked. "I failed to get the memo, or I must have forgotten already."

"Special Investigations Unit," Kat said.

Nick put his hands out and shrugged. "Sounds vaguely familiar. What are the official duties?"

"As the name implies, we primarily work on special projects for the director." Eli cleared his throat and dug through the papers on his desk to find a Fiji water bottle. He took a long gulp, then continued. "As you know, sometimes we get outsourced to the president, and even helped you with Operation Red Star. If you recall, we were highly skilled in getting you intel on a certain senator who tried to kill not only you but POTUS himself."

Nick nodded. "I recall, and I thought the Amazon gift card I sent you should have squared things up." He winked at the end of the statement.

"As I was saying." Eli smirked. "Very often, we get tasked with working on national investigations. The high-profile murders, robberies, kidnappings, etc., etc., etc. This way, the director has direct contact with the lead investigators and can interject via us if needed. He's a very hands-on director, and we get to help facilitate his all-in approach."

"If Agent Calvin could see you now," Nick said.

Eli frowned. "Jeez, Kat told you about that, too?"

"We might go out for drinks occasionally, and she may have spilled a few secrets."

Kat raised her hand. "Guilty as charged."

"After all," Nick said, "I have to know who I'm pulling into critical investigations."

"And is that why you are here?" Eli asked. "To pull us into one of your *critical investigations*?" The last two words were bathed in sarcasm.

Nick grabbed the black backpack on his right shoulder and placed it on the floor as they chatted. He unzipped the bag and retrieved a thick folder. "Why yes, in fact, that's exactly why I am here."

Eli and Kat exchanged curious glances.

With a wry grin, Nick walked past Eli's desk and placed the overflowing folder on Kat's desk. As he did so, he glanced back at Eli. "Your desk will turn this thing into D.B. Cooper, so I'd better let Kat keep this file safe."

"Pfft, whatever," Eli said as he pursed his lips. "I know where everything is on my desk. Thank you very much."

"What I'm about to request will require a little bit of bending the rules."

A wide smile formed on Eli's face. "Miss Goody Two-Shoes might get her panties ruffled, but I'm up for doing a little rule bending."

Kat frowned. "Depending on the request, I can get on board with some bending, as long as it doesn't lead to a break."

"Don't worry, if it all goes to hell, I'm in good with the one person on Earth who can give you a full pardon."

Kat looked down at the file. "What are you trying to get us into this time, Nick?"

Chapter Thirty-Nine

Manhattan

Geno called a few of his contacts within Manhattan and found out Sheryl was transported to Lenox Hill Hospital at Lexington and E 77th St. after the incident. After climbing into the Cadillac Escalade, his company car, Geno made his way down to the Battery before curving around lower Manhattan until he merged with FDR Drive. Since he spent most of his adult life, when not deployed by the military, driving in the city, he knew going through lower Manhattan and midtown would be a nightmare and take forever. The drive from One World Trade Center to Lenox Hill Hospital Emergency Department took less than twenty-five minutes.

Miraculously, he found a spot a block from the hospital, parked on the side of the street, and hurried into the main entrance.

Geno was immediately greeted with the smell of antiseptic, cleaning chemicals, and hand sanitizer as he snaked his way through a myriad of people who crowded the emergency department. After waiting several minutes, a worker directed him to the ninth floor, where the hospital's computer said Sheryl Hopping could be located.

The sights and smells of the hospital reminded Geno of his mother, Isabella. She worked as a nurse for most of his childhood, and he often accompanied her to work if the sitter was late or unable to make it. He spent many days as a young man in the waiting room watching as sick people entered, mourners gathered, and often children just like him passed the time as loved ones talked around them. The flood of memories brought back some bittersweet feelings from his time growing up.

Geno approached the nurses' station on the ninth floor. The brown-haired woman who stood at the counter looked like she had a long day, which is not abnormal in the eyes of any healthcare provider. He glanced from her face to her name badge, which read Heather Reaves, RN.

"Can I help you?" she asked in a kind but firm tone.

"Yes, you can. My name is Gary Hopping. I was told my sister was on this floor.

The look in her eyes suddenly turned into one of sadness and dread. "Um, yes, Mr. Hopping ..." She paused before continuing

"I know she passed away," Geno interjected. "They told me over the phone."

"Sorry for your loss," Heather said.

"Is she still here, or did they move her down to the morgue? I'd appreciate a few minutes to say my goodbyes." A tear formed at the corner of Geno's eye. Those drama classes his mom forced him to take in high school paid off from time to time.

Heather stammered slightly. "We are a little behind at the moment. Your sister is still in room 95, down the hall, fifth door on the left. You can have as much time as you need." She walked around the desk, gently touched Geno's shoulder, and walked side-by-side with him down the hall to where Sheryl lay in the hospital bed.

Geno looked somber as they stepped into the room. Sheryl lay in the bed, deep cuts and a softball-sized bruise visible on her face, the result of her deadly impact from not only the touring bus but also a cab. The color had already left her face. Death's natural progression continues unabated, as it was designed.

"I'll leave you with your sister, Mr. Hopping. If you need anything, let me know." Heather lowered her head and touched Geno's arm on her way out of the room.

As soon as she left the room, Geno moved closer to the body. Besides the hospital bed, a brown two-drawer nightstand that looked like it came out of the 1970s caught his attention. While he glanced over his shoulder to make sure no one was walking by the door, his left hand pulled open the dresser's top drawer. Geno looked down at the open drawer, and lying on top of her large teal purse was a white iPhone. The screen looked cracked as he picked it up.

Paydirt.

As he touched the phone's splintered glass face, the screen brightened, and the Face ID activated. Geno moved closer to Sheryl and hoped that even with her head trauma, the iPhone security feature would still work.

Holding the phone in front of Sheryl's face, Geno breathed a sigh of relief as the Face ID activated and the iPhone apps filled the display screen. Next, he removed the small device from his pocket, smaller than a 9-volt battery, and connected it to the lightning port. Immediately, a screen popped up on the display, and Geno clicked the *copy all* option. Unsure how long it would take, he stayed close to the body, his back to the open door. That way, if anyone walked by, they would not be suspicious of him with the phone.

Five minutes into the data transfer, a man's voice resonated down the hall. It sounded like he was getting closer.

Geno raised the phone and acted like he was deep in conversation. The voice grew quiet, but footsteps entered the room behind him. After speaking for another few seconds and even starting to fake cry, he lowered the phone out of view.

Geno turned and came face to face with a man in a long white coat. The name badge hanging off the left breast pocket read, *Dr. Joel Miller.*

"Mr. Hopping, I'm sorry for your loss. The nurse mentioned you were in here paying your last respects."

Geno wiped away the fake tears and sniffed up a glob of snot from the lower part of his nose. "Yes, Doctor. My brother called to check on her. I answered her phone, which was ringing in the drawer, and delivered the horrible news. The two of them were very close. He's devastated."

The conversation went on for a couple of minutes. Dr. Miller spoke about the extent of Sheryl's injuries and how the physicians couldn't save her because of the trauma she sustained. While the doctor spoke, Geno looked down to see that the file transfer was completed. As quickly as he could without seeming rude, Geno dovetailed the conversation into how he needed to check on his elderly mother and break the news to her.

Dr. Miller said he understood.

Geno gave Sheryl one final embrace as he removed the device and slipped her phone back into the drawer. He turned and thanked Dr. Miller for the care shown by the hospital staff as he left the room. As he walked past the nurses' station, he said that he appreciated Heather and the rest of the staff for their kindness to his sister. She hugged him and wished him well.

Six minutes later, Geno walked out of the hospital and placed a single call. "I have the data from the phone, and I'm headed back to the office to analyze it."

Chapter Forty

Washington, D.C.

Marcus lay on his side and propped his head with his bent arm. His fierce gaze watched Merci as she peacefully slept beside him. Her lip quivered slightly as she breathed out, while her eyelids twitched.

He didn't agree with her decision to accept the contract, but true to his words, he never told her what to do. Besides loving Merci unconditionally, he respected her independence and knew if he tried to take that away from her, without a doubt, she would cease to be the amazing woman he fell in love with. Also, he rightly figured she may castrate him in the middle of the night, á la Lorena Bobbitt, if he crossed the line and tried to control her. He had no desire to find out if a surgeon could reattach his manhood.

Years before, he rescued Merci from a life of hell on the streets of Paris. She only had one request as their connection intensified while she perfected her particular skillset at an astonishing pace.

Let me be free, and always allow me to stay that way. Don't be like the rest of them and try to control me.

He could still hear her words echo as he stared at her flawless silhouette under the thin silk sheets.

Marcus watched her sleep for several minutes before slowly sliding out of the bed and going over to the dresser positioned against the far wall opposite the sleigh bed. He opened the drawer and moved a stack of handsomely folded shirts to the side, revealing a small red box.

With the box in his hand, he looked back and made sure Merci was still fast asleep. As he made his way out of the bedroom and toward the kitchen, he retrieved a Montblanc ballpoint pen, a piece of stationery, and an envelope from the desk in the living room.

A high-top bar separated the kitchen and living room, and he sat down at one bar stool. Placing the box next to the paper and pen, he flipped open the ring box, revealing the platinum band De Beers classic round 3.23-carat diamond engagement ring.

Marcus picked up the pen and tapped it slowly on the counter, making little sound. His thoughts spun around in his head like a washer's spin cycle as he tried to formulate the right words to say to the woman he loved.

How do you express admiration, unconditional love, and deep desire without it coming across as a cheesy Hallmark card?

Forty minutes later, he finished the letter and even dabbed a drop of his cologne on the paper. It was a scent she picked out in Paris the weekend they first made love many years earlier. Tri-folding the letter, he gently stuffed it inside the envelope. Then, he wrote her name as elegantly as he could in cursive and sealed it with a wax seal kit he retrieved from the desk.

Marcus returned to the bedroom, put the sealed envelope with the engagement ring box back in the dresser drawer, and covered them both with a stack of shirts. Next, he slid back into bed and crawled under the sheet. He snuck in close to her and wrapped her up in a firm embrace.

She let out the quietest of moans as his body intertwined with hers.

Chapter Forty-One

One World Trade Center

Mr. Joshua sat in his office and examined the packet one more time, carefully studying every photo in the detailed material. At least to him, it seemed pretty straightforward, and for someone as skilled as Merci, there was very little chance the task could not be executed.

With the floor empty of personnel since everyone had already gone home for the day, the sound of the elevator made his head turn upward. Mr. Joshua got up and stepped out of his office. He watched as Geno proceeded down the hall toward him.

As Geno got close, Mr. Joshua indicated he wanted him to enter the office and gestured to the chair next to his desk.

"Tell me what happened at the hospital." He spoke while an expression of unhappiness covered his face.

It took Geno about ten minutes to thoroughly explain what transpired. He even went further back and told Mr. Joshua about the search of the apartment and the fatal incident with Sheryl in the streets of New York City.

"How long will it take to analyze the data you retrieved from her phone?" Mr. Joshua asked.

"Hard to say, but I would assume several hours at the minimum. Not really sure what I'm looking for yet." Geno pulled the thumb drive from his pocket and flashed it so Mr. Joshua could see what he collected at the hospital.

"I talked with the boss at length. You need to find any evidence that she did or did not reach out to anyone about the file she took from the conference room.

Also, check the metadata, trace her locations, and see where she went. There are a lot of unaccounted-for hours from when she took the file to us getting it back. Are you able to track all of that?"

"Yes, it will take a bit of time, though. But I have software that can pinpoint where she went, how long she stayed there, and even who she called. Plus, if she used Apple Pay, I can find out what she bought. However, it won't let me know any transactions she made with her debit or credit cards, but I have someone who can get that data for us."

"Good." Mr. Joshua bit his lower lip. "We need to be fast, but discretion is necessary, so only outsource what you must. And above all, time is working against us. I fly out to Washington, D.C., in an hour. I need to know by the morning if we have a big problem, or if our problem was just eliminated."

Geno nodded. "Copy that."

"You're gonna need to pull an all-nighter."

"Already planned on it. America is not the only thing that runs on Dunkin'. I'll be okay. Caffeine is my friend in situations like this."

"Good," Mr. Joshua said.

Geno cleared his throat. "One more thing. There's a good chance the staff will know about Sheryl's death when they come in tomorrow morning. News like that travels fast, and I'm sure the news reported on the fatal accident tonight. Now that the hospital believes her brother visited, they will release the name overnight. Others will know soon enough."

"I'm aware of it. Spoke with the boss, and we already have an announcement ready to go out first thing in the morning. We can handle it."

"Whatever you say," Geno said as he stood and approached the door. "I better dig in and see what I can find."

"Keep me in the loop, and if you find anything abnormal, let me know ASAP, okay?"

Geno nodded. "Will do."

Before going down the hall to his office, Geno headed to the break room to inject caffeine into his system. The obese man was rarely thoughtful toward his employees, but the coffee machine was one thing he did not skimp on.

Geno turned on the PrimaDonna Elite Espresso machine and made himself a double shot. As he walked to his office, he saw Mr. Joshua disappear inside the elevator as the doors closed behind him.

Inside his office, Geno fired up his MacBook Pro and connected the flash drive. It took several minutes to download all the data from Sheryl's iPhone to his laptop. While waiting for the data transfer to be completed, he opened several programs to help analyze the data contained within her phone.

His cellphone vibrated. The caller ID said one word: *Boss*. "Yes, sir," he said as he answered the call.

"You find out anything yet?" The obese man's voice was almost drowned out by the raucous sounds of boisterous talk and laughter in the background.

"Just downloaded the data onto my laptop. As I told Mr. Joshua, it will take a while to decipher what data I have and what it all means.

Sitting at Emilios Ballato's in Little Italy, some twenty-odd blocks away, the obese man did little to hide his annoyance. Dinner that night was with several high-end clients. Two of them each had hundreds of millions of dollars, while the third was part of the *B Club*, as exclusive a financial class as one can get. "Geno, I've told you how important this is. I need answers from you. Not tomorrow, but tonight. No excuses, only answers."

The line went dead as Geno turned his attention from the iPhone to the data on his laptop. Before he dug into anything else, he used a custom EXIF tool to compile all the data points the phone collected to see where Sheryl had gone in the past thirty-six hours. For someone with a small social network, she moved around lower Manhattan quite a bit. It took almost ninety minutes, but he quickly had a full map of Manhattan showing her precise locations during that time.

As Geno looked at each waypoint from the metadata, one spot stood out above all else. She spent more than a few minutes at the FedEx office store at the corner of Seventy-Eighth Street and Lexington Avenue.

That can only mean one thing.

"Shit!"

CHAPTER FORTY-TWO

THE WEST WING

Nick looked down at his watch as he exited the Eisenhower Executive Office Building and entered the West Wing. It was pushing midnight, and his energy tank hovered just above empty. He sent Sam home a few hours earlier and decided he would sleep in his normal spot, the worn leather couch in his office.

As he reached his office door, noises echoed down the hall. The White House is never quiet, but late at night things do tend to be less robust. A Secret Service agent stood ten feet down from his office. The man in a blue suit with a coiled earpiece had his back to the wall.

Nick approached the stoic agent, like a sentry guarding a treasure, and gestured toward the Oval Office. "Preacher in there?"

Special Agent Matthew Persson nodded. "You bet, Jordan. Been in the Oval for going on over two hours."

"Everything okay?" Nick asked as he looked at his watch. "That's not like him to be down here so late."

Matt shrugged. "Don't know what to say, bud. The doors have been closed the whole time. Said he needed to catch up on a few things. I've been tasked with holding up this load-bearing wall." Matt winked as he said the last word.

"Thanks." Nick smacked his palm against the thick material used to construct the wall. "I'd get you a chair but the director would fry your ass if he saw you sitting down on the job. So keep holding up that wall. You're doing a phenomenal job keeping the old place from falling down."

Nick turned around quickly and missed the middle finger thrust his way in a playful manner.

In three long strides, he approached the northwest door leading into the world's most famous office, knocked three times, and opened the door without waiting for a response. "Mr. President, sorry to disturb you."

"Fortunately, you didn't catch me with my pants down," the most powerful leader on planet earth said in a dry tone.

"Well, it wouldn't be the first time an occupant was in a compromising position in this office, sir." Nick didn't wait for any snide comments or inappropriate jokes about interns or blue dresses. "You're burning the midnight oil tonight, huh?"

President Thomas Collins looked up from the papers on the Resolute Desk. "Guess you could say I'm working Body Man hours tonight." A tall glass of sweet tea sat on a coaster next to the black telephone on the left side of the desk. Beside it sat a plate of fresh cookies, which were baked especially for the president by the White House pastry chef.

"Jeez, I'd advise against that, sir. There are better ways to spend an evening." Nick chuckled as he said the last few words. "I see it's a cookie and sweet tea kind of night. This must be dire."

The president released a deep sigh. "Probably better than a highball."

"Not sure about that, Mr. President, you know one of your predecessors, number thirty-four, used to enjoy a highball as his drink of choice. Although the Resolute Desk was in the Broadcast Room during his term."

President Collins shook his head and smiled. "I've heard Ike was a fan of those drinks, although I can't say I knew the desk was in that room during his time in office." The president ran his hand along the smooth surface of the desk's side. "You're just a wealth of knowledge when it comes to this place, aren't you?"

"To protect the office, you must understand it, sir." Nick cleared his throat. "I'm no expert by any means, sir, but I know a good deal of the history within these walls as well as the men who resided within them."

"If these walls could only talk. Right, Nicholas?"

"That would be a problem, sir. These walls have heard not only historic conversations but also every dirty little secret the American people would be better off not knowing."

"Roger that." The president became silent as his gaze moved around the oval-shaped office.

Nick watched his glance but said nothing.

"You heard about what happened in the Taiwan Strait a few hours ago?"

"Yes, sir," Nick said.

"Of course you would. The Body Man knows everything that's going on." A smirk formed at the corner of the president's lips.

"Can't do my job very well if I find out too many things after the fact, sir. But considering how Mogul's men got the drop on me, trust me when I say without a doubt I don't know everything that's going on."

President Collins shook his head slowly. "I know offering international geopolitical advice is not in your job description, but do you have any thoughts on the best course of action for Taiwan?"

"China is flexing its muscle, Mr. President. We all know they will make a play for the island eventually. They keep pushing the envelope and seeing what type of reaction they will get. The former president talked tough but generally let them get away with the flex. I would not assume to tell you how to do your job, sir, but I'd keep the Chinese president on a short leash. The Red Dragon thinks in terms of centuries and millennia. Unfortunately, our government often focuses on sound bites and TikTok clips more than the long game."

"It's a chess game dealing with them for sure, and I feel like after the recent blunders by several previous administrations, we are far too many moves behind."

Nick shrugged. "There's always a way to run the board, sir."

"Elements within Section Seven have made some interesting observations and suggestions."

"They often have a good pulse on these incidents, sir. I'd certainly suggest giving serious thought to whatever it is they are suggesting." Nick had stood just in front of the desk the entire time they talked.

The president gestured to one of the cream-colored couches in the center of the room. "Would you mind reviewing the brief they sent a little while ago, and giving me your thoughts. I mean it's not like you sleep or anything."

"Sure. I could use a cup of coffee, though."

The president pushed the lowest button on the keypad of the black phone. Three seconds later, a voice came over the speaker. "Yes, Mr. President?"

"Need a pot of coffee in the Oval, Carl. Light roast with half-n-half and sugar, please."

"Right away, sir," Carl, one of six White House butlers on permanent staff, said in response.

"A cup would be plenty, sir. I may want to go to sleep eventually."

"Nonsense, Carl would be insulted if I asked for just one cup," the president replied. "Besides, aren't you the one who always says life's a journey and not a destination? You can help the president out on his journey by offering me your two cents."

"Good to know you listen to a few things I say, Mr. President."

"My reactions may have slowed, but my hearing and memory are still top-notch, Nicholas."

Chapter Forty-Three

Arlington, Virginia

Arlington Memorial Bridge

A stiff breeze blew from the east as it raced across the Potomac River and blanketed the bench where Mr. Joshua sat. The cold chill pierced his thick overcoat and thin pants. He did very few things without a specific intent, and chose the place to conduct the dead drop with Merci for a distinct reason.

Six groupings of quadruple skull boats cut through the water as they proceeded down the river in front of him. Not someone who spent much time on the water as a youth, Mr. Joshua admired the tenacity and skill rowers possessed as they got up at the crack of dawn and pushed their bodies to perfect their craft. As the group passed, he took another bite of the harissa bacon egg and cheddar cheese croissant he picked up at For Five Coffee Roasters in Rosslyn, five minutes away. He washed the food down with a sip of dark roast Nicaraguan coffee.

Mr. Joshua arrived in plenty of time before he expected Merci to arrive. Since he knew she would likely be there early to recon the area, he was on the bench overlooking the river an hour before the scheduled dead drop.

His back faced the George Washington Memorial Parkway some fifty feet away. The view in front included the backside of the Lincoln Memorial. In the distance, the Washington Monument jutted into the sky like a finger pointed toward Heaven. As he turned to his right, he could see the top of the dome comprising the Thomas Jefferson Memorial.

Every thirty to forty-five seconds, a runner would make their way down the path that followed the river's contour. As he watched one attractive blond jog the trail, he realized he missed running on an actual path. These days, because of his extensive travel and insane work hours, he rarely ran outdoors, sticking to the treadmill at the gym in his high-rise Manhattan apartment or various hotel fitness centers.

As Mr. Joshua looked around at his surroundings, he thought about what he discovered when he dug into Merci's background. He knew as much as one could know about hers contracts since she entered the professional assassin ranks before he hired her for the hit on Chuck Brown. Some stories were possibly just that, figments of someone's imagination, but thanks to the dark web and loose lips, he could piece together a fairly accurate bio on her. Something about how she operated piqued his interest, and it was more than her mixture of beauty blended with deadly precision. From what he read, she could be provocative yet lethal, and demure while also calculating.

Few people in the seedy world away from his investment banking life knew Mr. Joshua's real name was Prescott. His Wall Street father had no clue about his double life. Even though he worked for the firm his father founded, the day-to-day management was handled by a team of professionals in the C-suite. These days, his father spent most of his days sailing the Mediterranean or traversing the globe. The work bored Prescott, and he only followed his father's footsteps due to the immense pressure on him. He convinced senior management and his father to let him work remotely most of the time, facilitating the vastly different work-flow he performed secretly with The Fulbright Group. Mr. Joshua, or Prescott, whichever persona he pretended to be while living a double life, only cared about one person: himself.

On his iPhone, he pulled up the file that detailed the hit Merci conducted on Danny Frazier, The Body Man's apprentice under the previous administration. The dossier provided proved to be falsified to get her on board with the assassination. Based on the details in the report, Danny's body fell less than ten feet from where Mr. Joshua currently sat. This plan he concocted would either royally backfire or give him the leverage he wanted to have over her. Even though the obese man did not think it wise, Mr. Joshua did what he felt was best, not what others suggested.

As he looked down at his watch, he could sense eyes directed his way. He felt her presence before he turned and locked onto her fierce glance.

CHAPTER FORTY-FOUR

MANHATTAN

Geno approached the FedEx store at the corner of Seventy-Eighth Street and Lexington Avenue. The smell of herbs, spices, garlic, and onions emanated from the falafel food truck beside the entrance. He paused and went over the plan of action again in his head before stepping inside.

Good cop, or bad cop? He opened the glass door and walked toward the counter.

A lanky girl with hot pink hair, a hooped nose ring, and a large neck tattoo worked behind the counter. Before she could say anything, Geno had the fake detective badge out and flashed it so the girl with the nametag of Liza could see it. He pointed to the array of cameras behind the counter. "I'll need to get a copy of your surveillance video."

"Excuse me?" the girl asked.

"I think you heard me, young lady. I need a digital copy of your security footage." Geno watched out of the corner of his eye as a thin man with hair down to his shoulders stood at the other end of the counter and shifted his eyes toward Geno as he demanded the video.

Liza's look could best be described as incredulous. "Yeah, I don't think so. You got a warrant, pops?"

Geno explained to her how he didn't need one while he glanced over to see the skinny worker. The man looked nervous.

"Sorry, 5-0, not getting anything without a warrant. I know how the law works. My uncle is a defense attorney." She glanced over at the other worker. "I'm taking my fifteen-minute break." She looked back at Geno. "Get a warrant and you can get your surveillance footage." With that, she removed her FedEx apron, placed it on the desk behind the counter, and walked out the front door.

Geno motioned with his finger for the nervous, scrawny man to come over to where he stood leaning against the counter. "Get me the footage," he demanded in a harsh tone. In a matter of seconds, he sized the man up, who looked like he might be a stoner, or at least indulged from time to time.

A bead of sweat formed at the man's temple. "I can't. Liza is the supervisor here. She calls the shots until our manager gets in later."

Geno read the man's nametag. *Kevin Fields.* It was time for bad cop to take over. He pulled out his phone and faked dialing a number. "I'm calling my precinct, Kevin, and going to run your name. Twenty bucks says you have a record, and if you do, I'll bust you for possession on the spot."

Kevin's expression changed from concern to downright terror. "Man, I don't touch that shit anymore! I'm clean, bro."

Geno's voice came out like an unhinged snarl. "Let's get this straight. I'm not your, *bro*!" He stressed the last word. "I don't give a damn what you say, because I'll still haul your skinny ass to the station and put you in central holding for the rest of the day and even overnight." He paused. "Or you can go to the back and get me the security footage from the past five days and keep your mouth quiet. Your call, Kevin. We can do this the easy way or the less-than-optimal way. If you do this for me, it will be like I was never here."

With a quiver in his lip, Kevin replied, "Man, I don't know how to pull up that data from the computer. I'm not some techie dude. And even if I did, there's no way to transfer the data."

Geno removed the flash drive from his front right pocket and swung it in front of Kevin's narrow face. "Well, what do you know? I just happen to have a device we can use, and I even know how to download it from the server where it's likely stored." Geno gestured with his hand toward the rear of the store. "I'll follow you back there, Kev."

Sixteen minutes later, Geno stepped onto the sidewalk and was hit by a fresh wave of the falafel smell that permeated the block.

Liza sneered at him as she approached, back from her morning break. "See you back here later with a warrant, 5-0?"

Geno rolled his eyes. "Yeah, sure. I'll also bring some peroxide to fix that rat's nest you call hair." He turned and walked in the opposite direction of the FedEx location. The back of his head could feel the dirty look his snide comment generated.

CHAPTER FORTY-FIVE

ARLINGTON MEMORIAL BRIDGE

Merci approached the dead drop location from the south with her senses on a heightened state of alert. She had exact latitude and longitude coordinates, plus the instructions said a park bench would be present serving as the pickup spot. Concealed inside her coat pocket, her hand firmly gripped the hidden Sig Sauer pistol. She did not know what she was about to walk into and took no unnecessary chances.

Inside her ear was a small transmitter that relayed audio and contained a microphone to transmit her words.

"I'm less than two hundred yards from the GPS location. What do you see?" She waited for Marcus's response.

Set up half a mile away, Marcus looked through the Leupold scope mounted atop his Barrett M82A1 rifle. The location chosen for the dead drop was quite clever, considering it allowed for very few overwatch locations. With Arlington National Cemetery due west, the Pentagon southwest, and the Potomac to the east, Marcus had to be resourceful to find a place to set up his hide site. "For the record, I don't like this location. I'm too far away and have a very limited line of sight."

"You've said that several times already. So, do you see anything or not?" Merci's voice did little to hide her displeasure in stating the obvious.

"There are several trees in the way. I see a park bench, but I don't think it's the right one. It looks like the bench referenced by the GPS location they gave you is out of my direct line of sight because of obstructions. I can't get any closer or move anywhere that will give me a clear field of view. If I do, I'll have to ditch the rifle and only use binoculars. But I don't think that will be wise since it offers no added protection."

"Keep your eyes open. If you see any suspicious movement, let me know. I'm going to move closer."

Marcus pleaded, "If someone is at the bench, promise me you'll bail."

"I know what I'm doing."

As Merci made her way around the slight bend in the trail, the bench where the dead drop would take place came into view. A big problem suddenly occurred when she saw that the bench was, in fact, not empty. She slowed as her eyes focused on the person who sat at the precise location the GPS told her to go. The person's back was toward her since the park bench faced the Potomac. Cautiously, she approached the spot where the drop was to occur.

"Someone is sitting on the bench," Merci said.

"Copy that, I don't have eyes on them."

Merci's expression shifted to a frustrated look. "I'm going to approach."

"Be careful," Marcus said. "Remember, it could be a setup."

Merci did not reply.

As she approached the spot, memories flooded back to her, and she diverted her eyes from the bench to a place in the grass near the trail just past where the person sat.

That was the exact location where she shot Danny Frazier. He should have died that day, but a scream from a woman on the Arlington Memorial Bridge startled her, and she missed her intended mark by a fraction of an inch. The measurement might have been small, but it meant the difference between life and death.

As she wrestled with her feelings of failure that day, she turned her attention back to the person sitting on the bench. Merci was now less than twenty feet away from where they sat. Whoever was on the bench suddenly turned around and faced her.

Their eyes locked. Her grip on the Sig intensified as her pulse quickened.

Mr. Joshua. The name didn't leave her tongue but spun around in her head like an electron orbiting the nucleus of an atom.

"What the hell are you doing here?" she asked Mr. Joshua with a distinct hiss in her voice.

Inside her earpiece, Marcus's voice echoed. "Who? Who is there?"

Mr. Joshua smiled.

CHAPTER FORTY-SIX

ONE WORLD TRADE CENTER

Back at his office, Geno began the arduous task of downloading the surveillance footage to his MacBook Air. Fortunately, the software FedEx used to record the multiple camera video feeds interfaced well with the program he installed. Within twenty minutes, his analysis of the footage began. With a hot cup of coffee next to the mouse, he dug into the hours of video.

The program used advanced facial recognition software, so even though the image from the surveillance cameras was slightly grainy, he quickly narrowed down the frames containing Sheryl Hopping.

When Geno poured his second cup of coffee, he isolated Sheryl's seventeen minutes inside the store.

Now came the arduous part. He watched the real-time footage of Sheryl from several angles in its entirety, which took over an hour. Then, once he felt comfortable with what occurred, he went frame by frame, pausing and zooming in where necessary. Another two hours passed, and three more cups of coffee were consumed, as well as several trips to the bathroom to relieve himself.

One thing was clear from the images: Sheryl had the FedEx staff make copies of at least part, if not the entire, document she handed over. Geno immediately recognized the worker as Liza, who was no help when he requested the video footage.

Based on his analysis of the videos, it appeared that three copies were then placed inside mailing envelopes.

Who did she send them to? His pulse raced.

This is not good at all. The obese man was going to be royally pissed off. He had to go back to the FedEx location and get the mailing information. Kevin wouldn't be too thrilled to see him again.

He picked up the phone and called a contact at the NYPD. Geno needed the full jacket on Kevin Fields, if one existed. Fifteen minutes later, he had his answer. *Bingo, China white*, he said to himself.

Next, he called another person, one who could get him anything at any time if the price was right.

The remaining question was whether to tell the obese man before or after he returned to the location. Geno decided to rip off the Band-Aid and go to his office as he left for the return trip to the FedEx store.

⸻◆⸻

The obese man displayed a most unpleasant face, like a toddler sucking on a lemon, as Geno explained what he found when he visited the FedEx store, and then after he reviewed the security footage.

"You're positive Sheryl made three copies?"

Geno cleared his throat and sipped from the water bottle in his left hand. "Yes, sir, it is clear on the surveillance footage."

A growing hue of red spread across the obese man's face. "And you think those three copies got mailed out?"

"It appears so, yes."

"To where? And who were they addressed to?" Spittle formed on his lips as he said the last few words.

"No clue. The video is grainy. There's no way to read anything as small as the address or name on the mailing label."

"Then why are you still here and not at the FedEx store getting that critical information?"

Geno stammered. "I ... uh ... well, I thought you should know."

The obese man raised his hand and pointed his pudgy finger at Geno. "Know this, if those copies aren't retrieved intact, without the addressee opening them, there will be hell to pay." He shook his finger back and forth. "Got it?"

Not needing to be told twice, Geno pivoted and headed for the door. "Got it," he said as he exited the office and made his way to the bank of elevators.

CHAPTER FORTY-SEVEN

ARLINGTON MEMORIAL BRIDGE

Mr. Joshua smirked as he connected with Merci's fierce gaze. "We finally meet in person." The words were said in a smooth, drawn-out tone.

"What the hell are you doing here? I won't ask a third time."

In Merci's ear, Marcus asked again, "Who is it?"

Mr. Joshua stood, turned to face her, and put his hands in front of his body. The gesture was meant to assure her that he was no threat. "Merci, I come in peace. I have the intel packet on your target."

She did little to hide the disdain in her voice. "Look, Mr. Joshua, I don't know what game you are playing, but in my world dead drops involve items being exchanged in a secret place, without meeting in person. The contract I agreed to was clear. This was a dead drop, not a meet and greet." Since Merci couldn't say anything without giving away the fact that Marcus was close by, she reached into her pocket and clicked the FOB three times, the pre-planned code to let him know she was okay.

She heard two clicks in response, acknowledging he received her message.

"Hmm, Mr. Joshua. So you know who I am. I don't recall my name being on any of the electronic correspondence we exchanged for this job or the previous one. But impressive. You did your homework. Kudos."

"Oh, I know all about you, Prescott."

The smug look on his face transformed into one of genuine surprise. "What did you call me?"

Now, Merci displayed a smirk. "Your real name is Prescott Avery. The son of an investment banker. You grew up in Connecticut until your parents sent you off to a well-to-do boarding school in upstate New York when you turned eleven. After your primary education, you graduated from Columbia University near the top of your class with a degree in economics. You still hold a position in your father's firm, but spend most of your time working for The Fulbright Group. Should I go on?"

Mr. Joshua's face turned a shade of red. "I must say I'm at a loss for words. I always try to stay anonymous when hiring a client for sensitive jobs. You clearly have good sources."

"I've been burned before when I didn't do my due diligence. I learned as much about you and TFG as possible before I accepted either contract."

He thumped his balled fist against his broad chest. "Respect. To be clear, though, The Fulbright Group is not paying you. We secure professionals with a specific skillset, such as yourself, on behalf of our clients. Of course, we work very hard to respect their privacy and never reveal who hires us."

"You're a middleman?"

"Precisely."

"So, who decided to have me followed in western North Carolina? You, someone else at TFG, or possibly your client?"

"What I can tell you is the person was instructed only to observe. They were no threat to you at any point during the operation. This was a valuable contract that needed to be completed successfully. Someone other than me decided it was necessary to have you watched. The person who followed you has been eliminated."

Merci shook her head. "I don't like being micro-managed. If I'm hired to do a job, I should be allowed to complete it without interference."

"That's reasonable." Mr. Joshua nodded.

"Am I to assume something similar will happen with this new contract?"

"No, you proved yourself with Chuck Brown's termination. I don't foresee any reason that would be necessary."

"Before you give me the intel packet, I have a question for you."

Mr. Joshua contorted his face. "Okay, I guess. What is it?"

"Where did you come up with the name, Mr. Joshua?"

He smirked. "Not a fan of eighties movies, I take it?"

"Ah contraire. I love them. Let me guess." Merci paused. "You named yourself after the movie *Lethal Weapon*. Mr. Joshua, who was played by Gary Busey in the film, was part of the Shadow Company, a group of mercenaries who smuggled heroin. Fancy yourself an eighties wannabe badass?"

Mr. Joshua clapped. "Very good. You know your movie trivia after all."

"Spoiler alert, it didn't turn out real well for Busey or members of the Shadow Company at the end of the movie. But none of this explains why you are here in person and why this wasn't handled electronically."

"What I have to give you is highly sensitive. The client did not want electronic breadcrumbs."

"And a paper trail would be better?"

"There will be no paper trail, Merci. Once I show you the intel I brought, the info will be burned right here near the Potomac. You'll need to memorize what I'm about to show you. I am under the impression you have a nearly photographic memory. Have I been misinformed?"

"You have not. I can memorize whatever you brought for me within minutes."

"Glad to hear that."

She motioned toward the bench. "Should we take a seat and go over whatever I need to memorize?"

"Sure thing. And you can tell Marcus to stand down. He won't need the Barrett M82A1."

Merci's eyes grew noticeably wider, but she said nothing.

Mr. Joshua sneered. "Like you, Miss de Atta, I do my homework as well and know exactly who I hire on behalf of our clients and who they work with and even who they screw. You don't go into a situation without redundancies and escape plans, nor do I. In this game, we both know those who don't have foresight end up six feet underground in a hurry."

CHAPTER FORTY-EIGHT

THE WHITE HOUSE

FIRST FAMILY RESIDENCE

Once a week, Nick had a standing invitation for breakfast at the president's family dining room in the northwest corner of the second floor. The room is across from the first family's private kitchen, where the first family can prepare their own meals and at least have the illusion of being in their own home. Often, the president invited his wife, Ali, to have breakfast with him and The Body Man. Most weeks, if she could not join them, she at least made the meal. A magnificent cook in her own right, Ali loved baking for her family and friends.

This week, she planned an outing at a local women's shelter, so she made Thomas and Nick breakfast before heading out with her Secret Service detail.

The President of the United States having a regular meal with the person whose job it is to protect the office they hold was not the norm. The connection shared by Thomas Collins and Nick Jordan didn't fit any of the regular patterns established since the role of The Body Man began under the Kennedy administration.

The morning's discussion started with the passing of Clint Hill, a retired Secret Service agent who was known for throwing himself atop the convertible seconds after President Kennedy's 1963 assassination in Dallas. Clint found the notoriety he received to be a heavy burden over the years. Nick and many other agents who make up the United States Secret Service considered Clint a legend. His books were required reading for any new hires. The president told Nick how he met former Special Agent Hill at an event when he was vice-president and even had the privilege to enjoy a drink with him. Yes, it was called "The Clint," one of First Lady Jackie Kennedy's favorite beverages. Nick shared with the president that he tossed back a few himself with Clint over the years, and Clint even gave him one of the cards he always carried that had instructions on making the famous drink. A card Nick still kept in his desk.

Next, they discussed sports, recent book releases, and some D.C.-centric gossip.

Nick used the napkin to get the last bit of homemade strawberry preserve off the corner of his lips. "As usual, sir, the first lady outdid herself with breakfast."

The president smiled. "She's a fantastic cook. She picked those strawberries herself and made six months' worth of preserves from scratch. Actually, her specialty is baking, but it's a little harder for her to get into it here at the White House. When we are back home in Dana, she bakes up a storm. You should see her on Christmas morning. You would think she was planning to feed the whole county."

"I know this is a major subject change, Mr. President, but with the Kennedy versus Byolyze case starting soon, the Secret Service has increased the security presence here at the White House and on your detail."

"Uh, that. And yes, the director read me in last night about the changes." The president's smile quickly faded. "I was really hoping all that nonsense was behind us, but with a case of that magnitude reaching our top court, it will incite a lot of hostility around the nation. Depending on which way the justices swing, this case could have long-lasting ramifications for our healthcare system and the economy as a whole. And by the way, you are at my breakfast table. Do not call me Mr. President. TC or Thomas is fine. But not, Mr. Collins, that was what we called my dad. Don't I tell you that almost every week?"

"Yes, Mr. President, you do. And every week, I ignore you. I hold the office in way too high regard to refer to the occupant in any way other than the term, *Mr. President*. Sorry, sir, that's just the way it has to be in my book."

"Well, considering I'm an accidental president, can't you make an exception?"

"Accidental? How do you figure, sir? You were duly elected by almost eighty million citizens."

The president frowned. "No, Charles Steele was duly elected. I was only the undercard on the ticket."

"Your name was on the ballot as well, Mr. President. Even if it was below Mogul's."

"Nobody is voting for the vice president, Nicholas. They are merely the insurance policy if POTUS kicks the bucket while in the office. We are pretty much like the spare donut tire. Nobody ever wants to pull the spare out of the hidden compartment in the trunk and use it unless they absolutely have to."

"Jeez, it's almost as if you didn't want the job, sir."

Thomas nodded. "Truly, I didn't."

"But, sir, you did run for vice president."

"Correct, and don't get me wrong, I always wanted to serve my country. As you know, my dad was an elected official in Hendersonville, North Carolina, when I grew up. Fast forward years later, and after my kids went away to college, I had a hankering to serve the community in some capacity." President Collins appeared lost in thought momentarily as he thought back to his political beginnings. His dad had passed several years prior and never saw him reach the highest office in the land.

Thomas Collins continued. "I had a lot of contacts in the community and ran for mayor at the urgings of my dad. To my surprise, what do you know, I actually won. Four years later, the congressman for my home district, the eleventh, retired, and I was asked to run by leaders in the community. I did not expect to win, but once again, I took the seat by a large margin. I proudly served western North Carolina as their U.S. Representative in the House for three full terms. Then, halfway through my fourth term, Charles Steele tapped me to be his running mate as vice president. Yeah, I never saw that coming. I might have been more shocked than the rest of the nation. Most reporters outside my district and a large swath of the nation collectively asked, *Who in heaven's name is Thomas Collins?* Charles and I didn't see eye to eye on many things, but I felt obligated to serve my country once again. Like I've said repeatedly and sincerely, I never had aspirations to go for a high office in our government; it just happened. That, my friend, is why I'm an accidental president."

Nick shook his head. "Sorry, sir, I believe the whole story except for the accidental part. I believe in fate, not luck, and I don't believe anyone accidentally rises to the role of President of the United States. What happened to you is what occurs when preparation meets opportunity." Nick smirked. "Accidental is when you are walking on a perfectly manicured lawn, and you somehow step in the one spot that has dog crap."

The president shrugged. "Some might say that's karma, or maybe you should look down more often and avoid said dookie."

With a chuckle, Nick replied, "Maybe, sir. And I'm not sure I've heard someone refer to it as dookie in ages."

President Collins pushed his chair back from the table with a wide smile. "I could sit here and chew the fat with you all day, Nick, but unfortunately, I have a busy schedule." He extended his hand across the table. "There are world leaders who need my hand-holding. House and Senate leaders who want to butter me up for some pork-laden bills, and of course, more spots in the world ready to catch on fire than fire extinguishers in our arsenal to put them out if they all ignite simultaneously. But ... the beat goes on."

Nick took the extended hand and returned a firm shake.

"Same time next week, Mr. Body Man?"

"Yes, Thomas." Nick winked. "I mean, yes, Mr. President."

Chapter Forty-Nine

Manhattan

Geno made one stop at the West Village on Perry Street before he crossed to the other side of Manhattan and once again visited the FedEx store at the corner of Seventy-Eighth Street and Lexington Avenue.

He had his game face on. It was time for Mr. Bad Cop. Within a few steps inside the store, his eyes locked on Kevin Fields.

Kevin's eyes appeared wide as saucers as Geno made a straight line through the store to where Kevin stood beside the counter. At the moment, there were no other customers inside.

Going around the counter, with a snarl spread across his face, Geno pointed his finger at Kevin and poked it into his bony chest. "We got a problem here, Kev."

Kevin swallowed hard, as if his mouth didn't have enough saliva. "A problem. What do you mean?"

"I reviewed the security footage," Geno stated. "And now I'll need the address where the three envelopes were sent."

Kevin shuddered, his nerves clearly getting the best of him. "I, um, I can't do that. Pretty sure you need a warrant to access private data like that. Don't you?"

Geno let out a large gasp of air. "We playing that game again, like the shit Liza pulled on me earlier." As he said it, his right arm swung up, and his hand forcefully grabbed the scruff of Kevin's neck.

Kevin flinched as Geno applied firm pressure.

Next, with his left hand, Geno removed a small one-inch by two-inch plastic baggie he purchased in the West Village on Perry Street and dropped it on the floor. The bag landed a few inches from Kevin's Converse high-top sneakers.

"What the hell is that?" Geno asked as he pointed to the baggie next to Kevin's shoe. "Did you just drop that?"

Kevin shook his head as fiercely as he could, but considering Geno still had a firm grip on his neck, the movement was severely restricted. "Yo, yo, yo, that's not my stuff, man. I swear. I don't do that trash anymore."

Geno released the scrawny man's neck from his vice-like grip, reached back to his belt, and removed a set of handcuffs affixed to the loop of his pants. "You're in a heap of trouble now, Kev."

"Yo, man, it's not my stuff. Please! I'll do anything. I can't go back to the clink."

Geno shrugged and said, "Pull the billing info and addresses for the three mailing envelopes I need, and I'll be on my way."

"But I could get fired if my manager knew I provided someone's personal data. My boss is on a lunch break, but will be back any minute."

"Then I suggest you work fast, Kev. Or I'll drag your ass back to my station, and you know what will happen next."

Kevin took four minutes to pull up the invoice and tracking information on the three envelopes Sheryl mailed. He handed it to Geno, his hand trembling.

"See, that wasn't hard." Geno grabbed the printouts. As he turned to walk out the door, he pointed to the bag of heroin that remained on the floor. "Oh, and you can keep that for your troubles. Goodness knows you might need it after the day you've had so far."

Kevin did not reply but grabbed the plastic baggie and stuffed it in his pocket.

⎯⎯⎯◦◦◦⎯⎯⎯

Once outdoors, Geno examined the invoice and tracking details for the three envelopes. Before he got to the end of the city block, he placed a call.

"What did you find out?" the obese man asked in a perturbed tone.

Geno sighed. "She mailed out three envelopes to various states, but sent them ground service; none of them have arrived at their destinations yet."

"They must be intercepted. Get your men assembled and get those envelopes. None of them can be received by whoever she mailed them to. Do you understand?"

"Copy that, boss."

"If any addressees get them, you'll need to intervene and undo the mess she created. The contents of those envelopes cannot be seen in the light of day under any circumstances. All hell will break loose if they do."

The line went dead. Geno looked down at his cell phone as he removed it from the side of his head. *I don't get paid enough to deal with this horseshit.*

Chapter Fifty

Arlington Memorial Bridge

Merci did not like the idea of sitting on a park bench alongside Mr. Joshua, but she didn't feel threatened by him, at least not physically.

"You good?" Marcus asked in her earpiece. Merci reached into her pocket, felt the Sig, but gripped the FOB and clicked the button three times. The pre-planned code assured Marcus that everything was going fine.

She scanned the area around where they sat. Nothing looked suspicious. She felt remarkably at peace out in the open with very little in her direct control.

"I'm going to reach back around and remove the file I've brought for you to review." Mr. Joshua knew she would come armed, so he moved very slowly as his hands went behind his back and removed the folder stuffed between his belt and shirt.

Merci watched his movements. With her right hand still in her pocket, she gripped the Sig just in case he did something stupid.

Mr. Joshua placed the file on his lap, his hands resting on top of the quarter-inch-thick sealed envelope. Several seconds passed in silence as he looked at Merci and back at the file. "You can take as long as you need, but most of what's enclosed are pictures, so I don't believe you will need long to review the contents." He tapped the envelope as he finished speaking.

Merci removed her hand from her pocket. "Let's have it then. We can stop dicking around playing all this cloak and dagger nonsense and see what you are paying mc an cxorbitant amount of money to do."

Mr. Joshua handed over the envelope but didn't immediately let go as Merci pulled it toward her.

She gave it a firm tug before he finally released his grip. *What game is he playing?*

Merci bent the metal clasps away from the envelope and unclasped the flap, sliding the contents out. In the first picture, atop the stack, a shudder ran through her body. Imperceptible to the naked eye, she wasn't about to allow anyone to see how she reacted. In fact, she showed no reaction on her face as she methodically went page by page through the packet. It contained about ten pages of text and over twenty photos in all.

She knew the mark as soon as she looked at the first photo.

Inside, she seethed with righteous anger. *I should have known better than to accept a contract without knowing the target.* Outwardly, she showed zero emotion.

Mr. Joshua watched as she reviewed the packet, one page after another. "Take her alive, and when, or if, I give you the word, kill her. Do it in the way detailed on page six. If that's unnecessary, I'll give you further instructions." Mr. Joshua spoke the words like a convenience store worker stating the total of a purchase. With no emotion, he spoke in a matter-of-fact tone.

"Thirty-six hours to complete it?"

"Maximum," Mr. Joshua said. "The sooner, the better, but I know this operation will take time to organize and familiarize you with the target's location. Everything you need is in the intel packet. Do you need to look at the pages one more time?"

Merci shook her head. "No, it's been memorized already." She slid the papers back inside the envelope and closed it again.

"Good." Mr. Joshua put out his hand, and Merci returned the packet.

—◦—

Twenty feet away was a picnic table and a permanent galvanized steel grill. He walked over to the grill, placed the closed envelope under the metal grate, removed a small can of butane lighter fluid from his coat pocket, doused the packet, and lit it on fire. Several times, he squirted more fluid on the disintegrating papers. It took several minutes, but once the last of the papers burned, Mr. Joshua walked back to the bench and sat down.

Merci said nothing. She looked straight ahead toward the ripples in the Potomac's flowing water.

He stared at her for over a minute before he finally spoke. "So, we don't have any problems?"

"How do you mean?" Merci asked.

"Well, I know you have certain rules you typically follow, and this contract may require you to violate those said rules."

Merci shrugged. "A job is a job. I said yes, got paid, and now I'll deliver the results you expect."

"I'm glad to hear that. Contact me as soon as you have her. The phone number was in the packet on the last page."

"Yes," Merci replied. "I know the number."

Mr. Joshua stood. "Are you leaving first, or am I?"

Merci shook her head. "Go ahead, I need to sit here for a few. The peacefulness of the water helps me organize my thoughts and determine my plan of attack."

"Very well, I'll be hearing from you soon." Mr. Joshua walked away from the bench, but several feet away, turned and paused. "Your time starts now, Merci," he said as he gestured toward his watch. "Thirty-six hours and not a minute more." Not waiting for a response, he spun on his heels, walked away, and followed the path under the Arlington Memorial Bridge. A black Infinite QX80 Luxe pulled up along the side of the road on the George Washington Memorial Parkway as he crossed under the bridge. Mr. Joshua climbed into the vehicle. It sped off a few seconds later.

On you, Merci thought as she watched Mr. Joshua get into the car. Her eyes focused on the driver as the car pulled away from the curb and merged into traffic. *My plan of attack on you!*

"Babe, speak to me," Marcus pleaded in a firm tone from the earpiece she wore.

Chapter Fifty-One

The West Wing

After breakfast with the president, Nick went downstairs to his office. As he opened the door, he saw Sam sitting behind the desk in the cramped office space, reviewing a thick stack of reports.

"How was breakfast with Preacher?" Sam asked.

Nick smiled as he sat on the worn leather couch. He stretched his arms over his head and let out an audible yawn. "It was good. The first lady made a phenomenal meal as usual."

"She normally does." Sam picked up the detailed itinerary from the side of the desk. "His schedule looks pretty slammed today."

"Yes. Mainly phone calls with world leaders. Things appear to be heating up in Taiwan, which is not encouraging. Plus, the Gaza and West Bank situation is like walking on broken eggshells."

"You think China will invade soon? That's what the media has been stating for a few months."

Nick exhaled a deep breath of air. "I don't know, Sam. The media has its own agenda. The intel reports aren't promising, but President Collins continues to show strength in that region, which makes me believe it gives China pause. Weak presidents tend to invite conflict, while ones that convey strength usually help to keep the vultures at bay."

"You headed home or sticking around here today?"

"Nah, I'll be around. I got enough shut-eye on the couch last night. I'm good. You can join me in the Situation Room in fifteen minutes if you'd like. Meeting with one of the duty officers to go over the hotspots that are making the most noise recently around the globe."

"Thanks, I think I will." She bit her lower lip and paused for a moment. "Does it ever seem weird to you that Preacher is so strait-laced?"

Nick furrowed his brow. "How do you mean?"

"I mean, from what you told me about Mogul, and even the other president's before him, the occupants of the office seem to give The Body Man role more trouble. Yet, Preacher, I think, can best be described as fairly predictable and boring."

"Ha." Nick let out an audible laugh. "After getting abducted and almost killed by the men Mogul hired, I, for one, am grateful we have an easier occupant of the office this time around."

"Guess I never thought about it that way."

"I'll take predictable and boring over what I went through with the previous administration. My concerns about the office these days are from outside sources. Especially the list Luke and I found at the Black Sea. The implication of what is happening could have dire consequences for the presidency and the American public. That's why I can't go home and just relax. Until the threat is understood and dealt with, there's no rest for the weary. That includes not only me, but the rest of the team as well."

Sam nodded. "I get it."

"You've had to take on much more of an active role day-to-day with the president and monitoring what's happening around here since my focus is often elsewhere."

"Glad to play my part, Nick. Fortunately, I didn't have much social life before I joined the Secret Service, so I guess I don't know what I'm missing anyway."

"Same here, Sam. I never wanted an ordinary life."

Sam winked. "After your time on that oil platform, I bet you might tell others to be careful what they wish."

"Yeah, that's for sure cause you just might get it. Hey, want to grab a cup of coffee at the mess before the meeting? I want to discuss some stuff and pick your brain about a few things."

"Yeah, sure, java sounds good right now. I've only had a cup so far today. Dare I ask how many you've thrown down already?"

"Not enough," Nick answered.

They headed down the hallway to the far stairwell, which led them to the basement, where the White House Mess and Situation Room were located.

"Any chance you're headed to the Lincoln Memorial after the meeting with the duty officer?" Sam asked.

"Probably." Nick smirked. "I know it's predictable, but the sixteenth president expects me to visit him as often as possible. Besides, with the current threat, I have my own armed guards pretty much everywhere I go outside the White House property."

"Who would have thought The Body Man would ever have his own Secret Service detail?"

Nick frowned as he opened the stairwell door and gestured with his arm that Sam should go first. "I don't like it, not one bit. The sooner we can get to the bottom of what is happening and return to some semblance of normalcy, the better. I love being a protector, but being protected is not in my repertoire."

"Pulling out the big words, are we?"

With a smirk Nick replied, "I know one or two and use them from time to time."

They grabbed an empty table in the wood-paneled dining room as a Navy steward came over to take their order.

Minutes later, the woman returned with cups of coffee for both of them.

Sam took a sip before she placed the cup on the saucer adorned with the White House logo. "Okay, what did you want to discuss with me?"

Nick raised his eyebrows. "Oh, where to begin ..."

CHAPTER FIFTY-TWO

MIDTOWN MANHATTAN

Geno knew time worked against him, and every second counted if he would successfully retrieve all three FedEx envelopes. He made four brief calls and told his regular crew, Matteo, Leo, Gus, and Trey, to meet him at Peter Dillon's on E 40th St. and Lexington Ave in an hour.

The bartender nodded as Geno eased onto an empty barstool. "Jeez, you're here early. We just opened. What'll it be?"

"My normal Guinness, Paulie," Geno said.

A couple of minutes later, Paulie slid the Irish beer across the thick mahogany bar to where Geno sat. "You look tired, buddy."

With a deep sigh, Geno let out a breath. "Been a long few days, my friend." He held up the richly colored pint. "Cheers."

"Sláinte," Paulie replied. "You drinking alone today?"

"Nah, the lads will be here soon."

"Don't see the five of you together for a pint too often anymore," Paulie said.

"Yeah, it's harder for all of us to make it up here every week. The job down in the financial district keeps me busy, and the others are doing their own things most of the time."

"Is it a good gig you got? You're with The Fulbright Group, right?"

"I am. And yeah, it's a solid way to earn a living."

The two men engaged in small talk for a few more minutes. Geno finished the pint and gestured to an open table in the back of the bar. "Pour me five more, Paulie, and bring them to the back. The lads should be here any minute."

"Aye, I can do that."

"Throw it on my tab. I'll settle up before I leave."

Geno walked to the back, and within five minutes, the four men who made up his regular crew arrived. All of them appeared glad for the pints that awaited them.

———◈———

It took Geno about ten minutes to fill in Matteo, Leo, Gus, and Trey on what had occurred since they helped him search for the document and chase down Sheryl Hopping outside her apartment. By then, Paulie dropped off another round of Guinness at the table. Geno indicated the second round would be enough. He needed the men to get moving soon, and they would need their wits about them.

"We got three FedEx envelopes and five of us, boss," Matteo said. "How you wanna split this up?"

"I'm sparse on details right now," Geno stated with pursed lips. "I made a few calls, and I've got a contact tracking down the details on the three people Sheryl mailed the files to. As of right now, all I know is their names and addresses. Also, I have detailed tracking information, so we have a ballpark of when they should be delivered. Needless to say, we don't have much time."

"We got an odd number," Trey said. "Who is going where, or are we all going together?"

Geno shook his head. "Can't happen. These FedEx envelopes got sent all around the country. We have to team up and hit the three locations simultaneously. The addresses are in Seattle, Phoenix, and Miami."

"We get to choose who goes where?" Gus asked.

"Maybe," Geno said. "Have you been to any of those three cities before?"

Gus nodded. "Yeah, I got a cousin, Burton, who lives in the southeast Phoenix area, Chandler, Arizona, to be exact. I've been out there a few times to golf with him and even attended the Waste Management tournament a few years back.

There are so many drunk blokes at that spot, oh, and they seem to be playing golf as well." Gus grinned as he said the last few words.

"I've been out that way, too," Trey replied. "My ex used to like Sonoma. We flew into the Phoenix area a bunch of times."

Geno raised his arms slightly from the table. "There you go. Gus and Trey. You have the FedEx package on its way to Phoenix." He looked down at his smartphone. "According to the online tracking, it's in Chicago. You both need to be in Phoenix before it arrives and intercept it."

"And what do we do when we find it?" Gus asked.

"Boss wants it destroyed. Don't open it, don't toss it. Burn it onsite."

Trey looked at Gus. "We can do that. How do you want us to get the Phoenix? Commercial?"

Geno shook his head. "Boss told me to charter three jets out of Teterboro ASAP. They'll be fueled and ready for us when we get there. Commercial takes too long, and we could have delays. This is a no-fail scenario. What Sheryl mailed to these three individuals cannot be opened under any circumstances."

"And if somehow they get it before we arrive?" Trey asked. "What then?"

Geno turned stoic. "We'll figure that out on the fly if it occurs." He looked down at his phone. "That leaves us Miami and Seattle." He looked up at the phone and locked eyes first with Matteo, then with Leo. "Which one you lads want?"

Matteo spoke up first. "I'm cool with Seattle. My sister lived out there."

"Yeah, I'd say Seattle, too," Leo responded a second later.

"Okay," Geno said. "Then it's settled. I'll take Miami."

"My sisters lived in Bellevue. It's a nice place," Matteo said.

"Maybe Bill Gates will let us bunk at his pad." Leo poked Matteo with his finger. "Doesn't he have some hundred million plus mega mansion out that way?"

"Yeah." Matteo nodded. "It's on Lake Washington in Medina. I drove close by it when I took the 520 bridge into Bellevue. I tell you fellas, the view as you are driving down Interstate 5 early in the morning with the sun rising and Mount

Rainier jutting into the air on the horizon. Well, let's just say it's a thing of beauty. Also, there's some great Thai food around Richmond Beach."

"So, when do we head to Teterboro?" Leo asked.

Geno looked down at his Movado Bold Verso watch. "We've got ninety minutes to be on those three planes and be on our way."

"Do we get to tell our wives and kids where we are headed?"

Geno frowned. "No dumbass, you ain't telling anyone where we are going. The five of us, Mr. Joshua and the boss, are the only ones who know anything about this. And it needs to stay that way. Tell the ladies in your life, your parents or kids, nothing. Tell a story about pulling an overnight job out of town if they ask. Say whatever, just don't tell them the truth."

The four men looked back and forth at each other and slowly nodded.

"Good, let's get to work and destroy those three FedEx envelopes," Geno said.

Sixty minutes later, on the way out, he swung by the bar and settled up with Paulie for the rounds of Guinness.

"We'll see you back here soon, Geno?"

"Karaoke still going strong on Friday and Saturday nights?"

"The Pope is still catholic, right?" Paulie asked.

Geno nodded. "Yeah, and he's from Chi-town. Of all places, who woulda thunk it?"

Paulie shrugged. "Won't matter the Bears will still suck this year, even the Holy See can't fix their dismal play."

"Long live the Giants," Geno said in response as he fist bumped Paulie and walked out the door.

Chapter Fifty-Three

Georgetown

After leaving the dead drop with Merci, Mr. Joshua had his driver bring him across the Potomac River to the Ritz-Carlton on South Street in Georgetown.

"Park the car, Rocco," he said to the driver. "Go grab a bite to eat, but don't venture too far."

Rocco nodded. "Whatever you say." After Mr. Joshua got out, he pulled around the curved driveway and exited the property on the hunt for a place to grab an early lunch.

Instead of going to his room, Mr. Joshua sat in one of the oversized leather chairs in the living room. Even though the space didn't open and serve food or drinks for several more hours, one of the Marriott servers brought him an old-fashioned. As he sipped on the drink, his cell phone rang.

Mr. Joshua glanced around the space, and seeing he was alone, answered the call. He kept his voice low, considering he sat in a public setting.

"How did it go?" The obese man asked in his typical out-of-breath voice.

"Fine," Mr. Joshua answered. "Just like I told you."

"She didn't balk at the target?"

"Didn't bat an eye. I told you she is a professional, has been paid to do a job, and will complete the contract as instructed." Mr. Joshua took another sip from the glass containing bourbon, bitters, orange peels, and sugar.

"How about her handler, lover, whatever the hell he is?"

"Never saw Marcus. I had two spotters though. They saw him in the distance. He had a rifle trained in my direction but was no real threat. I told her to have him stand down."

The obese man cleared his throat, an obnoxious gargling sound coming from the phone's speaker. "And she agreed to the timeframe?"

"She knows it must be done within thirty-six hours and that her time started immediately. Based on her past success rate, I'd be surprised if it's not done within twenty-four hours."

"There's something else," the obese man said.

"What?" Mr. Joshua asked.

"Sheryl Hopping made three copies of the file and mailed them via FedEx."

Mr. Joshua made a *tsk-tsk-tsk* sound. "That's not good."

"I know. Geno retrieved the FedEx tracking numbers. He and his men are splitting up to retrieve the files before the people she mailed them to can get their hands on the information."

Mr. Joshua sat up straighter in the oversized chair. "Were they just random people, or did she send them with a specific intent?"

"Geno is looking into the recipients. I can't imagine it was random. They must be someone she knew in some context."

"Do we need more men? Should I make some calls?"

"Not yet. Geno said he and his crew could take care of it. Also, the fewer people who know anything about this, the better."

"Understood."

"You staying put for now?"

"Yes, I have a room at the Ritz. I need to be close to make sure everything goes according to plan. Plus, I'll need to contact Justice Brown as soon as it's done."

"The Ritz, huh? Splurging a little?"

"I don't do low end. Never have, never will. Blame my father for giving us the finer things in life. Besides, the client pays for all this, and they have deep pockets."

The obese man's voice took on a firmer tone. "This plan of yours better work. Securing her vote for our client is imperative. You were clearly misguided by how she reacted to the death of her husband."

"A miscalculation on my part." Mr. Joshua took the last sip of the old-fashioned. The large round cubes clanged inside the thick tumbler as he shook the glass. "I knew Chuck Brown was a dirtbag, but even so, I figured his death would sway her."

"Clearly, you have never been married to someone you hate or who hates you in return."

"What? Did any of your three ex-wives try to have you killed?"

"I think two of them would have if they were smart enough to orchestrate such a thing. Fortunately, I married them for their bodies and not their brains. But they definitely tried to bleed me dry, like I was some walking, talking ATM. All three learned the hard way once the naughty stuff ends, so does the financial faucet."

"Pretty sure most ex-wives try to bankrupt their ex-husbands. It's in the unspoken ex-wives rule or something," Mr. Joshua said.

"Probably. But for whatever reason, and to their great dismay, I just wouldn't die. Eventually, my heart will explode, but not while I was with any of them."

Mr. Joshua couldn't hold his tongue with that setup. "You have a heart?"

The obese man let out a slight chuckle. "It's hard, but there. Just make sure this works. We won't have another chance to secure her vote, and none of the other justices can be swayed to our client's side."

"I know what I'm doing. Find what someone loves the most and take it away from them. Trust me, it'll work. Mary Brown will be putty in my hands within thirty-six hours." Mr. Joshua disconnected the call before the back and forth continued anymore. Plus, he needed another stiff drink.

Chapter Fifty-Four

Washington, D.C.

Merci climbed into Marcus's Aston Martin. She looked straight ahead and did not utter a word as the vehicle pulled away from the curb and sped up to merge into traffic.

"Soooo ..." The word rolled off his tongue in a drawn-out manner. "You're not gonna tell me how it went? I could only hear part of the conversation from your mic, and you didn't say very much. Who is the target?"

Merci said nothing. With her fists balled, she did not attempt to hide her frustration. She didn't show it with Mr. Joshua, but she could be herself with Marcus.

They drove in silence for almost ten minutes. As he pulled onto Wisconsin Avenue NW, she finally broke her silence.

"You're not going to your place, are you?"

Marcus scrunched his face. "Um, yeah, why wouldn't I?"

"We can't go back there. Not right now at least."

"Why the hell not?" Marcus asked.

"Because of who they want me to target."

He let out a deep sigh. "Sorry, babe, you're not making any sense. Are you going to tell me who the contract is for? Or at least show me the intel packet?"

Merci shook her head. "No, Mr. Joshua burned the packet after I memorized the details. The only proof of what they want me to do is right here." She jabbed her finger into her temple. "Give me a few minutes to process things. Until I do, it's not safe to return home, not yet."

"I mean, is my car safe?" Marcus tapped the steering wheel.

"Umm, I think so. You check it for trackers, don't you?"

Marcus nodded. "Yeah, of course, babe. It's clean. I have a device that detects stuff like that. I use it every morning before I go anywhere." He pulled up to a stoplight and diverted his eyes to her. "You gonna tell me what's going on, or not?"

Merci put a finger in the air. "Thinking. Hold tight."

"You got it. But I need to know where I should go, or do you want me to drive around the district while you process your thoughts?"

The light turned green, and Marcus sped up. Instead of asking more questions, he simply drove at the posted speed limit and approached Washington Circle Park.

A thought occurred to Merci. "I got it."

"What?" Marcus asked.

"Where we need to go. Take me to the Lincoln Memorial."

"Lincoln? Why there?"

"I'm not there to see the statue of the sixteenth president."

Marcus pursed his lips. "Then why the memorial?"

Merci did not respond.

It took a minute, but suddenly the perplexed look on Marcus's face changed. "Oh, I get it. I know who you want to find. Shit. This must be bad. Really bad."

"It's not good."

"What's the chance of him being there at this very moment?"

Merci bit her lower lip and raised her shoulders. "Not sure, but I guess we'll find out soon enough."

"You could call him. He did give you his number after all."

"This is more of a face-to-face kind of discussion, but yes, if he is not there, I will ring him and tell him we have to meet ASAP!"

Chapter Fifty-Five

The Lincoln Memorial

Nick stood at the base of the twenty-eight white Georgian marble blocks used to create the statue of President Abraham Lincoln. His time with ole Abe became a common ritual after the events on the oil platform under Mogul.

His gaze left the chiseled form of his favorite president and moved around the neoclassical chamber to the various faces belonging to the tourists who flocked to the site twenty-four hours a day, three hundred sixty-five days a year.

There were four Secret Service agents close by to protect him, but they knew to keep their distance.

The Body Man position proved to be a lonely existence for anyone who accepted the position. One of the hardest parts centered on the fact that virtually nobody knows about the role or the inherent risks the person who holds the job faces. Most people can find someone with a similar job, and they have a shared bond over their responsibilities. That's not the case with The Body Man. Fewer than fifteen have served in the role, or as the apprentice, since the Kennedy administration. It really is a more exclusive role than being one of the less than fifty men who have occupied the office that The Body Man swears to protect.

The stress of the past year took its toll on Nick physically, as it does on any person who becomes The Body Man. Things improved over the past few months, but Nick was by no means back to normal after the events in the Gulf of Mexico. His ongoing therapy seemed to help, but it did not alleviate all the symptoms.

Getting out of the White House daily and walking seemed to help. Although having a ritual can be dangerous in his line of work, Nick needed time at the National Mall, particularly the Lincoln Memorial, as often as he could get away.

As he watched the throngs of tourists make their way up the steps and pose for pictures or read the words in the chambers near the Lincoln statue, Nick took great pride in seeing the people's reaction to being in such an amazing architectural spot.

His eyes shifted to his watch. *I better get back.*

Nick stood at the edge of the chamber and glanced down at the eighty-seven steps that led to the reflecting pool. The Washington Monument in the distance and far behind the memorial to the first president, the U.S. Capitol, toward the horizon.

Something inside him stiffened before he took the first step downward. He sensed her presence before he saw her. Almost as if she gave off some biometric signal his body could pick up on before his eyes had time to recognize her physical form.

As his eyes narrowed, she stood on the seventh step from the plaza level.

"*Merci de Atta,*" he said in a whisper. Beside her was Marcus Rollings.

They both stayed in place as Nick approached. He paused two steps above where they waited and crossed his arms. "Well, I must say, I didn't have seeing the two of you on my bingo card for today. I have a sneaking suspicion you're not back in Washington to take me to L'Auberge Chez Francois for a high-end French dinner."

"Sorry, Nick, not this time." She looked first at Marcus and back at Nick. "When I tell you why I'm here, you'd wish you skipped that bingo game."

The agents tasked with protecting Nick converged where he stood as Merci spoke to him. With a hand wave, Nick instructed them to stand down, and they backed off.

"You wanna chat here in the open or find a quiet place near the reflecting pool?" Nick asked.

Merci moved her arm away from her body. "This is your church. You lead the way."

CHAPTER FIFTY-SIX

THE REFLECTING POOL

Nick led Merci and Marcus to a spot near the Reflecting Pool on the side closest to the Korean War Veterans Memorial. He indicated they should sit on the bench while he stood facing them with his arms crossed. "Okay, let's have it. Why did you track me down here on the National Mall?"

"Two words: Chuck Brown," Merci said.

Nick shook his head quickly. "Oh, for fuck's sake, that was you?"

Merci pursed her lips and lowered her head. "Yes, but it gets worse."

Nick didn't try to hide the frustration in his voice as the anger spread over his face. "President Collins gave you both full pardons for any illegal acts committed up to that point, but that wasn't a get out of jail free pass for any future crimes. He's gonna be pissed when I tell him what you did. Wait, what else did you do? I mean, besides the incident in Paris."

Merci looked up at him. "You know about that?"

"Umm, yeah. Interpol has a new warrant out for your arrest. Of course, I know about it. That's my job to know about stuff that may have ramifications affecting the Office of the Presidency."

"Didn't think about that, but it makes sense," Merci said.

"You said it gets worse. So, what is *it* if it's not the hit in Paris or Chuck Brown?"

"Look, for the record, the guy in Paris was a pimp, who nearly killed me a half dozen times and sold me into the flesh trade when I was a teenager. And Chuck Brown was a piece of shit. You know it, I know it, Nick. If you think for a second I regret sending either one of those fucks to bake with the devil, you're wrong."

Merci jumped to her feet and was face-to-face with Nick, albeit several inches shorter.

Marcus stood as well and placed his hand on her shoulder. "Okay, babe, you need to chill. Let's all take a step back. This won't help solve the problem."

"Tell me what you did next after killing Justice Brown's husband, Merci. Are you about to complicate my life even more than it already is now?"

"No … well, I don't know. I'm here to save a life, not take one." She pointed to the bench. "Can we sit down? I don't like you standing over me like some father figure getting ready to scold me for disobeying a direct order."

Nick put his hands out to de-escalate the situation. "Okay, okay, I'll sit. But you need to tell me what the hell you've gotten yourself into."

The three of them sat. Nick in the middle with Merci to his right, and Marcus to his left.

"Fair enough." Merci spent the next ten minutes in explicit detail bringing Nick completely up to speed.

"Okay," Nick said. "I don't agree with what you did, but let's hear it. Who was this next extremely lucrative contract put out on?"

"Abigale Hudson."

"Who?" Nick and Marcus both said the word at the same moment.

"Justice Mary Brown's seven-year-old granddaughter."

Nick had a confused look on his face. "I thought you never targeted children. You told me that was the line in the sand you would die to protect."

"Yeah, that's why I'm here, Nick. Like I said, I accepted the contract before I knew who the target was, and as soon as I found out they wanted me to abduct and likely kill Abigale, I came straight here to see you. I'll die to protect that little girl, not kidnap her or take her life."

This was the first time Marcus heard who the target was, and he was as shocked as Nick.

Nick buried his head in his hands but said nothing.

"You may think I'm a monster, Nick, but I'm not. I might do wicked things for money, but I know right from wrong. Even if our versions of right and wrong don't have the same demarcation line."

"I need a minute." Nick raised his head from his hands, stood, and walked toward the reflecting pool.

Merci and Marcus stayed seated and watched him pace for several minutes.

Nick turned toward the Lincoln Memorial and thought for a minute before he spun around and stared at the Washington Monument. He tried to think through scenarios as fast as possible, but he knew who he needed to speak with next.

He walked back to the bench and let out a deep sigh.

"Looks like I hurt your brain," Merci said.

"You and a bunch of others are currently trying to see how hard they push me before I crack."

"Is it working?"

"Honestly, I think I cracked a long time ago." He grew quiet for a few seconds. "I need to speak with the president."

Merci stood. "Good, we will go with you."

Nick shook his head. "No, I mean, not yet. I need to talk with him first. Then I can bring you into the conversation."

Merci pointed to Nick's Rolex on his wrist. "There's a deadline for this job, Nick. Like I said, the clock is ticking. If I don't grab her, my employer will find someone else. We need a plan to save Abigale, and time is working against us."

"I know, Merci, that's why I need to talk with the president. We are talking about the interference of a landmark Supreme Court case. This isn't some lower court larceny case; this Kennedy vs Byolyze case will literally have global consequences."

"I get it, Nick. I had no clue how deep all this went until an hour ago."

"Let me talk with President Collins. And after he and I chat, we will bring you into the conversation." Nick reached into his pocket, fished out the brass-colored key, and handed it to her. "Look, I have a permanent suite at the Hay-Adams Hotel, room 7124. I rarely sleep there, but I think you and Marcus should crash there for a little bit while I sort things out. You know where the Hay-Adams is, right?"

Merci rolled her eyes. "Duh, of course I know where it is."

"Let me guess, you killed someone there?" Nick asked.

"Nope." She pointed her thumb toward Marcus. "But I screwed him there a handful of times. It's high-end digs. The Egyptian sheets are some of the nicest ones in the city."

"Whatever," Nick said. "You two can bang like love sick teenagers while you're there. I don't care. Just stay put. I'll call when it's safe to come to the White House. Like when I snuck you in through the tunnels at the St. Regis, the Hay-Adams has a passageway leading to the same underground tunnel. You'll come in that way after I speak with the president."

"Got it," Merci said.

Nick turned to leave. "Oh, and don't open the fridge. The mini bar is expensive as hell, and I don't want you blowing my expense account." He said the last few words with a smile as he winked.

She waited until he was about thirty feet away before she yelled. "JUST FOR THAT I'M TAKING A BITE OUT OF EVERYTHING IN THAT MINI-BAR AND I'LL SPIT IT OUT IN THE TRASH CAN!"

Nick didn't turn around and did not reply. Instead, he raised his arm above his head and extended his middle finger skyward.

"You're a real piece of work sometimes," Marcus said to Merci as they started for his car.

"What can I say? Guys have balls. I like to bust them."

CHAPTER FIFTY-SEVEN

GEORGETOWN

Mr. Joshua enjoyed another old-fashioned before he went to his elegantly decorated suite on the top floor of the Ritz. After thirty minutes inside the suite, he was tired of working at the desk on his laptop. He called and had Rocco meet him out in front of the hotel and take him to 33rd and O Street, only a handful of blocks from Georgetown University.

Rocco dropped him off a block south, and he entered the townhouse from the back entrance. He couldn't risk getting out of the vehicle on O Street and Justice Brown seeing him somehow. He had a direct line of sight from the third-story bedroom to the front of Mary Brown's townhouse.

Four men were set up in various rooms of the rented townhouse. Many flat-panel monitors showed live video feeds inside Mary's house. Every room had video and audio capabilities. In addition to her house, a camera and microphone sent a live feed from her chamber inside the Supreme Court. There were also surveillance cameras at her son's house in Pimmit Hills and her daughter's residence in Falls Church.

"Where is she, Allen?" Mr. Joshua asked the tech who was set up inside the rental home's master bedroom and had the largest display of monitors in front of him.

"She's at the Supreme Court, sir," Allen Rigsby said. He had worked with The Fulbright Group for several years, an absolute wizard regarding surveillance, something he perfected while working at the Central Intelligence Agency for over ten years. When he grew tired of the bureaucracy and red tape, he found that the private sector paid a hell of a lot better. "They are hearing oral arguments until lunch, and then in the afternoon, her schedule indicates she will be in her chamber reviewing opinions. I wouldn't expect her back home before seven or eight tonight."

Mr. Joshua nodded. "And how about her daughter and Abigale?"

"Jenn Hudson is home in Falls Church at the moment. Abigale is at her Montessori School, the Valleybrook Campus." The tech looked at his watch. "Jenn will leave in a few hours to pick up Abigale from school, unless she heads out early to run an errand. That's if she keeps to her routine. She's fairly predictable."

Mr. Joshua's eyes darted from monitor to monitor. "Everyone is a creatures of habit, huh?"

Allen shrugged. "Most people are. It makes our job easier since tracking them and finding patterns happens quickly. Although even the most regimented person breaks pattern from time to time." He patted the computer. "That's where technology and AI come in handy. We can anticipate many variables based on the data we feed into the system."

"Where do you expect Merci to acquire her? Home, school, or in-transit?"

Allen scrunched his nose. "Hard to say with certainty. Based on our models and purely considering risk versus reward, I think the Montessori School is a no-go."

"Why so?"

"Well, for starters, they have a fairly secure campus because of the nationwide school shootings. This isn't some run-of-the-mill public school. They have several resource officers, and even a fenced-in property. It creates complications and would require advanced planning. She won't have that luxury with the limited time frame you gave her."

"That leaves in-transit or home."

"Correct. In transit or a public place is always a probability, but again, not knowing the Hudson's schedule will make that option problematic. She won't have enough time to establish patterns or follow the family to attain the intel to orchestrate a kidnapping in broad daylight. You gave her basic info, but she won't trust it completely. Someone with her skill set will want to observe and track the patterns on her own. Merci is smart. She wants to control as many variables as possible to limit her exposure and mitigate risks from unknown sources."

"That leaves the family home as the most likely target," Mr. Joshua said.

"It's the safest bet. With minimal observation, she'll see the house is not guarded. The security system is one of those shitty ones advertised on late night network television and cable stations, which any run of the mill hack can easily bypass. There are no guarantees in this business, but if I'm in Vegas and have to place a large wager, my money is on the abduction happening at the house." Allen paused. "And late at night or very early in the morning as well."

"Why do you say that?"

"Merci is not afraid of the dark. I would say operating in the cloak of darkness is her friend. She knows people are much more vulnerable when asleep or tired. Hell, I bet she could disable the security system, get into the house, and have Abigale out without anyone knowing based on her skill set."

Mr. Joshua raised his eyebrows. "They do have a family dog to contend with."

"Bo is a nine-year-old golden retriever. Anyone with her résumé can easily deal with a dog, especially a friendly breed like that. Or she'll eliminate the dog, problem solved. Although I doubt that is her style."

"Pretty good assessment, Allen."

Allen rubbed the top of his bald head. "You didn't hire me for imaginary hair, did you?"

"No, no, I did not." Mr. Joshua looked over the monitors once more. What Allen said made a lot of sense. Merci could adapt and think quickly on her feet, but time limited her options if she was going to fulfill the contract in the allotted time. "So, you think she'll abduct her at the house later tonight, or in the early morning hours?"

Allen looked away from the screen and turned toward Mr. Joshua. He replied with a concise two-word answer: "I would."

Chapter Fifty-Eight

The Oval Office

Nick made his way through the West Wing, his usual stoic look visible across his fatigued face. Scenarios of how things might play out raced around his mind like a full field of cars vying for position at Daytona International.

Matthew Persson stood like a sentry across from the northwest door leading into the Oval Office.

Nick made eye contact with Matt as he approached the closed door.

Matt recognized the expression. "All good, boss? You look like the rival quarterback after Bobby Boucher lines up across from them."

"Yeah," Nick replied with a smirk. "Just another day trying to stop the latest imminent threat with no waterboy around to help make the game-winning play." He pointed to the Oval Office. "Preacher has company?"

"Yes, sir. You'll need to check with Patricia, but the doors have been closed for over thirty minutes. Nobody in or out."

"Thanks, I will," Nick said. He fist bumped Matt as he continued past the closed door.

Nick stopped beside the desk of the president's administrative assistant.

"Yes, Mr. Jordan?" Patricia asked.

"Who is Preacher in with?"

"SecDef, they will probably be there for another twenty minutes. Lebanon started lobbing missiles at Israel an hour ago, and the Israelis are threatening to turn the whole country into a parking lot."

Nick's expression relayed the importance. "When it rains, it pours. This can't wait."

Patricia nodded and pressed the intercom button on her phone.

"*Mr. President,*" she said.

"*Yes?*" the president asked in a slightly annoyed tone.

"*Nick Jordan, sir. It's urgent.*"

"*Let him in.*"

Nick thanked her for the intrusion, opened the northeast door, and walked into the Oval Office. His eyes darted from the president sitting behind his desk to the SecDef sitting in one of the two rosewood chairs across from him. "Mr. President, and Mr. Secretary, sorry for the intrusion, but this can't wait." Nick stepped around the resolute desk, leaned over, and whispered several words into the president's right ear.

The president's eyes focused on the intel report before him but grew wider as Nick spoke.

President Collins cleared his throat as he shifted his gaze from the report to Curt Wastradowski, the Secretary of Defense. "Curt, not to cut you short, but this matter also requires immediate attention. If you'd be so kind to go down to the Situation Room and call the Israeli prime minister, tell him we will have a video call in twenty minutes to de-escalate these growing hostilities between Hezbollah and Israel." He paused and looked at Nick, who now stood beside the desk. "Is twenty minutes enough time, Nicholas?"

"I think it will have to be, sir. We can't have the Middle East on fire again this week."

The SecDef stood, nodded to both men, then left via the northwest door and headed to the Situation Room, sure to close the door as he departed.

President Collins shifted his focus back to Nick. "Okay, give me the 30,000-foot recap. But first, tell me how bad is it, really?"

"Bad enough that I think we need to get all nine justices in protective custody sooner rather than later, sir."

The president frowned. "Happy, happy, joy, joy," his only retort.

—◆—

Nick spent several minutes telling the president everything he knew about what occurred.

After Nick finished, the president didn't respond immediately. He picked up his pen and tapped it dozens of times on the large pad that protected the surface of the historic desk from scuffs or scratches.

"Merci has no intention of completing the contract, correct?"

"No, sir. She came to me to get Abigale and the rest of the family in protective custody. But she didn't want to tip her hat. This Mr. Joshua gave her thirty-six hours to abduct Justice Brown's granddaughter." Nick looked at his watch. "That gives us about thirty-four hours to do what we need before they know she didn't complete the contract."

The president continued to tap the Montblanc pen on the pad. "What do we know about this Mr. Joshua, and The Fulbright Group?"

"At the moment, only what Merci told me. But I've got Abby digging into them now. We'll know everything we need about their organization very soon."

"And you don't want to pull the U.S. Marshals in on this pronto?"

"We will, sir. Just give me time. I want to contact Frank Halter, the Marshal, first."

The president furrowed his brow. "What about the fact that Merci claimed her intel indicated there could be a mole within the U.S. Marshals at the court. How can you be sure the Marshal's team is all clean?"

"That's just it, I can't, sir. But I can vouch for Frank Halter. I've known the man for years. I grew up in the same town as him and even worked landscaping for him when I was in college. If the Marshal is dirty and is the source of the leak, all the justices are in danger. Besides, I'm good at sniffing out a rat. I cleaned house after the trouble we had in the West Wing with Mogul. I believe the Marshal can be counted on, sir, since I know and trust the man. He won't like being told he may have someone crooked on his team, but I can gently break the news to him. Again, it's not proven yet, but we should take Merci's concerns seriously."

"That's all the assurance I need regarding the Marshal, Nicholas." The president looked at his watch. The silver Breitling Navitimer Automatic watch was a gift from his wife for their thirtieth anniversary. "I've gotta get down to the Situation Room and keep the Prime Minister from starting World War III. Let's meet back here in ninety minutes. Make a few discreet calls and get the assets on standby that we'll need to pull this thing off. Sneak Merci and Marcus into the Oval. They need to be involved in what we decide."

"Agreed, sir, although I think the meeting should occur in the DUCC, not in the West Wing. Too many ears are perked up around here. I don't have any issues with your staff, but we can't afford a leak with what is at stake."

"Your call, Nick. Make it so!"

Chapter Fifty-Nine

At Cruising Altitude

Neither Gus nor Trey ever flew on a private jet before the Phoenix flight. An hour from landing, Geno called and relayed the info they needed to retrieve the FedEx envelope. On the brief call, Geno explained that Sheryl mailed the FedEx envelope to Clarissa Hart, a television reporter who worked for the local ABC affiliate KNXV Channel 15. The good news was that Clarissa lived alone, appeared to be single, and worked the afternoon/evening shift at the television station. The bad news was that the package tracking said it might not be delivered until nine p.m. Based on their limited info, Clarissa might be home before the FedEx delivery arrived at her place.

Geno explained to both men that no matter what, they must retrieve the envelope, and its contents could not be read by anyone, including either of them.

"What's the connection between Sheryl and Clarissa?" Gus asked before the call ended.

"Clarissa was her college roommate," Geno said. "I've not had the time to do a deep dive, but they've stayed in contact over the years. Maybe Sheryl figured if something happened to her, Clarissa could get the information in the file out. But that's just a guess."

"And you have no clue what is in the file?" Gus asked.

"No, I wasn't read into the contents. It's none of my business, nor any of yours. Just get the FedEx delivery before Clarissa and send me proof it's destroyed." Geno took a deep breath and let it out in a slow exhale. He didn't enjoy repeating himself. "Look, like I said at Peter Dillons. Take a video of the unopened package being burned. That way, the boss knows no one saw the contents, and it's been destroyed. That will cover both of our asses. You got it?"

"Yeah, we got it. You already in Miami?"

"Yes, I got a hotel at the Seminole Hard Rock in Hollywood. The envelope I'm going after will not be delivered until tomorrow. Go figure why the one mailed to a closer location takes the longest to arrive. That's global shipping for you, I guess."

"How about Matteo and Leo?"

"They are still in the air, about an hour behind you. Their envelope is supposed to be delivered by tonight as well. I'm diving into their target location, and I'll be calling them soon to fill them in. You just worry about Phoenix. I'll handle the rest. The rental car is ready for you when you arrive. I'll send you detailed info in a secure email when you both are on the ground."

"Copy that."

"Don't screw it up," Geno said. "Get the envelope, destroy it, and don't do anything that will attract the fuzz."

＊＊＊

After his call with Gus and Trey, Geno finished his research on the Washington State FedEx envelope. Once he had enough details, he made an almost identical call to Matteo and Leo. All four men received the same warnings, and Geno hoped the subtle threats would keep them all in line. He trusted his team as much as one can trust people who work for them. But he also knew they each had a reputation for being loose cannons. The promised bump in their normal hourly rates and bonus for completing the job without incident would hopefully keep them on the straight and narrow.

Chapter Sixty

The White House

Nick met Merci and Marcus as they stepped through the thick steel, vault-like door underneath the Hay-Adams Hotel.

Merci looked around the tunnel as they followed Nick. "Wow! I'm having a flashback."

Nick looked over his shoulder. "Yeah, doesn't seem that long ago I was escorting both of you through this tunnel under much different circumstances."

"At least we know Mogul won't be waiting at the boiler when we get to the end," Merci said.

"Nope, you saw to that last time," Nick snickered.

Two minutes later, the tunnel opened to an expansive room in the White House basement complex. The boiler to the right of where they entered was no longer in operation. Merci stared at it more than once as they proceeded past that spot.

On the far wall was a bank of three elevators. Nick motioned for them to approach the middle one. He pushed the illuminated button to the right of the brass trim. Five seconds later, the elevator doors opened, and Nick stepped inside.

It looked like countless other elevators with cherry wood paneled walls and dark-brown carpet. A control panel to the left of the doors only had two buttons with letters in bold, *U* and *D*. Nick pushed the lower button.

As the elevator descended, Nick looked over at Merci and Marcus. "I'm assuming you are wondering where we are going?"

"Definitely curious. Thought maybe the Oval or Situation Room, but since we were already in the basement, I didn't think you'd be bringing us farther down."

Nick half smirked. "Oh, you are both in for a treat. You get to see something few civilians will ever see in their lifetime."

As the elevator descended quickly as their ears popped. Nick asked, "Either of you ever heard of the Deep Underground Command Center?"

Merci and Marcus both looked at each other and shrugged. "No clue," Marcus said. "It sounds important, though."

⸺◆⸺

Built in complete secrecy during a previous administration, the Deep Underground Command Center or DUCC, replaced the Presidential Emergency Operations Center or PEOC built during the Franklin D. Roosevelt presidential administration under the East Wing of the White House. The PEOC became antiquated and showed its faults during the terrorist attacks on 9/11. Those events necessitated the planning and eventual construction of the high-tech DUCC, which to this day is not acknowledged by any federal government employee.

⸺◆⸺

As they stepped out of the elevator, Nick led them both to the wall on the left.

Three biometric stations were stacked vertically along the wall: a hand scanner, a microphone, and a retina scanner. Nick used the three devices to authenticate his identity. As he completed the final verification, a sound indicated the locking mechanism had disengaged, and the massive blast door slowly opened.

It took almost twenty seconds for the enormous door to open fully. Once inside, Nick led Merci and Marcus down several long hallways. They passed over a dozen armed agents along the way. The halls were wide enough for two people to walk side by side with arms outstretched, with numerous rooms lining each passageway. At the end of the final hallway, Nick knocked on the door with the presidential seal affixed to the side of the door jamb.

"Enter," a firm voice said as Merci immediately recognized the voice behind the closed door.

Chapter Sixty-One

Deep Underground Command Center

Nick pushed the door open and motioned for Merci and Marcus to sit on the oversized rustic leather couch to the left. Across from it was another identical couch, while straight ahead was a cigar chair.

As expected, the president sat in the leather cigar chair. He nodded as Merci and Marcus took a seat. Nick joined them on the couch. Across from them were two men whom neither Merci nor Marcus recognized.

Nick was the first to speak. He directed his words to Merci and Marcus. "I'd like you to meet David Kline. He is the Director of the Secret Service." He motioned to the man who sat on the opposite couch but closest to the president. "And beside Director Kline is Frank Halter, the Marshal of the Supreme Court. Essentially, the Marshal ensures the safety of the court itself and the protection of all nine justices."

Nick looked at the director and the Marshal. "Gentlemen, this is Merci and Marcus."

"I know who they are," Director Kline stated. The disdain in his eyes was clear as day. "I've read their jackets."

"I don't want to be here any more than you do," Merci said, reading his expression.

"Sir, this woman is a threat. My job is to mitigate risks to those I'm tasked to protect. Do you think it safe to have her in this enclosed space with you after what she did to Mogul?" Director Kline glared at the president.

Merci's eyes narrowed. "Look, Kline. I'm a threat to assholes who sexually abuse children, beat their wives to an inch of their life, or dabble in the flesh and drug trade. Are there any men like that in this room?"

President Collins put his hands out as he looked at Nick, then back at Merci. "Everybody, take a chill pill." He focused on Merci as he spoke. "Are you a threat to me, Miss de Atta?"

Her head moved from side to side in a slow, drawn-out motion. "None whatsoever, Mr. President."

President Collins turned slightly. "Nick, are you concerned with Merci being in this room?"

"No, sir." Nick shook his head. "She's here to protect a life, not take one."

"Yet, she took a contract and killed Chuck Brown," Director Kline said. "She's not exactly a Girl Scout or model citizen. Plus, Interpol has you on a watch list since you allegedly killed a man at the Arc de Triomphe recently." He turned to the president. "Surely, we are not going to just look past that. Are we, sir?" The director glanced back and forth between President Collins and Nick.

"Yes, I killed a fucking pimp in cold blood. The same man who pulled me into the sex trade and nearly killed me more times than I can even count. You want to have me led out of here in cuffs and extradited to France for doing the women in the City of Light a favor? Go for it, bro!" Her face turned a darker shade of red as she got worked up. "And Chuck Brown was no saint. Wanna know what kind of lowlife he was and how he treated women?"

Nick raised his hands. "Look, this discussion is over. Director Kline, with all due respect, I don't give two squirts of piss what you think about Merci at this moment. Nor what she obviously feels about you. We can debate what Merci did till the cows come home, but that won't protect Abigale Hudson. If Merci simply rejects the contract, they will hire someone else to complete what she started. And time is working against us. Every minute we debate the morality of what Merci does for a living is another minute closer to bad things happening here on our soil and to our citizens. For now, we can leave what occurred to the words of Fritz Heider. *The enemy of my enemy is my friend.* Like it or not, regardless of what she did in the past, Merci is a friend to everyone in this room. We need to leave it at that and move on."

"Exactly. Enough of this squabbling, David." The president's facial expression looked stern. "I filled you and Marshal in with as much as I know while waiting for everyone to arrive. Next, the six of us will come up with a solution to this impending crisis. Someone paid The Fulbright Group, who in turn hired Merci. The purpose of her actions against Mary Brown's family was to manipulate Mary to vote their way on the Kennedy vs Byolyze case. We are going to figure out a way to put a stop to all of this." President Collins looked at everyone seated on either side of him on the leather couches. "Are we *ALL* clear?"

All five heads nodded in unison.

President Collins turned to Nick. "You're running this operation, Nicholas. Like you said, time is of the essence, so let's figure out this plan."

Nick stared at Frank. "Knowing what you've been read in on so far, what are your primary concerns, Marshal?"

"The well-being of all the justices, including Mary Brown and her family, of course. The unbiased sanctity of the court process is paramount as well. I'll do whatever is best for the nine justices and the court."

Nick's gaze shifted to Director Kline. "I know you're not comfortable with Merci's involvement. You made that abundantly clear, but can we count on the Secret Service being all in on whatever is agreed upon in this room today?"

Director Kline nodded. "In for a penny, in for a pound. I might have strong reservations regarding Miss de Atta's trustworthiness, given her past actions. But I have no such reservations with the office of The Body Man. Whatever is decided in this room today, the Secret Service will do our part."

Nick sighed. "Good, we need to formulate a plan and be ready to execute it immediately. So, let's get to work."

Chapter Sixty-Two

Hollywood, Florida

Seminole Hard Rock Hotel

Geno set up two laptops and two oversized monitors in his suite at the Hard Rock Seminole in Hollywood, Florida. The thirty-six-story guitar-shaped hotel tower included six hundred thirty-eight luxury suites and guestrooms. A frequent guest at the hotel, the casino host comped him a spacious suite on the thirty-second floor. Since Geno knew the envelope he had to retrieve wasn't scheduled to be delivered until the next day, and he liked to play poker any chance he got, staying at the Hard Rock proved to be a straightforward decision.

His cell phone, which sat next to his computer mouse, vibrated, shifting his eyes away from the tracking data he was analyzing on the dual monitors.

The caller ID on his iPhone simply read, *Boss.*

"Your guido ass better not be on the floor slinging cards with the sharks," the obese man said in a harsh tone.

"Negative, boss," Geno stated. "I'm in my room monitoring all the tracking numbers and giving instructions to my guys."

"I hope so. This isn't one of your gambling spree weekends down in Florida."

"Copy that."

"What's the status? Do you have any of the envelopes yet?"

"No, Gus and Trey are on the ground in Phoenix. The envelope is supposed to be delivered later this afternoon, and they've taken measures to track the person who Sheryl sent it to and get it before she arrives back home."

"This is the one going to the television reporter?"

"Yes, they should have it in a few hours. I checked the tracking. It's on the FedEx vehicle and scheduled to be delivered by around 7:30 p.m. Mountain Standard Time. She'll still be in the studio when it arrives at her condo."

"Hope so. What about the one mailed to Seattle?"

"Matteo and Leo landed. They are in transit to the delivery address now to scope out the place."

"This one is the lawyer?" the obese man asked. "How did Sheryl know this guy?"

"It looks like they dated many years ago when he lived in the city." Geno pulled up the bio he created on the flight from New York City to Miami and read it to his boss. "He left New York and moved to Seattle to start a law practice after they broke up. From what I can tell, he's a successful trial lawyer who takes on mainly criminal cases, including capital murder charges. Wins a hell of a lot more than he loses. Based on my online research, he and Sheryl continued to stay in contact even after their romance fizzled. Sending whatever it is to a lawyer was probably a smart move on her part."

"Probably, but I don't like lawyers. We have a team of them who represent TFG on an ongoing basis. I'd rather see them all at the bottom of the ocean, but I guess in our litigation crazy society, they are a necessary evil. Just tell your men to be careful around this guy. Get in, retrieve the envelope, and don't interact with him. They are crafty creatures and just like a shark smells blood from a mile away, lawyers can sense bullshit when they see or hear it."

"If all goes to plan, they'll never actually interact with him, but I'll remind them of the dangers when I check in with them soon."

"How about you? Who did she send it to in Miami again?"

"Her cousin lives in Sunny Isles Beach, a block from the ocean. His envelope got delayed for some unclear reason. Won't be delivered until sometime tomorrow afternoon."

"Okay, yeah, this one is the retired fed?" the obese man asked.

"Yeah," Geno said in his thick Italian accent. "He worked at the FBI for over twenty-six years. Twenty years served as a special agent in the Criminal Investigative Division (CID) located in Los Angeles. He took down some pretty big crews, including the McCauley, Shiherlis, Cheritto, and Trejo Families."

"Those were big crews, I read all about them. Sounds like you need to watch your six around the cousin."

"He's an old man now. I can handle the situation."

"Those old retired pricks are the ones you really need to keep an eye on. They've got nothing better to do, and once a hunter, always a hunter. You sure being there solo is a good idea? I can send someone else down. Mr. Joshua is in Washington, but I can send one of my other guys to give you another set of eyes."

"Thanks for the offer, but it's not needed. Besides, once the guys in Phoenix and Seattle complete their part, I can have them fly here. I plan on retrieving the envelope either in transit or when he's not home. This isn't my first job. My team has this handled, and I know what I'm doing."

"Does he know about Sheryl's death?"

"Yes, the extended family has been notified, including her cousin."

"Call me as soon as the envelopes in Phoenix and Seattle are intercepted and destroyed."

"You'll be my first call."

The phone line disconnected, and Geno looked back at the bank of monitors. He even had tracking dots on a real-time map that showed where his men were in relation to the last FedEx envelope scan and the addressee's location. Geotags proved to be a game changer when it comes to the world of tracking people or possessions.

⸻◆⸻

A knock at the door caused his head to snap up. He retrieved the pistol from the desk and approached the door. Using the peephole, he saw a Hispanic woman in a server's outfit behind a silver cart draped in a white tablecloth. *Damn, I totally forgot I ordered room service forty minutes ago.*

Geno tucked the gun under his waistband and pulled his shirt over it to conceal the weapon. He opened the door and let the server in. The smell of the pasta, sausage, and garlic bread filled his nostrils as his stomach let out a low growl. She left the cart near his king-sized bed, and he noticed her eyes linger on the monitors. He had activated the screen saver button before he moved to the door, so the monitors showed nothing.

"Thought I was getting away from work and they dragged me back in," Geno said with a warm smile. "Hopefully, I can finish this and hit the tables soon."

The server smiled but said nothing.

Geno looked at her name tag which read, *Lupe*.

Lupe's eyes widened as he pulled the wad of cash out of his pocket, slipped a fifty-dollar bill from the thick cash roll, and handed it to her.

"Muchas gracias, senior!" Lupe said with a wide grin.

"De nade," Geno said in response as she left the room.

With Lupe gone, he set the pile of food near his keyboard, inhaled several mouthfuls of pasta, and returned to work.

CHAPTER SIXTY-THREE

GEORGETOWN

Mr. Joshua leaned against the dresser and watched Allen flip the images between the camera feeds from Justice Brown's chamber and the Hudson house. Allen pulled up the surveillance footage at the Valleybrook Campus and even had a camera angle that showed the door leading into Abigale's classroom.

There was nothing of importance going on at any of the three locations.

"How can you look at these feeds for so long? My eyes would bleed," Mr. Joshua said.

Allen pursed his lips. "I mean, it's the job. Ninety-eight percent peace and quiet with hardly anything going on, followed by two percent balls-to-the-wall action. That's surveillance in a nutshell. And the two percent action is being generous."

"I can get behind the action part, but not the peace and quiet moments. I'd be bored out of my gourd if I had to stare at video images all day." He pushed away from the dresser and paced around the room. "I don't think Merci will grab her today, do you?"

Allen tossed his hands upward. "She has over twenty-four hours to go. She's likely doing reconnaissance. Like I said earlier, I'd expect her to grab Abigale at the house, either really late tonight or early in the morning. The probability of her snatching her from the school is very low. Too risky, a whole lot more variables to contend with."

"What about the tracker on Marcus's Aston Martin? Any idea where they are?"

"Nope. It pings overnight, so right now they could be anywhere."

"How about the camera hidden across the hall from Marcus's apartment?"

Allen toggled the image on the main monitor. "No movement since very early this morning. They did not go back to his place after you met with them."

"You think that's odd?"

"Nope. Like I said, I'm sure she's doing reconnaissance so she can decide where to intercept her target." Allen switched the camera feed to Falls Church. It showed the outside of the Hudson's home. He used his mouse to rotate the angle. "I don't see any evidence of Marcus's car near their house. Of course, they could have switched vehicles. But there's nobody parked anywhere on the road, and the cars in the neighbors' driveways are the same ones that were there earlier today."

Mr. Joshua continued to pace the room. "I think I'm going to run out and grab a bite. You want anything?"

"Sure, one thing I learned while I was a fed is you never turn down free food when on a stakeout."

— ◦ —

Five minutes later, Mr. Joshua climbed into the black Infinite.

"Where to?" Rocco asked.

"Need some grub, but want to check out the target locations, too."

"Which ones?"

"All of them," Mr. Joshua said. "The school, and Hudson's home. Hell, even the Supreme Court."

"I can't imagine Merci would go there. Abigale won't be at the Supreme Court."

"Yeah, I know, just need to drive around. Being stuck in that townhouse watching computer monitors makes my eyes loopy."

"You wouldn't last long in a real stakeout, boss," Rocco said.

"Don't want to. I'm a fiend for action. Idle hands have never been my strong suit."

Chapter Sixty-Four

Washington, D.C.

The Tunnels

Underneath Washington, D.C., lies a maze of tunnels and subterranean roadways few ever get to see. If the Secret Service wants to move the President of the United States around undetected, they can easily accomplish the task via any number of these passageways beneath the capital city. However, politicians make their living by optics, and it doesn't play well on the national media to transport the president in secret outside the purview of the general public. A picture may be worth a thousand words, but a politician is mainly concerned with how many votes that image generates.

***

After their meeting in the DUCC below the West Wing, Nick led the Marshal, Merci, and Marcus via the elevator up to the White House's basement level. From there, they took a flight of stairs two levels down and entered a tunnel marked with the color green within a circle. Nick indicated they should all climb into the oversized electric golf cart with three rows of seating.

"How many tunnels are under the White House?" Merci asked.

Nick smirked. "That's classified."

"Well, I've already been in the blue square, red triangle, and now the green circle tunnel."

"Tip of the iceberg is all I can say."

The tunnel was wide enough to fit four golf carts side by side and high enough for a large box van. With offshoot tunnels or alcoves every three hundred yards, the president's full motorcade could easily navigate the subterranean passageways. Periodically, they would drive past what looked like massive blast doors. While currently open, they looked like they could be closed if the need arose.

The green circle tunnel roughly followed Pennsylvania Avenue, about thirty feet above them. As the electric cart scooted down the passage, the fluorescent lights passed by overhead quickly as he increased speed. Nick turned slightly left when they reached a fork in the tunnel, The passageway followed Constitution Avenue above them. The green circle marks on the walls changed at the fork and were replaced by a star shape with the letters *SC* in the middle of the star.

As Nick stopped, he indicated that everyone should get out.

"Where are we?" Marcus asked.

Nick raised his eyebrows. "Under the Supreme Court."

"And if we had stayed in the green circle tunnel?" Merci asked.

"That one leads to the U.S. Capitol but continues until it reaches Joint Base Andrews." He paused. "But you didn't hear that from me. Like I said, there's a maze of tunnels under this city. They are convenient for transporting things or people we don't want to be seen."

"That's pretty wild!" Marcus exclaimed.

"There's a reason government departments fail audits and hammers seemingly cost ten thousand dollars a pop while nails are a hundred bucks a piece, according to watchdog sites," Nick said.

Marcus smiled. "I thought that was to pay for all those super secret underground cities the conspiracy folks say the government is building for when the nukes get launched."

Nick displayed a sheepish expression. "I didn't say what all the money was being spent on, did I?"

As they passed through the heavy blast door that could be closed to seal off the *SC* tunnel from the subbasement of the Supreme Court, the Marshal pointed to a hallway to the left of where they entered. "Why don't you all get comfortable, use the first room on the right. I'll be back with her as fast as I can."

The Marshal stepped inside, pushed the button and disappeared as the elevator door closed, while Nick led Merci and Marcus to the room indicated.

Ten minutes later, the door opened. The Marshal led Associate Justice Mary Brown inside the room, which contained a large mahogany conference table with an oversized leather chair at each end and five similar chairs on either side of the table. Nick sat at the far end of the table in the head of the table spot, while Merci sat to his right and Marcus sat to her right.

When the Marshal and Mary entered, they took the seats opposite Merci and Marcus, with Mary taking the chair to Nick's left.

Nick looked at the Marshal and raised his eyebrows. "What did you tell her?"

"Very little. I figured you would want to do most of the talking."

Mary looked back and forth from the Marshal to Nick, but her eyes settled back on the only person she knew in the room, the Marshal. "What's this about, Frank?"

He gestured toward the head of the table. "The gentleman to your right is Nick Jordan, Madam Justice. In private circles around Washington, he's known as ..."

Mary cut him off mid-sentence. "The Body Man, yes, I know who he is. President Collins mentioned him in private a few times. I've also seen him in the background at important events occasionally."

"I see," the Marshal said.

Her gaze pivoted back to the head of the table. "And why are you here, Mr. Jordan?" Her eyes then shifted to the two people who sat across from her. By the look in her eyes, it appeared she didn't know either of them. "And who are your associates?"

Nick took a sip from the glass of water in front of him. "I'm here because of a very serious matter, Justice Brown. We have some tough things to discuss, which are matters of life and death. As for the two of them ..."

At that moment, Merci changed the script they all agreed to stick with. "My name is Merci de Atta. I am a professional assassin, and I'm the woman who killed your husband. I was also contracted to kidnap and likely kill your granddaughter, Abigale." She spoke the words in a clinical tone. "However, I have no intention of fulfilling that contract."

Mary's mouth dropped open as she audibly gasped.

"Subtle," Nick quipped. "Real subtle, Merci. Good one."

Merci stared back at Nick. "We don't have time for subtle, Nick. Time is working against us, and the sooner we rip off the bandage, the sooner we can deal with the loss of blood."

The Marshal grabbed Mary's now trembling hand. "Mary, this is going to be a lot to take in, but we have a plan to keep you and your family safe. Just breathe. Above all, you have to trust what Nick has to tell you. I have full faith and confidence in Nick, and so can you."

Chapter Sixty-Five

United States Supreme Court

Mary Brown took the shocking news remarkably well. It's fairly rare to have someone sit across from the person who killed their spouse, and they have minimal reaction. After the initial shock wore off, Mary remained stoic, and her face looked neutral. Because of her years on the bench, Mary had remarkable poise and excelled at hiding her emotions while shielding those around her from what she felt inside. Where some might be angry at what she heard, Mary displayed an intense calm instead.

For almost fifteen minutes, Nick laid out a detailed assessment of what occurred since her husband Chuck was found dead until the moment the five of them met.

Mary asked a few questions as Nick spoke, but mainly listened. Several times, she looked at Merci, but mostly those glances proved fleeting.

As Nick transitioned to discussing what happened next, Mary put her hand out to stop him. She looked toward Merci, but her eyes focused back on Nick. "Can I ask her a question?"

"Merci, my name is Merci, and yes, you can ask me whatever you would like."

Mary's gaze narrowed as she locked eyes with Merci. "Why? Not why did you kill my husband? I get it's your job. Honestly, I don't hold any ill will for what you did to Chuck. You did me a favor. But why did you suddenly embrace a sense of morality and decide not to fulfill your contract? Why risk everything to protect my granddaughter versus abduct and/or kill her?"

Merci bit her upper lip. "This might be hard for you to understand, or even believe, but I have standards. There are lines I won't cross, and lives I won't take under any circumstances. Most people would consider what I do for a living to be morally reprehensible, but endangering the life of a child, any child, is something I'd never consider. As Nick explained, I had no idea who the contract was for until after I had accepted it. As soon as I learned Abigale was my next target, I reached out to Nick immediately. You might not believe me, or fathom how I can do what I do for a living, but everything Nick said is the God's honest truth. It might seem trite considering what I've done in the past, but I would die to protect Abigale. Even some of those who society might consider monsters live by a code. My code is simple. I never harm kids under any circumstances. Children are innocent and should be protected at all costs. I know what it is like firsthand when monsters prey on the young and weak."

Mary looked down at the mahogany table and said nothing for a solid minute. When she slowly looked back up, her gaze met Merci's, and she said only two words. "Thank you."

A prolonged silence filled the room.

Next, Nick told her the plan they had concocted with the president and director of the Secret Service when they were in the DUCC.

"Hold up," Mary said. "You can't take me into protective custody unless the entire operation is done at the same time."

"Why is that?" Nick asked as his eyebrows shifted downward.

"The man from The Fulbright Group who hired Merci ..." Mary paused.

"Mr. Joshua?" Nick interrupted her.

"Yes, Mr. Joshua had my house bugged as well as my chambers here in the Supreme Court."

"That's not possible," the Marshal said incredulously.

"Oh, but it is," Merci countered. "Like I told you when we met with the president, the intel they gave me to retrieve Abigale was very specific, and some of the details they provided had to come from the inside."

The Marshal shook his head. "I know what you said, but I trust the men and women in the Marshals Service."

"As any leader would," Nick said. "But the president was clear. He wants the Secret Service to take the lead on this. I know the U.S. Marshals roll up to the Justice Department, and the Secret Service runs through Homeland Security, but the president makes the final call. He wants the Secret Service to coordinate the protective detail for now. If Mary is correct and Mr. Joshua and members of The Fulbright Group have eyes on her house and her chamber, then she absolutely cannot go into protective custody right now. We need to orchestrate a simultaneous protective raid of sorts."

"Can we at least bring the Attorney General into the conversation?" the Marshal asked. "This is getting above my pay grade."

Nick nodded. "Yeah, I'll talk to Preacher. We can loop in the AG."

"And to be clear," Mary said. "I know they have my house bugged. Mr. Joshua even contacted me via text and threatened me when I was going to secretly meet with a friend. Trust me, they can hear and see what I do at home. Without a doubt, he has the same access to my chambers here at the court. Mr. Joshua repeated back verbatim what I had said while here at the court."

"That being the case, we probably need to get her back to her chambers soon," Nick spoke faster as his eyes darted to the Marshal. "She's already been gone for a while, which may cause flags to be raised, and things need to run as they normally do to not alert Mr. Joshua to what is going on."

"Finish telling her the plan, and I will get her back upstairs," the Marshal said. "The four of us can either meet back here or we can return to the White House."

"Yes." Nick nodded. "We will need the Secret Service director's input and get the president to sign off on it if we are going to alter the plan to do this whole thing simultaneously. I'll need more Secret Service personnel as well."

Mary nodded, too. "Fill me in on the plan you concocted with the president, and I'm especially curious as to where you plan on sequestering all nine justices and their families."

"Well, it isn't Club Med, but the place the president decided to keep you and the others is not a bad place to spend time. It's secure, and I assure you Mr. Joshua and his associates will have no access there."

⸻ ◆ ⸻

Mr. Joshua entered the master bedroom, placed a brown paper bag on the nightstand, and observed Allen staring at the bank of screens.

"Anything happening?" he asked.

"Been pretty quiet since you left," Allen said. "Justice Brown left for a while with the Marshal, but they just came back."

Mr. Joshua's face contorted. "Is that normal? For her and the Marshal to go somewhere together?"

"I mean, it's not unusual. It certainly has happened since I've been watching her these past several weeks."

"Did either of them say anything out of the ordinary when they left or came back?"

"Nope. Pretty regular stuff. Just chit chat. Why?" Allen asked.

"I don't know. With Merci about to kidnap her granddaughter, I'm a little jumpy. I want to make sure we have control of the situation and nobody throws us any curve balls."

"Sure, I get it. Call your guy inside the Marshals Service and see if he heard anything."

"I will."

"Did you bring me something back to eat?" Allen asked. "I'm famished."

Mr. Joshua walked over to the nightstand and grabbed the brown paper bag with visible signs of grease along the base of the bag. "Five Guys, bacon cheeseburger. Just like you said you wanted it when you texted me the order."

"And fries?"

Mr. Joshua rolled his eyes. "Yeah, Cajun style."

"With a strawberry shake?"

Mr. Joshua handed Allen the greasy bag. "Yup, got it all. It's a lot of money for a burger, fries, and a shake. Plus, it'll probably knock a few weeks off your life."

"I'd rather live fewer days on this planet and die younger while enjoying what I want to eat, than be miserable on some diet as I dream of what I can't have anymore."

Mr. Joshua sighed. "The American dream lives on ..."

Chapter Sixty-Six

Phoenix Metro Area, Arizona

After landing in Phoenix, Gus and Trey got the rental car and drove by Clarissa Hart's condo in the Maple-Ash area of Tempe, Arizona. They needed to see the location with their own eyes and did not want to merely rely on Google Earth images. Next, they drove fourteen minutes from her condo to the ABC 15 station, where she worked, on N 44th Street. Gus approached her Jeep Rubicon, bent down like he was tying his shoes, and placed a tracking device on the undercarriage within the wheel well. That way, they would know her exact location when the FedEx truck arrived later with the envelope.

Once they had made the drive several times and felt comfortable with the area, they grabbed a bite to eat. Several blocks from Clarissa's place, they found a large shopping area with just about everything, including an AMC movie theater, several big box stores, and dozens of chain restaurants. The suburban setting allowed them to blend in rather than sitting in the rental car outside her condo. Two guys in a parked car on a residential road for a long time would surely attract the wrong kind of attention.

Trey's cell phone rang. He looked at the caller ID: *Geno.* "Yup," Trey said as he answered the call and clicked on the speakerphone option.

"I just checked the real-time delivery information. There are eight packages before hers on the manifest, so the envelope will be there within twenty to thirty minutes. Are you both in place?"

"Three minutes away in an Applebee's parking lot. We'd stick out like a sore thumb if we sat outside her condo in the car for the entire afternoon."

"Copy that. Get in place. Is she still at the television station?"

Trey nudged Gus, who checked the GPS tracker location on the laptop. "Yeah, boss," Gus said. "Her Rubicon is still in the ABC lot. If she sticks to her normal routine, we should be good on time."

"Okay, tell me when you retrieve and destroy it."

The call ended.

Five minutes later, they found a parking spot fifty yards from her condo, which gave them a direct line of sight down the road in both directions.

Suddenly, the notifications *pinged* on the laptop. "Oh shit," Gus said. "Her Jeep is moving."

"She's early!" Trey exclaimed. "Is she headed home?"

Gus watched as the blue circle moved down North 44th Street and turned left on East Van Buren Street. "Can't be certain, but it looks that way."

Trey thumped his fist on the car's armrest. "We may need a distraction if she gets here around the same time as the FedEx truck."

Gus shrugged. "Yeah, we will have to improvise. Thoughts?"

"I got an idea." Trey reached into his pocket and removed the Wi-Fi-enabled earpieces Geno gave them before they left. He handed one of the transmitters to Gus. "Put this in your ear. I will retrieve the envelope when the driver arrives and leaves it in her doorway. You do exactly as I say."

⸻ ◦ ⸻

Clarissa Hart rubbed her temples in a circular motion, but it didn't help the throbbing headache. Fortunately, the station manager let her off early and another news anchor covered the rest of her shift.

Less than six minutes from home, she stopped at a red light on the corner of West Washington Street and North Mill Avenue across from the Marquee Theater. For the briefest of seconds, she closed her eyes, hoping that might help dull the unrelenting pain of the migraine. Clarissa's eyes opened as she felt a slight bump as her Jeep lurched forward.

Seconds later, a man stood by her door. His thick knuckles rapped hard on the glass. "I'm so sorry. Didn't mean to run into you."

The light turned green, and she took a right-hand turn, pulling over to the shoulder, with the vehicle pulling in behind her.

Clarissa got out and examined her rear bumper. She didn't see a scratch.

The man with a thick New York accent was apologizing profusely. "I'm so sorry. I thought the light turned green, and I let off the brake. It's a rental, and my car back home doesn't move forward so suddenly when you do that."

"I don't see any damage," Clarissa said. "We're good. I just want to get home."

Gus needed to keep her there longer. "Yeah, I screwed up and didn't get the damage coverage from Enterprise," he said in his distinct New York accent. He pulled out a wad of cash, peeled off five Benjamins, and handed her the money. "For your trouble. I'm in town to see my sister. She's in a hospice center in Tempe."

Clarissa's expression softened. "Oh my, I'm sorry to hear that." She tried to give the cash back.

Gus refused to take it. Just then, his hidden earpiece activated with Trey's voice.

I got the envelope. Meet me at the corner of West Tenth Street and South Maple Avenue.

"No, that's for your troubles, ma'am," Gus said. "I hate to cut this short and feel bad for bumping you. I'm glad there was no damage, but I really should get over to the hospice center. My sister doesn't have long."

Clarissa surprised him by stepping closer and giving him a warm hug. "Go see your sister. Again, I'm sorry our paths crossed during such a difficult time."

Gus smiled and returned to the rental while Clarissa climbed into the Rubicon and continued home.

⸺◆⸺

Ten minutes later, Gus and Trey were at Mitchell Park at one of the barbecue grills just down from the basketball courts. Trey took a picture of the sealed FedEx envelope to prove they had it, and it had not been tampered with. Next, he stuffed wads of newspaper he bought at a convenience store into the envelope and squirted lighter fluid on all of it. After he lit the match, he tossed it on the pile, and a whoosh was heard as the flames consumed it within a minute. He took another picture of the ashes, texted them, then placed a call.

Geno answered on the third ring.

"I sent you the evidence," Trey said.

"No complications?"

"Nothing we couldn't handle. We took care of it and Clarissa is none the wiser about what we did."

"Copy that. Drop off the rental car and get back to the plane. The pilot will bring you here to Miami, where I am. Good job, both of you."

Chapter Sixty-Seven

The White House

Nick leaned back in his worn office chair. A loud squeak ensued until he hit the position where the chair could bend no further. With his feet on the desktop, he let out a slow yet audible yawn. The meeting with President Collins, Secret Service Director Kline, and the Attorney General had just concluded, and all the details had been agreed to, although the process was not dissimilar to fingernails being removed by pliers at one point. A few egos were bruised, and not everyone got what they wanted. However, Nick was happy with the end result, at least on paper.

It had been one hell of a day so far, and by the looks of things, the night might not be any easier. He needed a few minutes to simply decompress and not think about anything. Reaching inside his pants pocket, he removed his iPhone and pulled up the Spotify playlist titled, *Save Me*. The playlist included a menagerie of songs by some of his favorite artists: U2, Shinedown, Bon Jovi, Dave Matthews Band, Coldplay, The Rolling Stones, AC/DC, Metallica, 3 Doors Down, Candlebox, and many other bands whose music helped bring a sense of balance to his mind when the rest of the world seemed bent on sending him on a proverbial highway to hell.

With his fingers locked together behind his head and his eyes firmly shut, he did nothing for almost forty-five minutes besides listening to the shuffled songs as their melodies echoed around his office.

The sound of his office door opening caused his restful moment to pause as he slowly opened his eyes. There stood Sam, his apprentice.

"It sounds like your day has been a bundle of joy. I just met with Preacher for a few minutes," Sam said.

Nick let out a deep sigh. "One of these days, maybe sooner rather than later, my days will be your days, and I will be the one sitting on some tropical beach deciding which fruity drink, paired with what main course and dessert sounds delectable."

"Yeah, sorry to disappoint you, but those days are still far off. You're too good a Body Man to walk away from the role. And besides, you'd miss all this craziness."

Nick rolled his eyes. "Miss it? Let's see, in the past year I've been abducted, tortured, shot at, and oh yeah, had a building dropped on top of me. I'm pretty sure sooner sounds like a great idea. I'm getting too old for this shit."

"You need to stick around at least until Preacher serves his last term."

"I make no promises, Sam. One day at a time is all I focus on nowadays."

"Sounds like, based on what Preacher told me, tomorrow is when everything will go down."

Nick slowly nodded. "Yeah, it'll be a late night getting all the pieces in place and coordinating all the simultaneous actions we must execute. I was just getting a little breather before I make calls and get everything lined up for the next twenty-four hours. It's gonna be bat shit crazy around here."

"Merci and Marcus?"

"They are back at my Hay-Adams suite. They know they need to lie low. Everyone else tied to the Supreme Court is following their normal schedule. Mary Brown is back at her townhouse. She'll be at the court tomorrow when everything goes down."

"Did you speak with Abby?"

Nick's brow scrunched together. "No, why?"

"She stopped by earlier and had some intel to review with you regarding The Fulbright Group and Mr. Joshua."

"Oh, damn, I totally spaced on that. The entire afternoon turned into a blur, and I forgot to check in with her. Is she still on the White House Complex?"

"Last I heard, she was working out of the office space at the Eisenhower Building."

"Good. I'll text her and see if she is over there. If so, I'll walk over and catch up with her."

"Smart idea."

"By the way, thanks for holding down the fort, Sam. I know I've been out of pocket recently and getting pulled in many directions. I'm not much of a mentor to show you the ropes when I'm always on the run and don't give you enough attention."

"Nonsense, you're doing a solid job, Nick. Besides, I think the role of The Body Man is not something you can necessarily be taught, at least not very much. You have to learn a lot of it on the fly." She had a quizzical look on her face. "Am I right?"

"You're not wrong," Nick said. "Go get some dinner and call it a night. There's really nothing for you to do here until morning. It would be helpful if you could be in by six a.m.

"Will do," Sam said as she grabbed her bag from the hanger behind the door and left the office.

Nick texted Abby as soon as Sam left.

Hey, you still around?

A few seconds later, the conversation bubble on the text chain popped up, and then her reply came over. *Yes, sir. I'm at the Eisenhower office space.*

Ok, stay put, I'll be there in ten minutes. You eat already?

Not yet.

Cool. We'll order anything you want via DoorDash. My treat.

I never pass up free takeout. BTW, I got the dirt on The Fulbright Group and Mr. Joshua. This shit goes deep.

Lovely. See you soon.

Nick slid his feet off the desk and sat upright.

Time to get back to work.

He opened up the top right drawer of his desk to get his wallet. As he picked it up, the challenge coin below caught his eye. Nick grabbed the coin and spun it around between his fingertips. It came in the mail, along with a handwritten note, about three weeks after the events involving Mogul in the White House basement. The coin and note were a gift from Joseph Lagano. In the letter, Jo-Jo, as he was known, told Nick he would have gotten along well with the Warrior, Peter Casha's twin brother. He was a NYC police officer who died several years before because of his exposure working on the pile of the twin towers rubble. The coin was two-sided, with one side featuring a Spartan mask overlaid with an American flag. Along the top of the coin, it said, FORTIS FORTUNA ADIUVAT. While along the bottom it read NEVER FORGET.

Not one for many attachments, Nick didn't collect many things in life. But the letter from Jo-Jo struck a chord, and he treasured the coin he received. That's why he kept it in the drawer, and every so often, he would take out the coin and read the letter. It normally helped clear his head when things seemed to be closing in. The coin reminded him that nobody knows how long their journey will last, and what they do during their time on this Earth seeps out through those they leave behind.

After he stared at the coin for a moment, he placed it back beside the letter and slid the drawer closed. Nick grabbed his suit jacket from the back of his chair and headed down the West Wing hallway.

CHAPTER SIXTY-EIGHT

SEATTLE, WASHINGTON

Matteo and Leo did not have a straightforward job of intercepting the FedEx envelope from the lawyer's office in Seattle. At least, not as easy as they would have hoped. When they landed at Boeing Field five miles south of downtown Seattle, the first issue they encountered was that the rental car waiting for them would not start. Matteo got worked up because of the disabled vehicle, and Leo had to calm him down before they made a scene. Instead of waiting for a replacement car to be delivered to the charter jet section of the airport, they called an Uber to get into the city.

Strike two occurred when the Uber driver pulled off the I-5 Freeway onto Mercer Street and promptly got sideswiped by a disheveled woman driving a black Honda sedan. The Uber driver wanted both men to stay to tell the cops what happened, but they refused and walked toward the lawyer's office. Several blocks away, they attempted to get another Uber and found the driver had reported them for leaving the scene, and Uber had locked out their account.

Fortunately, they flagged down a Seattle Yellow Cab that dropped them off in front of the Lake Union Building on Westlake Drive. Since they landed in Seattle, the only good news was that the envelope would not be delivered for two more hours. The bad news was that Sheryl mailed it to Dennis Cleghorne at his law office, and not his home address. FedEx would only deliver it during regular business hours, so somehow, Matteo and Leo needed to retrieve the envelope from the actual office as soon as the delivery occurred, without getting caught or alerting any law enforcement to their illegal activity.

As they stood outside the six-story office building, they concocted a plan. Leo was the one who wore pseudo-professional attire, so he went inside and took the elevator to the third floor. He walked by the suite where The Cleghorne Law Office took up the southwest corner of the floor. Ten minutes later, Leo came outside and sketched a diagram of the layout for Matteo.

Geno called and gave them an updated timeframe of when the FedEx truck was scheduled to deliver the package. They passed the time by walking part of Lake Union and grabbing food and coffee at a Starbucks a few blocks from the office building. They both knew they had to keep that part quiet or the other guys would give them shit for stepping foot in a Starbucks which was nothing short of sacrilege to lifelong New Yorkers who grew up like a percentage of Americans running on Dunkin'.

Five minutes before the FedEx truck arrived, they made their way inside past the Ticor Title Suite and headed for the third floor.

As the elevator door opened, the FedEx delivery person walked down the hall to the law office. Leo was a few steps ahead of him, and he entered the office's waiting area and went straight to the receptionist. Matteo held the office door open for the FedEx worker as he approached the counter.

An oversized bouquet of flowers sat on the counter, the card indicating who they were from was blank.

"What lovely flowers," Leo said as he made small talk with the attractive blond sitting behind the high-topped counter.

"I know," she replied. "And we don't even know who sent them or who they are for."

"My goodness, what a treat," Leo answered. Although, he knew damn well who sent them since he placed the order ninety minutes prior.

The FedEx delivery person placed three items on the counter, smiled at the receptionist, and told her to have a great day before he turned and left. Matteo stood just inside the doorway with a warm smile and reopened the door, but said nothing.

The blond stood and reached for the three FedEx envelopes. As she did so, Leo nudged the glass vase with his elbow as nonchalantly as he could muster. She reacted to the falling bouquet quicker than Leo expected, but not fast enough to prevent the vase from breaking as it hit her desktop. The water sprayed everywhere, and the flowers scattered on the floor and all over her workspace.

With the receptionist's back to him, Leo flipped through the FedEx envelopes, finding the one from Sheryl in the middle. He pulled it from the stack and handed it to Matteo, who was now at his side. Matteo tucked the envelope under his thin jacket and immediately left the office.

Leo profusely apologized and offered to help clean up the mess. She allowed him, and they quickly got the flowers and glass in the trash can using paper towels to absorb the water. Within less than five minutes, they had the mess under control.

"That was some unexpected excitement," the blond said. "I'm sorry, but who were you here to see again?"

"Scott Blackburn. He's handling my litigation."

"Scott Blackburn!" the blond exclaimed. "Oh dear, that is the law office on the sixth floor. This is Dennis Cleghorne's law office. I swear we get Scott's clients twice a week down here."

"You don't say," Leo said with a look of surprise plastered across his face. "Totally sorry about that. And again, my sincere apologies for knocking over the flowers. You've been a gem, though."

"Maybe the flowers were meant for the Blackburn office?" The blond asked followed by an innocent chuckle.

Five minutes later, Matteo and Leo were on the rocks close to Lake Union. There was no great place to burn the envelope, but they had strict orders. They took the before photo, stuffed the envelope between a couple of bowling ball-sized rocks near the water's edge, doused it with some butane they bought at a gas station a block away, and set the envelope on fire. Once they were sure only ashes remained, they took another photo and texted the images and the words, *It's done*, to Geno.

A minute later, he texted them back and instructed them both to head back to the airplane and that they were coming to Miami. Leo called a Seattle Yellow Cab, and within twenty minutes, they climbed aboard the private jet to start their journey back across the United States.

Chapter Sixty-Nine

Georgetown

The high-pitched buzzing sound emanating from the iPhone on the nightstand jostled Mr. Joshua from a deep sleep. He grabbed it and clicked the right-side button to silence the annoying sound. The display screen read 3:45 a.m.

"Yes," he said as he pressed the phone against the side of his head. "What is it?"

"You said to call when we had a location for the tracking device on Marcus's Aston Martin," Allen said.

Mr. Joshua blinked several times before the late-night fuzz dissipated as his mind returned online. "Yeah, that's right, the signal is sent at 3:33 a.m. I remember now."

"I triangulated the vehicle's location based on the signal we received."

"So, where's his car?" Mr. Joshua rubbed his eyes.

"About one and a half miles from you at the Hay-Adams Hotel."

Mr. Joshua cleared his throat. He needed a sip of water. "Are they staying at the hotel?"

"Don't know yet. I literally just got the signal a few minutes before I called you, and I had to figure out the location. Not had a chance to crack into their reservations system yet."

"Merci and Marcus are not amateurs. They won't be checked in under their names if they are at the Hay-Adams. They will use aliases. Check all the guests' names and see if you can check if any of the registered guests are them."

"Will do."

"Is Rocco up?"

"Not sure. He's bunking on the second floor. Why?"

"Get him up if he's sleeping. I want him to go to the Hay-Adams and confirm that he sees Marcus's car. If so, he needs to stay on that car and remind him he can't get caught. Merci almost lost it after what happened in Hendersonville. We can't have a repeat performance."

"Got it," Allen said. "I'll get the ball rolling. It's gonna get messy real fast once Merci grabs Abigale."

"Any activity at the Hudson house?"

"No, I just checked before I called. Everything there is quiet."

"Keep monitoring the house and call me if anything changes ASAP."

The line clicked off, and Mr. Joshua put the iPhone back on the nightstand before he rolled onto his side and fell back asleep within two minutes.

At 4:40 a.m., the annoying buzzing of his phone woke him up again. "Yeah, I'm here. What do you got?"

"Rocco is onsite. He confirmed the car in the garage at the Hay-Adams does, in fact, belong to Marcus. I procured him a parking pass for his rearview mirror so he can keep his vehicle in the garage with a direct line of sight on the Aston Martin. If Marcus and Merci get in the car, he'll know it. He also put a secondary device on the undercarriage. This one works a little differently, so when we send a signal, it returns the location coordinates. Again, it can't be detected since it is inactivated until we send the signal. The only downside is the radius is less than a mile, so we want to also keep a visual on the vehicle if possible."

"Smart move," Mr. Joshua said. "Any luck on the guest list?"

"No, all the guests come back as real individuals, so if any of them are aliases used by Marcus or Merci, they have a solid cover."

"Got it, I'm not surprised. I wouldn't expect either of them to make a rookie mistake." He paused. "The Hudson house is still quiet?"

"Silent as a mouse."

"When that changes, call me immediately."

Mr. Joshua hung the iPhone up, placed it back on the table, and stared at the ceiling, unable to fall back to sleep.

Things were moving in the right direction. Geno confirmed his men intercepted two of the envelopes, and all five men would converge on the final FedEx envelope near Miami later in the day. That took a few things off his mind. He wondered when Merci would grab Abigale, but he didn't let it bother him. After she snatched her, the fun would begin. Mary Brown was about to have her world rocked. She might not give a damn about her philandering husband, but she would change her tune as soon as her precious granddaughter was taken.

Mr. Joshua smiled widely before he dozed back off to a restless sleep.

Chapter Seventy

Falls Church, Virginia

Nick had no way of knowing how in-the-know Mr. Joshua and his men were to the day-to-day happenings with Justice Brown or her kids. This meant he and his team had to work off the assumption Mary and her family were completely compromised. They planned the operation to retrieve the family with as many contingencies as they could foresee.

After meeting with Abby the night before, Nick approached Jenn Hudson, Abigale's mother, while she was grocery shopping late at the Whole Foods on Hillwood Avenue. At first, she balked at the strange man and what he told her while in the produce aisle, as any rational person would. But when he handed Jenn the letter in her mother's handwriting, she knew he spoke the truth. It was a risk to approach her in a public setting since they did not know if someone tailed her at all times, but they had to take the chance to pull everything off. The Hudson family phones were most certainly bugged, as were any electronic devices they might use. That necessitated the in-person discussion.

Considering the dire nature of the situation, she took the news remarkably well.

Nick laid out the plan and what Jenn and the rest of her family needed to do. He told her she could not mention a word of what he said to anyone in the house, even her husband.

It would turn out to be the most anxious night's sleep of Jenn's life, and that included the fourteen hours of active labor she endured while pregnant with Abigale.

An email went out to Jenn Hudson from the Montessori School's Valleybrook Campus reminding her of the "Bring your parent to school event." This would act as a solid cover if Mr. Joshua's team were monitoring her emails and give a legitimate excuse as to why Jenn walked Abigale into school instead of using the school drop-off car line as she did every morning.

There was intense discussion back at the White House regarding how to co-ordinate the simultaneous events to secure everyone. But since they did not want to tip their hat, it was agreed they should get all the justices at the same time while they were in a hastily called meeting in the morning at the Supreme Court while the other Secret Service agents went out in pairs to retrieve the immediate family members of all the justices spread out around the D.C. metro area.

This meant Abigale would need to be placed in protective custody while at school.

Nick parked a few places down from Jenn Hudson as he pulled into the lot at the same time as her. He walked several steps behind Jenn and Abigale as they entered the school. He kept his head on a swivel as he looked for threats or something out of the ordinary. Of course, he had to do this while not looking like he was doing it. Something ingrained into all Secret Service agents while learning how to do the job at the James J. Rowley Training Center. Instead of going to the classroom, the three of them walked down the main hallway and out the back door, where two heavily armored black Suburbans pulled up to the curb.

Abigale initially seemed alarmed as they walked past her classroom, but her mother assured her they had a special treat planned and didn't want to ruin the surprise. Even after they climbed into the large SUV, the truth of what was really taking place was not revealed.

As Nick secured Abigale and her mom, a large contingent of Secret Service agents conducted simultaneous movements to tactically secure and shelter all vital personnel around the greater Washington, D.C. area.

At the same time, the nine Supreme Court justices were brought down into the basement level of the court by the Marshal himself, where a heavily armed team of Secret Service agents utilized the underground tunnels to get them out of the D.C. area with no one knowing of their movements. With the exception of Mary Brown, none of the other justices were given any prior information about the need to place them in protective custody, and even Mary knew very few details prior to being led into the basement. Even the Supreme Court clerks who work directly for the justices had no idea what happened until after the fact. Only after the nine justices were safely in Secret Service custody did the U.S. Marshals on site learn of the justices being placed in protective custody, but none of them, except the Marshal and the Attorney General, knew of their location.

⚬

The fleet of Suburbans met in Germantown, northwest of Washington, at a secure off-the-books government facility before continuing together in a heavily guarded convoy to Naval Support Facility Thurmont, located in Catoctin Mountain Park of Frederick County, Maryland. All nine justices and their immediate families would be guests at the presidential retreat known as Camp David until the president deemed it safe for them to return to Washington.

With everyone secure at Camp David, the president had one of his helicopters, commonly referred to as Marine One, but with the president not on board it was called Executive One Foxtrot (EXEC1F), to bring Nick and the Marshal back to the White House. The flight to the south lawn took just under thirty minutes, and as soon as they landed, Nick and the Marshal headed straight to the Oval Office.

CHAPTER SEVENTY-ONE

GEORGETOWN

After an early breakfast in his room at the Ritz, Mr. Joshua had one of his men pick him up and bring him back to the townhouse across from Mary Brown's place. During the brief drive, he called Rocco, who confirmed neither Merci nor Marcus had been seen, and the Aston Martin was still parked in the garage.

Mr. Joshua sat on a chair behind Allen just as he watched the security camera outside Abigale's school show mother and daughter walking from the parking lot to the school's front door. A man walked ten paces behind them but did not interact with them in any way. He pointed at the image. "So, Jenn is going in because it's bring your parents to school day?"

Allen nodded. "That's what the email from the school said."

"I thought Merci would grab her at the house. She's running low on time, and the school seems too risky." Mr. Joshua let out a loud gasp of air, a sound that reeked of frustration.

"Me too. I guess she'll either do it during the day or after school."

Mr. Joshua pulled his iPhone out of his pocket and started flipping through several apps. He looked back up, focusing on the screen in front of Allen. "Is that a live image from outside Abigale's classroom?"

"Yeah, why?"

"Have you seen any other parents enter the class?"

"Huh." Allen tapped his computer mouse several times. "No, I haven't."

"Shouldn't Jenn and Abigale be in the classroom by now?"

"Maybe they stopped by the restroom. It's just down the hall."

"What other camera images do we have onsite?" Mr. Joshua's pulse suddenly increased.

"Just the two, one camera that shows the front entrance, and the camera outside her classroom. We had to get in quickly to install those. Didn't think we needed to wire the whole building."

"Who do we have watching the school?" A bead of sweat formed at the corner of Mr. Joshua's temples.

"K.C. is a block away. It was too risky to have someone on the school property."

"Get him over there. Now!" The last word came out in a deep growl.

"I mean, he can't get inside. There's a resource officer at the front door. And every other door is locked. The school is pretty strict about security."

"Get him over there anyway." Mr. Joshua now stood and paced the floor. "We'll figure something out. Jenn and Abigale should be in the classroom by now, and since no other parents are entering the school, we may have a problem."

Three minutes later, Mr. Joshua's iPhone rang. He looked at the caller ID. It was his man assigned to the Supreme Court.

"Yes, what is it?" Mr. Joshua demanded.

"All nine justices just got ushered into the basement. Nobody is saying a word, but something's going on. This isn't normal. The Marshal is nowhere to be found. Even the court clerks are in the dark as to what is happening right now. Everyone is freaking out around here."

"Dammit!" Mr. Joshua threw his cell phone across the room, and it bounced off the sleeper sofa at the far end of the master bedroom, coming to rest in one piece on the carpeted floor.

"What?" Allen asked with a concerned look at the sudden and unprovoked outburst.

"We just got fucked. Merci must have double-crossed us."

CHAPTER SEVENTY-TWO

THE HAY-ADAMS

"I'm really sick of being in this hotel room." Merci got out of the chair and walked over to the window that looked out toward Lafayette Square. Dotted with billowing clouds, rays of sunshine pierced the gaps as the intense beams of light warmed her face. She had been acting anxious ever since she approached Nick. Being cooped up inside a hotel room didn't sit well with her, and the lack of control proved the hardest part for her to endure.

"Nick said to stay put until everyone is safe at Camp David. He will reach out later today, and we can hopefully get back to normal soon after they track down Mr. Joshua. Soon we will put this whole mess behind us." Marcus tried to offer words of encouragement. "Just a little bit longer to sit tight."

Merci turned away from the warmth of the sunlight. "Yeah, I guess." She let out an audible sigh. "I screwed up by taking this contract, didn't I?"

"Don't beat yourself up about it. What's done is done, and fretting over it won't help. Don't forget, your actions saved a little girls life. Besides, we've been stuck in worse places for much longer. The Hay-Adams is not a terrible place to lay low."

"Of course you're right. I don't handle it well when someone else makes all the plans."

Marcus sat on one side of the king sleigh bed with cherry wood. He patted the bedspread directly beside where he sat. "You could sit here and brood if you want."

She moved from the window, stood next to the bed, and bit her lower lip before her gaze locked onto Marcus. "I think I'm done," Merci stated.

"With what?" A confused look spread over Marcus's face.

She moved her arms around in the air. "With all this. Running around to cities, killing men for money. Stresses over whether someone will get me before I get them. All of it."

"Is this the retirement talk again?"

"I'm serious this time." She frowned as her hands grabbed the side of his face, and she got super close. "It's time for me to do something different."

"Babe, you know I support whatever you want to do. I love you no matter what. But you're a hunter. The chase is what keeps you going. I don't think you could make it doing anything else. You're not exactly the white picket fence, Suzie homemaker kinda gal."

"I didn't say that is what I wanted instead of my current occupation. But I'm sure I can do something different and prove you wrong at the same time." The fierce look in her eyes revealed an inner resolve.

His head moved up and down. "Of that I have zero doubt."

"Can you walk away from all this?"

"Me?" Marcus asked. "I've got many things I could do to occupy my time. You tell me we are done with this crazy lifestyle, and mean it for real, then I'm good with that. We have enough money put away to live for a hundred lifetimes, and not Al Bundy money. We can live high off the hog like the Ewing family for as long as we want."

Merci shook her head. "I would not want the drama that came with the Dallas family."

"Nor would I want the drama that comes with Peggy Bundy."

She smiled and let out the hint of a chuckle at his response. "You would be on board with being done?" Merci asked.

Marcus grabbed her hands and coupled them with his own. "We've had this conversation before. My answer is always the same. You're my ride or die, babe. If you want to do something different, I'm onboard. You say the word and I'd get on the *Titanic* with you, knowing full well I would die with the rats and third-class losers. Or even knowing you would get to fulfill all your dreams like that tramp Rose after she let Jack die of hypothermia." He couldn't help but laugh, knowing full well Merci despised the movie *Titanic*.

"Uggh *Titanic*! You just think Kate Winslet had a nice rack."

"Duh, me and ninety-nine percent of straight dudes. But she doesn't hold a candle to your knockers, babe."

"Well, aren't you just a sweet talker?" Merci responded with a smirk. "Well, I'm telling you it's time for a change. Once this settles down, we are packing up and going on a long holiday while we figure out what to do next."

"Maybe I can get you back to Blarney Castle to kiss that damn stone."

Merci rolled her eyes. "What I'd really like is to get some non-hotel food."

Marcus cocked his head. "Tell you what. Watch *Titanic* with me, and I'll consider sneaking you out of the hotel to find a proper meal. Deal?"

"You're insufferable." Merci punched his shoulder.

"At least I have one good quality."

Merci hopped onto his lap. "I'm sure there's something I could do to change your mind and take me out for a proper meal."

Marcus smiled widely. "You're gonna be the death of me, aren't you?"

"Most likely," she said before planting a wet kiss on his cheek.

Chapter Seventy-Three

Georgetown

And just like that, a meticulously planned attempt to sway the vote of a Supreme Court justice went to absolute hell in the matter of a few minutes.

One after another, Mr. Joshua learned that not only Mary Brown and her family but also the other eight justices and those closest to them were in protective custody.

Any leverage Mr. Joshua had dissipated like a proverbial fart in the wind.

Instead of throwing the iPhone as he did initially, he resorted to punching holes in the drywall. His knuckles bled after he continually threw punch after punch as the bad news mounted.

The one person he had not spoken to so far was the obese man. Mr. Joshua knew a call must be made at some point, but it would have to wait until he exhausted all his resources. No matter how the cards flipped over, at this point, all he held was a losing hand. He could not figure out any way out of the mess. The only person he knew to blame was Merci. He had no concrete proof she was responsible, but no other explanation for what happened made sense. She was the only person outside the TFG organization who knew they targeted Mary Brown's family. He tried to reach out to Merci, but she had gone dark and didn't respond. The fact that she must have played him caused his blood to boil. He should have realized it when he met with her near the Arlington Bridge. But she was good, damn good at deceiving everyone. The obese man warned him, but he did not listen. His pride got the best of him.

The only thing he knew for certain was that Merci had to pay for her betrayal.

But how? Then it came to him. Mr. Joshua picked up his iPhone and called Rocco.

"They've still not come out of the hotel, boss," Rocco said as he answered the call on the first ring, knowing what the question would be. "I'm almost out of Mountain Dew bottles to piss in, but I haven't left my vehicle."

"What do you have with you that can do some damage?"

"You mean like guns?" Rocco asked.

"No, I'm not talking about firepower, I mean something bigger."

The line fell silent for almost ten seconds. "I've got a limited amount of plastic explosives with me. You told me to be prepared if things went south, and we had to breach doors. I knew RDX would do the trick." Rocco paused. "Why?"

"How much do you have?" Mr. Joshua asked.

"Three kilograms, give or take," Rocco stated with a hint of concern.

"Where is it?"

"In a case, hidden inside a compartment within the trunk."

"Do you have a way of remotely detonating the explosive material?"

"Yeah. Of course."

"How close do you have to be to set the charge off?" Mr. Joshua asked.

"I mean, you'd ideally want to be far outside the blast radius, which is a minimum of five to ten meters, but with my device, you could be several hundred yards away to set off the blast. Again, why are you asking?"

Mr. Joshua's voice appeared noticeably deeper as he spoke. "Listen to me carefully, and do exactly as I say."

Chapter Seventy-Four

The Oval Office

Nick walked into the Oval Office exhausted, yet with purpose. He displayed no slouch of the shoulders or sag in his back. The president remained seated behind the resolute desk and gestured toward the chair just to his right. "Take a seat."

Patricia, the president's administrative assistant, closed the door after Nick entered.

President Collins stroked his chin. "Sounds like the team pulled it off, and everyone is safe. You did well, Nicholas."

"There were many moving parts, sir, but everyone went the extra mile and performed flawlessly."

"What do we do about, Merci?"

"Regarding the Chuck Brown hit?" Nick asked.

"Yes, she violated the agreement we had in place for her full pardon after the incidents with the Sanctum."

"That is one hundred percent true, sir." Nick didn't say anything else but stared at the bust of John F. Kennedy located behind the president's desk.

"Why do I sense a *but* is coming, Nicholas?"

Nick raised his shoulders and made eye contact with the president. "Actually, sir, your assessment is correct."

The president smirked. "And yet, I don't think you agree with me. After all this time, I have a good read on the current Body Man. I can sense you think the murder of Chuck Brown should be swept under the rug."

"Mr. President, it is already under the rug. The coroner reported Chuck died of a heart attack. In my book, it's case closed."

"And Merci operating on United States soil is no big deal for you?"

"I know two wrongs don't make a right, but Merci redeemed herself by coming to me and letting us know about the threat to Abigale and Justice Brown." Nick paused as his gaze fell on the JFK bust. "The man whose actions necessitated this role is seen by the American people as being from a time of idealism and glamor. Hell, they refer to his presidency to this day as Camelot. Yet a lot of stuff got swept under the rug while he was president. That only intensified in the administrations to come."

The president's gaze narrowed. "This is about Merci's actions, and not the flawed men who have occupied this office."

"Maybe, but I don't see things as black and white, sir. To protect the office of the presidency, I have to operate in a world shaded with gray. And in my mind, as despicable as Merci's actions might have been, they were offset by saving the life of a young girl. Which at the same time might have upheld the impartial ruling the Supreme Court will hand down for the Kennedy verses Byolyze case. Merci's actions have caused ripples we don't yet feel."

"So just make it all go away?"

"Merci's part, yes. To keep the office protected, I believe I must do so. But as for Mr. Joshua and The Fulbright Group, that is another story."

"Dare I ask what you are thinking?"

"Sir, we need to find this Mr. Joshua and his associates. Intel indicated they are likely still in the D.C. metro area, but I can't imagine they will stay here long. By now, they must know Abigale and Justice Brown have been placed in protective custody, especially since the FBI confirmed Mary's house and chamber at the Supreme Court were bugged. They located cameras and microphones. Trust me, Mr. Joshua and whoever he employs knows everything just went to hell."

"Good. Let them sweat. Nervous people make mistakes."

"Abby has tracked down a tremendous amount of details about the organization Mr. Joshua works for, The Fulbright Group. It's some dark stuff. Like many nefarious groups, they have a legit business side, and then they have these contract jobs where things get murky fast."

"They have offices in New York City, right?"

"Correct, sir. They have an entire floor at One World Trade Center."

"Have the FBI raided their offices?"

"Not yet, but they will. The director wants to make sure his special agents have everything they need. Nobody wants any potential case to get ruined if things aren't handled within the context of the law."

President Collins nodded. "Smart move."

"Until Mr. Joshua and his men are apprehended, we must keep the justices and their families at Camp David."

"Agreed." The president tapped is pen on the desk. "Where's Merci and Marcus?"

"Still at my Hay-Adams suite. I told them to lie low and stay in the hotel until we capture Mr. Joshua."

"I guess we dodged a bullet, didn't we?"

"Yes, sir, thanks to Merci."

"Or because of her."

"Mr. Joshua would have hired someone else if Merci didn't take either contract, Mr. President. And it's highly probable that whoever else took the contract would not have had the morals to protect Abigale Hudson as Merci did. I don't condone all her actions, but there's more to her than meets the eye, sir. Sometimes in life, you meet people who do the wrong things for the right reasons. We both know her background and what was done to her as a young woman. Nobody lives a normal life after having Hell's flames scorch their flesh."

"What they did to her was inexcusable. But that doesn't get her off the hook for taking human lives in retaliation."

"Mr. President, you know our country's history in certain parts of the world. Many would say we shouldn't throw rocks since we live in a glass house."

"Life was simpler when I was teaching Sunday school at First Baptist of Hendersonville, Nicholas."

"Cain killed Able with a rock, according to the Good Book, sir. Humanity has been a mess ever since a certain naked someone took a bite out of an apple and handed it to a weak minded man." Nick smiled. "Or so the story goes."

Chapter Seventy-Five

The Hay-Adams

"The Body Man is gonna be pissed if he discovers we snuck out." Marcus looked down with a disapproving look as he spoke to her.

Merci sat on the sofa as she slipped on her shoes. She glanced up as she got them both on. "What are we, two dimwitted teenagers with no common sense trying to pull one over on our parents? Nick can just deal with it. And besides, I'm not sneaking out of anywhere. I'm a grown ass woman who wants to get a bite to eat outside this hotel prison cell I'm currently confined within. I can leave whenever I want, go wherever I choose, with whomever cares to join me."

Marcus puffed out his lips. "Duly noted, you rebellious adolescent!" He winked at her.

Merci let out a guttural *Ugh* sound, tossed her hair back with her free hand, before she added, "As if," with a smirk of her own.

With a crooked smirk, Marcus acknowledged the blatant Clueless reference, knowing it was one of her favorite movies.

She pulled her hair into a ponytail, grabbed her black sling bag, and put it on over her form-fitting sweater. "How do I look?"

With a broad smile, Marcus put his fingers up to his lips and made a kissing sound as he pulled them away from his face in a quick motion. "Sei perfetta, Tesoro," he replied in flawless Italian.

"Grazie, bello," she said in response.

"We need to make it back to Venice," Marcus said. "I could go for a prosciutto pizza and some gelato."

"Once this mess is behind us, let's do it. A world tour is in order as I consider my next phase of life."

Marcus pulled her in close, his strong arms wrapped around her waist.

Merci placed her head on his broad shoulder. He made her feel safe, and she had never felt that way with anyone. After at least a minute of his embrace, she tapped him gently. "I like you holding me a lot, but a full belly would also feel nice."

He let her go slowly, took a step back, and chuckled. "I swear, I don't know where you stick all that food."

Merci coupled her breasts. "Maybe here," she said with a wicked look.

"Don't get me started. Boobs are the downfall of most men."

"And women know that," Merci said with a wide grin. "Now, stop gawking at my tits, let's get the hell out of here and go eat."

"We're not going too far, just in case Nick calls."

"You're such a wuss," she said in a playful tone.

They exited the room and headed to the bank of elevators at the far end of the hall. Four minutes later, they were in the garage and climbed into Marcus's Aston Martin Vantage.

"Vroom, Vroom, Vroom," Marcus said through sputtering lips as he pulled out of the parking space.

◆◆◆

Rocco was scooping a large spoonful of yogurt as Marcus and Merci exited the door leading to the hotel.

Oh shit. He slid down into the seat to make it harder for them to see if they looked across the garage toward his car.

Rocco dialed Mr. Joshua, who fortunately answered on the second ring. Even though there was no way he could be heard outside the car, he spoke in a somewhat soft tone. "They just came out of the hotel, both Merci and Marcus."

"And?"

"They are in his car."

"Don't do it yet," Mr. Joshua said. "Wait until they're outside."

Rocco fumbled for the remote detonator in one of the cup holders in the center console after he put the metal spoon back into the yogurt container. His heart rate went from slow and steady to that of a locomotive climbing the Saluda grade in mere seconds. "Should I be careful about collateral damage?"

"No!" Came the enthusiastic response. "I don't give a shit about who else it kills. Just make sure you are nowhere near the blast radius." Mr. Joshua paused. "You sure there's enough RDX, and it will work, right?

"Plenty, more than enough, actually."

"Wish I was there to see the B-O-O-M!" Mr. Joshua exclaimed.

"Don't you worry, you'll hear it. All of DC will hear this mutha blow!"

⸻ ◄O► ⸻

Marcus navigated the garage's circular exit ramp and turned onto 16th Street, with Lafayette Square in front of him.

As they idled at the light, Merci slapped her leg. "Damn, I forgot my phone."

"You need it? I can go back if you want me to."

"Yeah, I'd better grab it, just in case Nick calls. He'll try my line first if he wants us." Merci sighed. "Tell you what. Drive around the block several times, and I'll jump out and run up to the room. It'll only take me a few minutes tops."

"If that's what you want."

Merci leaned over and kissed his cheek. "You're a jewel. I don't know what I'd do without you."

Marcus smirked. "I'm sure you'd get by. I'll see you again, just around the block."

She exited the car, closed the door, and walked towards the hotel entrance at a fast pace. To her right, a large box van was parked on the side of the road.

⸻ ◄O► ⸻

Rocco exited the garage in the black Infinite, which had been his home for the past twenty-four hours. He had both windows down to get some fresh air, which felt good as he pulled out of the garage.

As he turned right onto 16th Street, he saw Marcus's Aston Martin ahead at the light of the H Street intersection. Rocco scanned the area. No one stood on the sidewalks close by Marcus's car, although he could not see directly to the right because of a large box van parked at the curb.

Now is as good a time as any. His body tensed as he pushed the button on the remote detonator. The detonation was instantaneous and vicious. The shock wave shuddered his Infinite and even spider-webbed the glass of his windshield.

Rocco slowly crept forward in the vehicle since Mr. Joshua wanted him to verify that Merci and Marcus were dead.

The blast of the C-4 detonating in such proximity threw Merci against the side of the box van as her legs were swept away because of the concussive wave of energy. Her face and shoulder smacked against the side panel of the vehicle as she then slammed against the ground, landing flat on her back. It took her several seconds before she tried to stand. When she did, she stumbled toward the burning wreckage of Marcus's car. One glance was all it took. There was no way he could have survived the explosion and ensuing inferno.

Marcus was gone.

Merci turned toward the road as a black Infinite crept close to the wreckage and came into view.

The passenger window was down, and she immediately recognized the driver. The same man who picked up Mr. Joshua at the Arlington Memorial Bridge. At that instant, she knew the intended target of the car bomb was her. Pure unadulterated rage overtook her damaged and shaking body as she ran at the vehicle, ignoring the pain that pulsated across her bruised and battered body.

With the passenger window open, and in one motion, she dove headfirst into the vehicle, like a cheetah on top of an unsuspecting prey.

Rocco inched forward and, within a second of pulling up near the Aston Martin, realized no one could have survived the carnage the C-4 delivered.

Movement to his right caught his eye. Then someone leapt through the open window and into the passenger seat.

Instinctually, he reached down and withdrew the Glock from his belt holster, even got off two quick rounds. However, both bullets slammed into the floorboard as a strong grip forced his hand downward as he fired and then his attacker ripped the weapon from his grip.

As his eyes met Merci's, he understood he did not stand a chance against this ravenous demon now inside the car. He tried to fight back, but it was an exercise in futility. With his seatbelt fastened, his movements were severely restricted.

Merci angled the barrel downward as the driver got off two quick rounds. Next, she pulled the Glock from his grip and threw it in the back seat as she rained blows on the driver's face. The skin on her knuckles cracked and bled as she hammered his face like a meat tenderizer. The man tried to deflect her strikes with his arms and hands but could not return any blows.

Then she saw the metal spoon sticking out of the yogurt container in the cup holder. She gripped the spoon as one would a knife and jabbed it into the man's face, first into his eyes, which caused him to scream out like a dog being beaten to within an inch of its life. After she obliterated his eyes, she slashed the dull spoon at his neck. Blow after blow, puncture after puncture, until she was bathed in a sea of blood. Finally, after more strikes than she could count, she stopped. The gurgling sound from his throat ended, and whoever this man was, he was no longer part of the living world.

Merci felt no remorse. This piece of shit took everything from her, and in return she did the only thing she could. She ended his existence. Blood collected in her mouth, and she spat it into the mangled face of the corpse.

As she climbed out of the vehicle and stood upright, Merci looked like Sissy Spacek in the 1976 movie *Carrie* as she had blood all over her body. It even dripped to the ground from her fingertips.

Merci looked at the mangled car. She could smell Marcus's burning flesh amongst the plume of smoke as flames continued to engulf the vehicle. She needed to flee. Not because she feared law enforcement, but because she could not stand there and smell the burning flesh of her lover.

Across the street toward Lafayette Square, she saw uniformed Secret Service agents and other law enforcement officers running through the park to converge on the apocalyptic scene. Merci was not about to stick around and explain what part she had played in this.

She hurried back to the Hay-Adams with a steady pace and slight shuffle. The well-to-do guests who paid a premium for a world-class stay were about to see a bloodied woman walking through the lobby, a scene they would recount to everyone they knew in the coming days.

Merci didn't head for the hotel suite. Instead, she went straight to the staircase leading to the Hay-Adams' lowest level, ignoring the audible gasps from everyone she encountered.

Chapter Seventy-Six

Sunny Isles Beach, FL

Geno sat in the driver's seat of the white Ford Transit van he rented earlier in the day. Directly behind him sat Matteo and Leo, while Gus and Trey were in the third row. The van smelled like leftover fast food and also had a slight smell of wet socks. Not an uncommon odor when you put five men in a van when four of them had not showered in over twenty-four hours.

Mr. Joshua spoke with Geno a few hours earlier and told him about the shitshow going on in Washington. In not-so-cryptic words, he told Geno he and his men better not fail to retrieve the file from the FedEx delivery person.

The men debated whether to take the FedEx driver in transit or wait until the envelope was delivered. None of them were overly concerned that he was a retired FBI agent, but it did give them some pause. In the end, they constructed a simple plan and decided to grab the envelope as soon as it was left on the front porch. Rarely, if ever, do the drivers ring doorbells or knock on doors. Nine out of ten times, they drop it on the front stoop. If it's covered from the elements, they leave for their next delivery.

From what Geno could tell, Reggie Hopping, Sheryl's cousin, appeared to be home. He lived on Atlantic Island, a small sliver of land in Sunny Isles Beach that jutted into the Intracoastal Waterway. The house was modest by most standards, but still had to be quite expensive considering its location. For a retired fed, Reggie must have made wise choices with his money.

Geno parked the van a few doors down from Reggie's home and directly in front of a house for sale. He figured that would make it stand out less and not draw unwanted attention from a homeowner who might question why a van with five men in it was parked in front of their house.

As the FedEx driver pulled onto Atlantic Avenue, Geno turned to Matteo. "You're up. As soon as he drops it on the porch, you grab the envelope and high-tail it back to the van. Hopefully, Reggie will be none the wiser."

Matteo nodded. "And if the FedEx guy rings the doorbell?"

"We go to plan B," Geno said.

Fortunately, the FedEx guy looked to be in a hurry since he pulled in front of the house, jumped out of his delivery truck, and tossed the envelope on the wide covered front porch without giving the home a second look.

Before the driver pulled away, Matteo approached the house and already had the thin FedEx envelope in his hand as the FedEx van scurried down the road.

As Matteo turned to leave the porch, the front door opened.

The deep, billowing voice spoke harshly. "Hey, what the hell did you just take off my porch, you good-for-nothing punk!"

Matteo, who at times was known for being a hot head, made a fatal mistake as he turned back to the front door instead of running. "Go back in the house, old man, this doesn't concern you."

The sound of a shotgun being racked gave Matteo pause. But he compounded his error, and instead of running or de-escalating the situation, he reached under his shirt and pulled his own weapon.

"Drop whatever of mine you're holding, or I'll drop it for you." The old, grizzled retired agent threatened as he raised the shotgun about chest height.

Matteo raised his gun upward and moved his pointer finger from the slide to the trigger. Before he could get the weapon up, he felt an immense pressure tear into his chest as the slug struck him center mass.

The envelope fell to the ground, as did the handgun. Matteo's body followed the rules of physics and was hurled backward. His lifeless form flew off the porch and landed in the lush grass beside the walkway that led to the street.

Reggie racked the shotgun, the spent casing flying into the air and landing in the bushes, as he retrieved the envelope from the top step of his porch.

Geno watched the altercation, but sat frozen in his seat for several seconds. As the others in the truck protested, Geno bellowed out, "Oh Shit!" before he opened the van door and ran toward the retired agent's house.

With plans A, B, and probably C worthless, he would have to improvise.

The other three men were out of the van behind him with weapons drawn.

All four approached the house.

"He's gonna call the cops, so we gotta get in there fast and get the envelope," Geno said.

They all rushed past Matteo's corpse as they split into teams of two. Geno and Leo went around the back while Gus and Trey ran up the steps to the porch.

Reggie had already retreated inside and closed the front door as he saw the four men exit the white van and approach his home.

As Gus hit the top of the stairs, only a few steps behind Trey, who was within arm's reach of the front door, the window to his right of the doorway exploded as another shotgun blast took off half of Trey's head. Gus didn't wait for the next round to do the same to him as he dove off the steps and into the bushes below the porch. As he did so, another round careened over his head.

How many rounds does a shotgun hold? He remained on the ground, crawling around the side of the house. The shit just got real.

Geno and Leo heard the shots as they approached the back door, which looked out toward the waterway. With all the force he could muster, Geno kicked above the door handle, and the wood splintered as the door swung inward. He tapped Leo, who went into the house in front of him. They appeared to be in the kitchen.

Leo didn't pause. He ran past the stainless steel appliances and took two steps into the dining room. Two muzzle flashes exploded in front of him. The two .45 caliber rounds found his chest, and he dropped to the floor like an oversized sack of flour.

———— ◆ ————

Geno suppressed the urge to turn and run, but his instinct said if he did, he would likely get a slug to the back of the head. To the right of the kitchen was a long hallway that led to the front door, which now stood wide open. Geno slowly made his way down the hall. There was a living room to his left as he approached the front door. He pivoted into the living room, ready to fire as he tried to locate a target, but the room was empty. He turned back toward the front door and wondered if Reggie had exited the house.

Moving toward the door, Geno saw the stairs to the right of the door. He made a tactical error and checked the front porch before he cleared the stairway.

When he reached the doorway, he heard a creak behind him and turned just in time to see the muzzle flash as the round struck him in the upper back between the shoulder blades. Two more rounds struck repetitively.

❖

As Gus crawled around the side of the house and heard multiple rounds, he froze. *What do I do?* He did not want to barge into the house and end up dead like the others. Above where he crawled, glass broke, and he rolled over onto his back. Shards of broken glass rained down on him as he raised his gun toward the broken window. Gus saw the barrel of the .45 extended out by someone's arm and pointed at him. Before he could get off a shot, the gun barrel exploded, and Gus saw only darkness.

❖

Reggie waited for the local police to arrive, but first went back to the front room and opened up the FedEx envelope. He had to know what it was these five men were willing to die for in order to collect.

The letter from his now deceased cousin, Sheryl, sent chills down his spine. Next, he read the file she mailed to him. He knew only one person he could trust with the information contained within the envelope.

Before the cops arrived, he put the envelope contents in his safe.

For the next five hours, he went through intense scrutiny as he went step-by-step through the process of how five dead men littered his home and yard.

Fortunately, the police chief was one of his best friends, and the evidence of the men being armed and attacking his home was irrefutable. He did not reveal the contents of the FedEx envelope and had to make up a slight white lie when they asked about the FedEx delivery. He slid a bill inside the empty envelope and told the chief it was what his cousin mailed to him, although he acted like the FedEx envelope was not why the men entered the house.

An hour into the interview at the police station, the chief asked, "Couldn't you have left one of them alive so we could find out what they were trying to steal from you?"

Reggie assured him the FBI taught their agents the same way as the local police department. "If you draw your weapon to fire, it's to kill, not maim. A wounded aggressor can still be lethal. Dead men don't fight back, Chief."

The police chief could not find any fault with that logic.

Many hours later, Reggie was back at his house. His wife had passed away several years earlier from breast cancer, and his children both lived out of state, so he was alone at the house. The chief had sent over a few men to secure the house, board up the broken windows, and ensure the back door could be locked.

Later that night, after reading Sheryl's letter and the file several more times, he called the DC metro area. The person on the other end of the line, while friendly, seemed incredulous when Reggie said he had something for *the director's eyes only*. It took a lot of prodding, a promise of a thirty-five-year-old Macallan bottle, and a few other favors to be repaid sooner rather than later to get an appointment with the director of the FBI within forty-eight hours.

CHAPTER SEVENTY-SEVEN

THE WHITE HOUSE

Inside the White House complex, Nick heard the explosion a block away near Lafayette Square. The entire Secret Service security apparatus kicked into overdrive as the president's safety took priority over everything else. Within seconds, the eighteen-acre grounds went into a complete lockdown. Nick rushed to the Oval to check on the president, whom he found perfectly safe. There was a brief discussion about moving President Collins to the DUCC, but he refused.

With the president safe, Nick hurried back to his office. As he opened the door, his cell phone rang. "Yes, what is it?"

"Sir, it's Toby. We have a problem."

"Go ahead."

"It's Merci. She's at the secure door under the Hay-Adams, and requesting to be allowed into the tunnel."

"Buzz her in. What's the problem?"

"Sir," Toby's voice cracked. "She's covered in blood from head to toe."

The earpiece in his right ear transmitted some back-and-forth chatter between Secret Service agents, claiming the explosion looked to be a car bomb that went off across from Lafayette Square near the Hay-Adams Hotel. Uniformed agents were on the scene of the carnage.

Shit. They went after her.

"Let her in, Toby."

"But, sir. She's dripping with blood."

"Unlock the damn door, Toby, and let her in. Clear the tunnel and keep everyone away. I'll meet her down there and don't say anything to anyone. This is an Alpha Seven order, stand down, I'll take it from here."

"I just buzzed her in," Toby said.

"Copy that, I'm on my way."

⎯⎯⎯◆O◆⎯⎯⎯

About two hundred yards into the tunnel, Nick reached Merci. She moved slowly, considering her normal agility. He could see from a distance that she looked like absolute hell. Visible bruises covered her face and hands, and like Toby said, caked-on blood was visible all over her exposed body and clothing. It even matted down her usually pristine hair.

"What the hell happened out there?"

Merci's eyes burned red as she got close. "They killed him, Nick. They fucking killed him like a dog!" She displayed every visible sign of someone in shock, as one would expect after experiencing such a traumatic event.

Nick did something completely unexpected. He pulled her in close to his body and held her as she trembled uncontrollably. Even her teeth chattered. After a full minute embracing her, he pulled back slightly. "Can you tell me what happened?"

Merci collapsed in a heap directly under one of the long fluorescent light bulbs. After several moments, she sat up. She assumed the position of her legs crossed, elbows on knees, and hands covering her face.

With emotions overwhelming her, Merci wept.

Nick sat across from her and held her bloodied hands.

Her tears flowed freely, and finally, after there were no more tears to shed, she composed herself. Merci told him what occurred when she and Marcus exited the hotel suite until she met Nick in the tunnel, looking like an extra from a horror movie.

After she finished speaking, she fell into a somewhat trance-like state as she stared at the ground, the stress clearly taking hold of her by that point.

"We need to get you cleaned up," Nick said. "The White House basement has a full bathroom, including a shower. Agents use it if they don't have time to head home to clean up before their next assignment. As they walked side-by-side down the tunnel, he put his hand on her shoulder, the material sticky with blood. "We'll figure this out, Merci."

She didn't respond.

Minutes later, they were outside the bathroom. Nick got a towel and toiletries for her, and said he would track her down some clothes when she got out of the shower.

Merci turned before she stepped inside the bathroom. "I'm going to New York tonight. The Fulbright Group has offices in lower Manhattan."

"Yes, I know."

"I'm going there to kill Mr. Joshua and his boss. Figured you would want to know."

Nick shook his head. "Yeah, so that's not going to happen. You're in shock. I get it, but I can't let you kill them, Merci. I know they killed Marcus and tried to kill you. But we need them alive. Justice will be served, but not the way you think."

She glared at him, and the fire returned to her eyes. "You don't get it, Jordan. That wasn't a request. I am the Supreme Justice they both deserve, and I will render my judgement by taking their lives."

He didn't reply, but it was clear his body tensed. In a fight-or-flight situation, The Body Man didn't believe in flight.

Merci continued. "If you want to stop me, you'll need to put me down. If you won't or can't then stay out of my fucking way."

⸺◆⸺

Ninety minutes later, Nick and Merci boarded a Citation X at Joint Base Andrews. The private jet was bound for New York City.

"Are you sure you want to be there for this?" Merci asked.

Nick looked at her but said nothing.

"You're not gonna tell me what was discussed with the president?"

"No, Merci," Nick said as he shook his head. "No, I'm not."

They said nothing to each other for the next ten minutes as the plane taxied and climbed into the night sky.

"You think I should let them live?" She paused. "Not exact my revenge?"

"I don't believe for a second I could change your mind, Merci."

"You know if they are arrested, they will both lawyer up. Money is no object for either of them. They will both secure the best legal counsel money can buy and eventually walk. The other option is that they will end up like Epstein, since they have very powerful clients. But no matter what you think, they won't provide any of the dirt you or the president hope you'll get."

"Does it ever occur to you that maybe there are other ways to solve a problem besides killing someone?"

"Sure, there are many ways to resolve conflict that do not require violence. But this isn't one of those times. I won't be able to sleep until both those men take a dirt nap. Besides, I only have two more people to kill, and then I'm done."

Nick frowned. "Done? You? For good?" The questions rolled off his tongue.

"Yup, me. Done, for good." Merci nodded.

Nick rolled his eyes. "Forgive me if I don't believe you."

"Well, it's true. And besides, the president is letting me do this after all."

His gaze looked incredulous. "No, Merci. No, he's not."

She looked surprised. "Then who authorized me to go after them?"

Nick took his index finger and pointed it at his chest. "I did."

Merci's battered mouth opened slightly, but no words came out.

"You're welcome. Take your vengeance. I'm coming along to make sure only two more people pay the ultimate price for what happened to Marcus. This isn't going to turn into some John Wick bloodbath all over One World Trade Center and lower Manhattan. You get to usher two souls into the afterlife, and that's fucking it!"

CHAPTER SEVENTY-EIGHT

ONE WORLD TRADE CENTER

Mr. Joshua did not receive a warm reception as he stepped off the elevator onto the seventy-sixth floor. Most of the staff were already gone for the day, and the few remaining people seemed to ignore him as he walked down the main hall.

Even though the operation in DC turned out to be an epic failure, and the blame rested solely on his shoulders, he walked into the obese man's office with his head held high. Mr. Joshua wasn't about to make excuses or grovel at the feet of anyone. Especially not someone who might be three slices of Famous Ray's pizza away from a coronary.

The obese man looked up from the paperwork in front of him with a look of pure disdain as Mr. Joshua entered his office. "Sit." He pointed his stubby finger at the chair across his desk.

Over a minute passed in dead silence, the only noise the loud gasps from the obese man as he struggled to draw in a full breath each time. Finally, he spoke. "You really screwed the pooch, didn't you?"

"Me? You're throwing this whole clusterfuck on me?" Mr. Joshua asked.

"Yes, you. It was your idea to hire Merci. You are the one who said we could pressure Mary Brown via coercion and threats of violence against her family. Clearly, you were wrong on every count."

"That's not how I see it." Mr. Joshua thumped his balled fist on the chair's armrest. "You hired Merci years ago for the first time, long before I worked for you. When you told me to get the best to get the job done, I went by your recommendations and offered her a contract. The fact that she suddenly grew a conscience and would not kidnap a kid is not on me. That's on her."

The obese man was livid, but the back-and-forth bickering would solve nothing, and they needed to figure a way out of this mess if The Fulbright Group had any chance to survive the microscope they were about to find themselves under. "So, is that what you suggest we tell our client? The assassin we hired suddenly found Jesus, and she wouldn't complete the contract. You think they're going to accept that as an answer?"

"I don't think the client would care what we had to say at this point. They are ruthless, money hungry, and only care about their bottom line."

The obese man nodded. "That's correct. They won't even listen to any of our excuses. This isn't some group with limited reach and scarce financial resources. We are talking about an entity with billions of dollars at risk if this Supreme Court case does not go in their favor. We both damn well know what they are capable of doing to those who mess with their bottom line." He paused as he struggled to turn his large girth in the office chair and glanced toward the New York City skyline. "They will have us butchered, and that's only if we are lucky."

"I am fully aware of what they may do."

"And how do you suggest we handle the situation that's been created?"

"Still trying to figure that out," Mr. Joshua said.

"What about your team in Washington? Are they still in place?"

"I paid all of them before I left. They scattered like the wind. Allen was still breaking everything down at the townhouse when I left. But he's a professional. He knows how to destroy all the evidence and disappear for a while."

"And what about Geno? Have you heard from him? Did he destroy the third FedEx envelope Sheryl mailed?"

Mr. Joshua knew this was where the shit would hit the fan. "So, about that ..."

"What do you mean *about that*?" The obese man's voice rose a few octaves. He struggled to turn his chair away from the skyline and back to Mr. Joshua.

"I've not been able to get in touch with him. He went dark."

"I don't like the sound of that."

"No, it gets worse than that. Local television in Miami is reporting that there was a home invasion gone wrong, and five men are dead."

"Any you think it's Geno and the others?"

"The media is reporting that the homeowner whose house was broken into was a retired FBI agent. Apparently, he shot all five would-be robbers."

"And the FedEx envelope?"

"No clue. I've not even confirmed it was Geno's team, but the Miami Herald is reporting online that the incident took place on Sunny Isles Beach. That's where Reggie Hopping lives."

The obese man tapped his knuckles on the top of his desk. "Worst case scenario, Reggie opens the envelope, and he does what? Goes to the media with it? Can we pay off someone to bury the story if that happens?"

"If he goes to the media, that will be optimal. What concerns me is if he runs the file up through the chain of command at the FBI."

"But he's retired. What contacts does he still have?"

"Based on my research, he was well-connected in the bureau. He took down some heavy hitters while working major crimes at the field office in Los Angeles. He was very good friends with the special agent in charge back in LA, who is now at headquarters and works directly for the director of the FBI himself.

"Well, aren't you just a load of unicorns and rainbows?" The obsess man paused. "Are we dead men walking?"

"Not yet. I'm not giving up and rolling over."

"It will take a miracle for us both to survive this mess. At least your man killed Merci and Marcus with the car bomb, but I'm surprised he was so close to the explosion."

Mr. Joshua shook his head. "I told him to stay back. He either accidentally got too close, or the bomb was bigger than he anticipated."

As he spoke, the obese man went to his safe. He punched in the six-digit code and removed the original file Sheryl had taken and copied. The obese man ambled to the opposite end of the room, where an oversized cabinet was located. He opened the heavy doors to reveal a thick black box slightly larger than a full-size microwave. As he placed the file inside the device, he closed the thick door and pushed a button on the right side.

"What are you doing? Why are you destroying the file?"

"The client will want to know what we did with it. If the FBI gets their grubby hands on the file, we can deny to our client that it came from us. They won't know if someone else made a copy from their company, and that one fell into the hands of the feds. If ours is gone, it mitigates our risk. Maybe."

The small incinerator completely burned the file in about four minutes. Only a pile of ashes remained as the obese man opened the door and stuck a poker stick inside the space.

"Or." Mr. Joshua cleared his throat. "If we get scooped up by the feds, that evidence might have been leverage we could have used as a bargaining chip."

"If the feds grab us I don't think they will try and turn us against our client, but if they did I'll sell out anyone if it means I protect my own ass. You will do the same thing. What we need to be doing tonight is going through everything we have and making sure nothing points back to us with this client or any others. We might need to get my money's worth out of the incinerator tonight. Plus, we need to figure out the next steps."

"Looking for a non-extradition country might also be a good idea," Mr. Joshua said.

"That might be prudent if the government comes after us, but our client is not bound by national borders or extradition agreements."

"I'll head back to my office and see what's in my safe."

The obese man did not try to hide his displeasure. "It's gonna be a late night. I just hope we get to see the dawn."

Chapter Seventy-Nine

One World Trade Center

Merci and Nick sat in a large SUV within the parking structure under One World Trade Center complex. He was on his iPhone, and she could only hear one side of the conversation. He hung up, placed the phone in his tactical vest, and looked at her. "Okay, we are a go."

"And you're sure they are the only people on the floor?" Merci asked.

"Correct. Security cameras confirmed it. Mr. Joshua is in his office, and the obese man is in his. Wham-bam, we get this thing done."

Merci's eyes shifted to the side as she cocked her head at an angle toward him. "You know, in my line of work, wham-bam has other connotations."

Nick frowned. "Yeah, I don't want to know."

"It's nice having connections in government agencies to hack into security systems, isn't it?"

He nodded. "Sometimes it pays to be The Body Man."

"I bet," Merci replied.

"Trust me, other times, it doesn't!"

"I'll take you word for it."

Nick looked down at his watch. "You ready?"

"I am," Merci replied.

"We are going in via the service elevator to the seventy-seventh floor. It's clear as well. We will come down from the southwest staircase to the seventy-sixth floor. That's the most direct way to get us to where they both are while concealing our movements."

Merci nodded. "Understood."

"I made a few calls earlier. The Washington media is reporting that two bodies were in the car that exploded. Plus, another victim was in a vehicle near the one that exploded. No positive IDs have been released, but that at least should make Mr. Joshua believe you are dead, as well as his trigger man, who detonated the car bomb."

"Music to my ears."

"No shooting, right?" Nick asked. "Only use the weapons as a last resort?"

"Correct. A bullet would be way too fast. I want them both to suffer."

"Well, I don't want this to stretch out too long either. I've placed calls, and we own that floor, but if something happens and it attracts building security or NYPD, I don't want to have to pull my Secret Service badge and call in any favors. The fewer people who know we are here, the better. We get in, we get out, and nobody else gets harmed. Are we clear?"

"One hundred percent."

"Don't put me in some situation where you harm building security or other LEOs."

Merci reached over and put her hand on Nick's arm. She gave it a firm squeeze. "I want my revenge, which will only be on those two." She looked him in the eye. "I promise you, nobody else will be harmed. If someone else steps in, I will stand down. We've been over this already."

"Correct, but you also have a track record of disregarding authority."

"You're not my father, Nick, and I'm not your child. I'll stick to the ground rules we agreed to." She squeezed his arm tighter. "I swear on Marcus's soul."

She held very few things sacred in this life, and that was one of them. He opened the driver's side door and stepped out into the parking structure. "Okay, then let's fucking go!"

Nick and Merci found the seventy-seventh floor empty when they got off the service elevator and eased down the southwest staircase to the floor below. While on the landing, Nick called his man, who had eyes on the seventy-sixth floor security cameras, who told him Mr. Joshua was now with the obese man in his office.

Nick relayed the information to Merci. "They're together. You can kill two birds with one stone and mitigate one's attempts to flee or call for help."

Merci nodded. "Let's do it."

As they opened the door and made their way through the lobby toward the obese man's office, they stayed close to the wall and moved swiftly toward their targets.

⸺◆⸺

Mr. Joshua had only been back in his office for about forty minutes when his boss summoned him. It was the third time he had been called back to the office, and he grew tired of the constant bickering with the obese man.

As he stood there getting berated again, a faint *ding-dong* sound echoed throughout the office. None of the employees, except him and his boss, knew a sensor had been placed in the lobby and could be activated by the obese man after everyone left for the day. The sensor picked up movement and sent a signal that alerted him to someone's presence in the lobby.

"Who the hell is here?" the obese man asked.

"Nobody should be here," Mr. Joshua said as he exited the office.

Two figures clad in all-black, fifty feet away, approached his position quickly. He cursed himself for not being armed, and instead of darting back in with the obese man, he ran through the maze of cubicles toward his own office on the far side of the expansive floor. Inside his office, he kept an arsenal of weapons.

⸺◆⸺

Merci saw Mr. Joshua, in his suit, step out of the office and look in their direction. As she pointed with her left hand to the obese man's office, she said, "Secure him." Then, she reached for the sheath strapped to the side of her leg.

Within a fraction of a second, Merci had one of the three Alamo throwing knives out as she whipped it through the air at her intended target striking him deep into the semitendinosus muscle in the back of his leg just below his butt cheek. The razor-sharp knife cut into the muscle, lodging itself into the bone, which caused the leg to lock up.

Mr. Joshua lost his balance and tumbled face-first to the carpeted floor.

On the ground, Mr. Joshua reached behind him and wrangled the blade out of his leg as an intense pain shot through his body. As he rolled over onto his back, he sat up and seeing the figure approach cocked his arm back to throw the bloodied knife at Merci whom he recognized as she got closer.

How the hell is she still alive?

Merci saw his arm draw back but didn't slow her pace as she grabbed a three-inch-thick binder from the desk to her left in mid-stride and used it to deflect the blade as it whizzed toward her. With her right hand, she removed a second sheathed Alamo blade.

The blade's tip was pointed downward as it struck the plastic binder and harmlessly ricocheted off to land on the floor with no harm caused to Merci. She dropped the binder as she moved closer to her mark.

With precise accuracy, she threw the second blade, which struck Mr. Joshua in the sternum, lodging deep into the bone but not piercing any major organs.

Mr. Joshua fell backward, and his hands instinctively grabbed for the hilt, which stuck out of his chest. Merci was on top of him in an instant as she had a third blade out and stabbed him in both shoulders with lightning-quick motions.

He screamed out in agony as she took her balled left-hand fist and struck him in the side of his head, knocking him out with one blow.

As he lay there unconscious, she thought of all the heinous and perverse things she could do to his body to violate it before she ushered him off to the next state of reality. But at that moment, a strange feeling overcame her. She felt a presence, an almost imperceptible push back from an invisible force. In all her years of killing, Merci had never experienced anything like it. Almost as if Marcus was there somehow, telling her not to do what ran through her mind.

Merci climbed off him and didn't initially know what to do. An office chair inside a cubicle to the left caught her attention, and she pulled Mr. Joshua's unconscious body up and into the chair. She zip-tied his hands behind the chair, securing them to the frame while doing the same with his ankles. She rolled Mr. Joshua back down the aisle between cubicles toward the obese man's office.

◆

As Nick entered the obese man's office, he observed two things in a fraction of a second. First, the man behind the desk was beyond large, and held a cell phone in his hand. It appeared he was attempting to dial a number. The second thing Nick noticed was a Japanese-style Samurai sword on a thin shelf mounted to the wall. Even though the sword was sheathed, he could use that to his advantage. In one fluid motion, he had the sword off the pegs, holding it aloft as he approached the desk, and swung it at the phone in the obese man's hand.

The phone fractured into pieces as the sheathed blade hit the face of the phone, splintering into glass and chunks of metal intertwined with plastic across the office floor.

Next, Nick hurled himself across the desk and took the large, melon-sized head of the man with both hands and slammed it onto the solid desktop. The sound of cracking cartilage filled the room as sprays of blood from the large man's nose covered the desk.

Nick pulled the man's hands back behind the chair and, with a snarl, said, "Let it bleed." He pulled out flex cuffs and bound the obese man's hands as he waited for Merci. The bound man tried to protest even with the blood oozing down his nose and in his mouth, but Nick ignored the curses being hurled at him.

"Do you know who I am?" the obese man demanded.

"I do. Do you know who I am, tubby?"

"You're a dead man. That's who you are."

Nick laughed out loud at the comment. "Look, shit for brains. When Merci marches in here, your tough talk will die real fast. I'm a gentle teddy bear compared to her. She's an angel of death if I've ever met one."

"Merci is dead," the obese man said as he spat gobs of blood out of his mouth.

"Wow, you're in for a surprise, Lardo."

The obese man tried to argue, but Nick ignored the taunts and threats.

Two minutes later, Merci wheeled in Mr. Joshua. "What do you know? Great minds think alike. Looks like two pigs ready for the slaughter."

Nick pointed at the blade sticking out of Mr. Joshua's chest, and his head slumped down, almost touching it. "Did you kill him already?"

"No, I just had a little fun with him."

"How are you still alive?" the obese man asked.

Merci ignored the question.

"I'll step outside. Try to be quick about it." Nick walked around the side of the desk and approached the door.

"Don't go. I want you to stick around."

"Merci, I don't really want to see what you're about to do."

"There's nothing to see. I'm done hitting and stabbing and using my hands to take lives."

Nick frowned. "So what? You'll let them live after all this bluster about getting your revenge?"

"No, not exactly. Seeing them both strapped to these chairs gives me an idea. Did I ever tell you Marcus's favorite Christmas movie was *Die Hard*?"

"Don't think so, but that's a pretty common favorite flick for most dudes."

"Well, these chairs got me thinking."

"About what?" Nick asked.

Merci's expression changed to a devious smirk. "Remember what John Mc-Clane tossed down the elevator shaft?"

"Yeah, the office chair with the C-4 strapped ..." His eyes grew wide, but he didn't finish the thought.

"Exactly."

"You want to kill them by tossing them down a damn elevator shaft?" Nick asked.

"I think Marcus would appreciate the irony, considering it was his favorite movie."

They rolled both chairs into the lobby. Merci pried open the center elevator door and stuck a tool into the gap, keeping the hatch doors open.

"I'm not pushing them. This is your deal," Nick said as he backed away from the obese man's chair.

In front of the open doors, Merci smacked Mr. Joshua a few times until he came around, albeit still groggy.

"We can make a deal," the obese man said. "There's no reason to do this, Merci. Name your price. Money is no object."

"You've already paid me, fatboy," Merci said as she stood behind the chair and gave it a firm push. He was a lot of weight to push around.

The obese man screamed as his enormous frame and chair disappeared into the black void of the elevator shaft. His screams echoed through the space until finally a loud *thud* reverberated like the echo of a church bell in the shaft before everything went quiet.

Mr. Joshua watched in horror as his boss disappeared in front of his eyes, since she had slid his chair up toward the edge after she pushed the obese man over.

She spun his chair back around to see him one last time.

He looked at Merci with a snarl stretched across his face. "You know what you are, don't you. I'm sure you've been called it countless times."

"I don't like that word. I would advise you not to say it," Merci said in a firm tone.

"You bit—" he began to yell.

Merci knew it was coming and kicked him in the sternum, driving the knife farther into his chest cavity.

As he descended into the void like his boss before him, clear as day, Merci and Nick could hear the drawn-out word "B-I-T-C-H" echo through the elevator shaft before the loud crash and similar *thud* signaled Mr. Joshua's demise. Then silence.

"Told him, I don't like that word. Some dudes just don't listen to women."

They both stood there and said nothing for a minute.

Merci turned and looked at Nick. "Marcus would have liked that."

Nick shrugged. "Hell if I know, but even Bruce Willis might have approved."

Merci looked away from the void of the shaft as her eyes focused on Nick. "Well, it's done," she said.

"I'll make a few calls. I know people who can clean up the bodies from the bottom of the shaft and keep this whole thing out of the papers.

"Whatever it costs, I'll pay for it."

"Nah, I got it. These people owe The Body Man a few favors. These two are on the house."

Chapter Eighty

Washington, D.C.

Five Days Later

Merci was scheduled to be at the White House later that afternoon. She spent the morning packing up Marcus's apartment. Each thing she placed in the crate to keep or the boxes to discard was like a small dagger in her still-tender heart. The last room to go through was the bedroom. She brought in several boxes and started with the top drawer of his dresser. As she picked up the stack of neatly folded shirts, she uncovered the wax-sealed envelope, her name written in fancy cursive upon it, with a ring box under the letter.

Her hands trembled as she opened the box to reveal a De Beers classic round 3.23 carat diamond platinum engagement ring. Tears flowed down her face as she took the ring out of the box and placed it on her finger. Next, she broke the seal and pulled the tri-folded letter from the envelope. The paper smelled of his distinct cologne, the one she remembered picking out in Paris the first weekend they made love. Her hands shook as she read his handwritten words.

It was as if a ghost from an unseen realm spoke to her. She could hear his voice saying the words as her eyes danced across the page.

Tears continued to flow as her breaths came in broken gasps. She had trouble seeing the words with her eyes flooded with tears and her emotions encompassing her entire body.

Finally, she finished the letter and collapsed into bed, a shell of her former self.

Even the harshest of people have a soft spot, a way to touch their soul. At the same time, the essence of their being can be damaged so badly that it crushes their will to survive.

Merci sat next to Nick on one of the couches in the center of the Oval Office. The President of the United States sat on the other side of the room, with his arms folded, and an inquisitive look covered his face.

President Collins's dog Oliver sat by his feet, as a fire crackled in the fireplace.

Merci looked at the orange and white colored Brittany and smiled. "He's a good-looking dog, sir, and such a wonderful breed."

The president's expression turned into a smile. "Yes, my wife and I love our Ollie. He's like one of our kids since our children have all grown up, and usually stays in the family residence. With Ali gone today, he wanted to be close by. Ollie's a great dog and doesn't even bite the Secret Service agents, right Nick?"

The subtle jab was a slight dig at a former president whose dog had such a bad habit of biting agents that they had to ship the animal back to the president's primary home. His welcome at the White House was short-lived.

The three of them discussed the events that occurred in Washington and Nick and Merci's visit to New York City for the next thirty minutes. After that, they talked about the evidence given to the director of the FBI from Sheryl Hopping's cousin, which was sure to change the fate of the case. The FBI raided The Fulbright Group's offices after the untimely death of the obese man and Mr. Joshua. Their physical files and electronic storage yielded a treasure trove of useful data and intel.

"You have lived an interesting life, Merci," the president said. "You've taken much from others, but I also accept that you have lost a lot along life's journey."

A tear drop formed at the corner of her eyes and followed the contour of her cheek as it made its way down her bruised face. "I had a man who loved me unconditionally, Mr. President, who wanted me to step away from this life. But the hunt, the kill, it was like a drug to me ever since I got off the streets in Paris.

Really and truly, he saved me from that life. But I craved what I did, and did not want to give up the thrill of the chase. It wasn't the financial reward once I completed a contract, but the journey to get there that enticed me. And in the end, it didn't cost me my life, but it cost the life of the man I loved." Merci pulled the letter and ring box out of her sling bag and handed them to the president.

President Collins read the letter, then opened the box and looked at the ring. He handed the letter and ring box to Nick, who looked at the engagement ring before he read the letter.

"Like I told Nick, I've lost the taste for it all. I can't go back to how things were. Not now. Not ever."

"And what if we propose something far different?" Nick asked.

Merci shrugged. "I don't know, but I'm willing to listen."

"Look," Nick said. "I'm not gonna sugar coat it, Merci. You've done things that most would consider to be unforgivable. And at times, innocent people have paid the price for those actions, even if only indirectly. Just because some of the people who hired you in the past lied to you when securing your particular services, that doesn't absolve you from the actions you took against those who proved to be innocent victims." Nick never said the name Danny Frazier, but he didn't have to. They all knew who he was referring to. "But ultimately, your actions didn't take his life; someone else's did. Plus, after losing Marcus and saving Abigale, you paid a price far beyond what was necessary to make things right."

The president interrupted. "Nick has a proposal he, well, really we would like to make."

For the next five minutes, Nick laid out something Merci never saw coming. It intrigued her, even excited her in some ways. *But could I commit to something, anything, right now?* she wondered.

"You don't have to take our offer, Merci, but we want you to give it serious thought," President Collins said. "And if you accept and become part of Section Seven, you do so of your own free will. You are not forced to commit to it for any set period, and you can walk away on your terms whenever you choose."

"I'll give it wholehearted consideration, Mr. President. Truly, I will. But like I told you and Nick. For now, I have some unfinished personal matters to take care of overseas."

Both the president's and Nick's eyes grew wider.

She saw their hint of concern. "It's not anything dangerous or illegal. Just something I need to put to rest before I can move on to whatever comes next."

They all stood. "I can respect that, Miss de Atta," the president said as he reached out and shook her hand.

Nick did the same. "Call me when you get back stateside. Let me know what you've decided."

Merci, removed the ring from the box and put it back on her ring finger. "I will, thanks again. Both of you."

"I'll walk you out." Nick gestured to the door leading to the president's assistants. You can use the east entrance this time. I think we've forced you through the tunnels quite enough times."

Merci smiled. "Actually, like the role of The Body Man, I prefer operating in the shadows. I'll take the tunnel out if you don't mind."

Epilogue

Dublin, Ireland

Merci climbed aboard the Paddywagon Tours coach-style tour bus on the corner of Beresford Place and Gardiner Street Lower in the heart of Dublin, Ireland, only a block from the River Liffey. She wore designer jeans, a light green cashmere sweater with a matching scarf and hat. As the bus driver, Eduardo, drove across the O'Connell Bridge, he explained the various attractions, including Trinity College, Temple Bar, Dublin Castle, and the Guinness Storehouse. While his voice carried over the speaker, Merci's mind drifted back to the last time she and Marcus were in Ireland. Over the speakers, *I Still Haven't Found What I'm Looking For* lightly played in the background. The song was an eerie reminder of why she was back on the Emerald Isle.

Marcus had the idea of taking a day trip down to the Blarney Castle several years prior. Merci wasn't the touristy type, but she also knew when to pick her battles and when to go along if he really wanted something. So, she agreed, and they took the organized day tour from Dublin down the eastern portion of the country.

After leaving the White House, her journey started several days prior in London, where she spent two nights. Dinner at the Savoy Grill, followed by seeing Les Misérables, while also visiting The Tower of London, Westminster Abbey, and watching the changing of the guard at Buckingham Palace. Next, she took the train from King's Cross station to Edinburgh, Scotland, where she ate at The

Witchery, toured the Edinburgh Castle, and even followed the legion of Harry Potter fans as she explored Victoria Street and Greyfriars Kirkyard to get a selfie at Tom Riddle's grave. After Edinburgh, her journey continued as she flew to Dublin where her first stop was The Temple Bar to enjoy a pint before making her way to The Clarence Hotel where she spent the night. The hotel famously known since it is owned by Bono and the Edge from the band U2.

After a stop at the service station, the tour bus made its way onto the Rock of Cashel. The greenery of the lush rolling hills, coupled with the imposing structure ravaged by the harshness of time, yet still standing tall, impressed Merci once again as she walked amongst the stone walls. A light rain fell, and with no roof, she let the water drench her hair as the beads slowly moved down her face and collected on the already damp jacket. She put it on after exiting the bus to protect her favorite sweater. Moving through the graveyard, she was struck by the mixture of century-old headstones interspersed with recent additions. A reminder that no one beats the savage swipe of time, yet life continues for those endure. Thirty-five minutes later, she went down the worn, gravel path and stopped at a marker that read Bishop's Walk. Merci knew a few people with the same surname and wondered if they would ever enjoy a similar adventure. She took a picture of the sign and texted it to her friend Jacquelyn, who needed to visit this place one day.

With everyone back aboard, Eduardo directed the bus through the narrow roads of the quaint town toward the next stop, the city of Cork, the second-largest city in Ireland.

Merci breathed in the smells and took in the sights of the famed English Market, located in the heart of the bustling city. With each step, she moved deeper into the web of shops. A pig head caught her eye at one vendor's spot, while the multitude of fresh fish did the same at the next counter. The area reminded her of Pike Place Market in Seattle, where she visited many times over the years, several while she was with Marcus.

As she explored the English Market, she strolled by the fountain and saw the sign for The Mutton Lane Inn. Her taste buds told her she needed a sip of something, so she ducked inside the narrow opening. Inside, she was greeted by an intimate pub filled with boisterous voices. A few steps in, and to the right of the bartender, a man who looked remarkably like the famed United States newscaster, Walter Cronkite, sat perched on one of the wooden stools, reading a newspaper with his feet tucked under the stool next to his.

Merci ordered a Murphy's Irish Stout, as one does in Cork, Ireland, and found an open spot under a framed poster of the band U2 for their *War* album. As she sat at the round table on a stool, she looked to her left and met the warm gaze of an Irish gentleman. She smiled and dipped her head ever so slightly.

He extended his hand. "Hello, lass, my name is Tony Cronin, and you are?"

"Merci," she replied as she shook his hand.

"That's a pretty name, for an exquisite beauty."

Merci let out an inviting, feminine laugh. Getting hit on by older men came with the territory for her, but she sized him up quickly, knowing he presented no threat. She allowed his attempt at either kindness or flirtation. "Flattery will get you as far as to buy me another Murphy's."

"Aye, I can do that," Tony said in a thick Irish accent as he slid his stool closer to hers.

They carried on like long-lost friends for over forty-five minutes, and the conversation proved easy and inviting. She shared with him an abbreviated tale of some countries she had visited without hinting at the sordid acts that occurred while there on account of her career choice. For his part, Tony told Merci about his grandchildren and also about his time in the military. Tony even shared with her a story about his father, who passed recently, and how his dad was shot while in the service to his country.

Merci enjoyed the conversation immensely and could have chatted for hours, but her iPhone alarm cut Tony off mid-story. She turned off the alert. "I'm sorry, Tony, but the Paddywagon Tour bus waits for no one. I must get going."

Tony removed a challenge coin from his pocket and handed it to Merci, placing the round medallion softly in the center of her hand. "If you ever find yourself back in Cork, please reach out. I would love to take you out for a proper Irish meal and hear more about these travels of yours. My gut feeling is there may be more to your global adventures than you are letting on."

"An astute observation, Tony, and it's a dinner date at some point."

"Can I walk you back to the bus pickup near the River Lee on St Patrick's Hill?"

"I'd very much like that."

They exchanged a warm embrace at the bus, and then Merci climbed aboard. Tony made his way off to the car park with a little extra pep in his tired steps.

⸺◆⸺

Thirty minutes later, Merci stood in the lush green grass beside the large rock with a gaping hole that provided a magnificent vantage of the castle atop the hill. With the river flowing to her right, she gazed at the Blarney Castle in the distance. A rush of emotions filled her, not common for someone who compartmentalized such feelings. She rarely let them out of their hiding place to display on her face, and never in public. But she was alone at the moment. All the other Paddywagon tourists had made their way up the castle. Besides exhilaration, a deep sadness permeated her features as the loss of Marcus finally seeped out from its hiding place deep within.

Mist fell from the sky, almost as if the universe slowly wept in tandem at the loss she now processed. She moved from the green grass up to the base of the castle. With each step on the slick, narrow spiral stairs, her feet grew heavier, almost as if an invisible force tried to keep her from doing what she knew must be seen to completion.

Finally, she reached the top of the castle steps and out into the open. Nobody was up there with her except two workers. As she moved around the exterior walkway, she paused several feet before the actual stone.

Merci and Marcus had stood at this very spot, and he ribbed her for not wanting to take the plunge and kiss the Blarney Stone. She insisted at the time that it was a silly tradition and that in her line of work, "the gift of the gab" would only lead to an early demise. Marcus shrugged off such nonsensical talk and did as so many others have: he kissed the stone. On the drive back to Dublin that day, he gave her grief for not doing likewise.

⸺⸺◆⸺⸺

The two workers, one sitting perched on either side of the stone, with their legs dangling down the hole, smiled as Merci stood there, lost in her thoughts. Their voices pulled her back from the distant, raw memories.

"Are you going to kiss it, girl?" the one on the right asked. He looked to be in his twenties, with a square jaw and a thick accent. He wore an oversized raincoat. No doubt, he grew up in the area and knew what to expect weather-wise from the Irish countryside.

She nodded. "Yes, I must."

"Afraid of heights, are we, little lady?" the man on the left asked. Much older, he likely helped many people fulfill their quest and complete their journey atop the Blarney Castle.

Merci politely shook her head. "Mister, I'm not afraid of anything."

Both men laughed at the brashness of her comment.

"Sure, you're not, lass," the older one stated with a wide toothy grin.

Taking a step forward, Merci followed the two men's instructions, crouched down, and lay on her back. Her arms reached out and gripped the black bars as she lowered her head back down the opening toward the ground below. The stone was located on the bottom portion of the exposed wall, and the man on the right held her back to provide support as her face moved closer to the smooth stone. Countless souls have done the same motion over centuries. Be it the working man or woman, the very wealthy, celebrities, politicians, and even royalty, the Blarney Stone has attracted every walk of life.

As Merci's lips pressed against the cool, to the touch, wet stone, she felt absolutely certain her skin touched the exact spot Marcus's lips pressed against years before. A bolt of adrenaline pulsated through her body as she pulled her lips away from the stone.

Her final kiss goodbye to the man she loved.

The only way in which she could truly let go of him.

Marcus was now at rest, and she believed he had finally found his peace.

With that kiss, Merci could move on with her own life. She stood and looked at the overcast sky. There was a break, and a hint of majestic blue appeared directly above the castle. "I'll see you again, just around the block." As she said the words out loud, a golden eagle pierced the blue dot of sky and disappeared into the billowing clouds. She thought of Marcus walking around the house in his Van Halen T-shirt with the eagle on the chest. In her mind, he saw her kiss the stone, approved of it, and this was his way of saying he found his peace.

Merci looked down at the engagement ring, which she now wore on her left hand. The sight of it brought a tear to her eye, yet joy to her heart.

It's time for the phoenix to rise!

THE END

***

THE BODY MAN WILL RETURN ...
MERCI DE ATTA WILL RETURN ...

***

DOWNFALL
(BOOK 4 IN THE SERIES - SUMMER 2026)

AUTHOR'S NOTE:

Before I get emails and social media messages regarding unresolved plots in this novel, let me explain a few things. The events at the end of the second book in The Body Man Series, **BREACH OF TRUST**, opened a new can of worms for Nick Jordan and Operation Red Star. The end of that book goes straight into **DOWNFALL**, the fourth book in The Body Man Series, which comes out in the summer of 2026. **SUPREME JUSTICE** takes place at the same time as **DOWNFALL** and bridges the gap between both stories. Plot lines that are hinted at during **SUPREME JUSTICE** are settled in **DOWNFALL**. Get ready for an epic ride with all your favorite characters returning next summer.

ACKNOWLEDGMENTS

My 5th published work, *Supreme Justice*, began in December 2020. At the time, it had a different title, and was originally planned to be a stand-alone book for **Merci de Atta**. The manuscript got put aside in February 2021 when I received a publishing contract for *The Body Man*. For years I didn't think about Merci's story and finally picked it back up in 2024. By then a lot had changed and I decided to incorporate the ideas I had for Merci into the world of *The Body Man*. That's how the book became the third entry in *The Body Man Series*. As my Author's note states it is a stand alone story but also a transitionary book between *Breach Of Trust* and *Downfall* (Summer 2026)

Writing is a very solitary endeavor, yet people help in the overall process from inception to finished product. It's an honor to share in the achievement of publishing books with so many family members, friends, and writing acquaintances who have supported me over the years. I put these words in most my acknowledgments but it's good to remind my kids, readers, and especially myself that, ***"Life's a Journey, Not a Destination."***

Above all, thank you to **I AM** for the gifts **HE** bestows upon me and my family

Bruce and **Noelle**. I love you both. It's an honor to be your dad, and watch both of you grow into such amazing young people. As long as I have breath in my lungs, I'm here for you. Also, I love hearing you strum that Martin guitar, son and can't beleive it's already time for you to march off to college and blaze your own path

My **Mom – Patty** and **Dad – Tom** helped shape me into the person I am today

Jackie, Shawn, Meadow, Brett, and **Alli**. Love you all

Aunt Sue. You've always supported my dreams

Grateful for the rest of my **Family**

Supreme Justice is dedicated to **Donald "Donnie" Cheshire** a friend from college. Donnie was diagnosed with Wegener's disease as a young man. We met through a mutual friend and continued our friendship long after college ended. Considering he had a rare disease and knew he was likely to not live a long life, Donnie never complained. Not once. In fact, his attitude and spirit remained positive even when many others found life's everyday problems to be overwhelming. Not Donnie, he saw life as a gift and even though his time on earth was shorter than most, he inspired many with his positivity. Sadly, he lost his battle with the disease in 2016 and was gone way too soon. I've dedicated this book to him because even though he read only one of my early unpublished works, he never got to read about **Merci de Atta**. She would have been right up his alley. Giddyup my friend, until we meet up again beyond this realm

---

Max Council/The Pope our get-togethers are less often but I treasure them when they occur

TC Thompson/Mr. President Can't believe our son's graduated high school and are off to college this fall!

John Guarnieri Thank you for putting *A Tale Of Two Scribes* on your **SpearTalk Podcast Network**. Looking forward to what awaits in the coming years. Oh, and thanks to **Nando, Fernando Menotti,** for the podcast video edits/formatting

Thank you to **Eric Bass** of the band **Shinedown**. Thrilled that you released your debut album *I Had A Name* and can't wait until your other creative projects see the light of day

Kathy Lubin My friend and 1st editor

Grateful for the **Annual Latina Invitational Golf Trip Crew** & the **Troop 610 Dads**

I get a lot of joy when including cameos in the pages of my books. Some books get more than others. For *Supreme Justice* I included: **Sheryl Hopping, Kim Daub, Heather Reaves, Dr. David Richards, Matthew Persson, Lori Twining, Scott Blackburn**, and the chef for the president, **Drew Ward**

Special note of thanks goes to **Tony Cronin**. While visiting Cork, Ireland during November 2024, Tony was kind enough to meet up with me and my mom. That get together inspired the scene in the last chapter when Merci shared a pint of **Murphy's Irish Stout** with Tony at **The Mutton Lane Inn**. That last chapter from London to Edinburgh to Blarney Castle was more fact than fiction. And yes, I did kiss the stone while atop the castle, mom did not (ha) which gave me the idea for the Merci/Marcus stone plotline

One person who never got to share in my writing journey was **Frank Halter**. Frank owned one of the largest real estate companies in town while I was in college. He and his wife **Shirley** hired me to do yard work around their main house on the weekends and ended up providing me with steady work for several years. Frank was kind enough to help me get my first post college car right before graduation when my old clunker died (yes I paid him back with interest), and even placed a few calls which opened some doors that started my career in corporate America. Both Frank and Shirley passed away several years ago, but I wanted to include Frank in this work of fiction and made him the "Marshal" of the Supreme Court.

⸺◦⸺

Thank you to **Kashif Hussain** at **Best Thriller Books** for the *Babylon Will Rise* review

I read a lot of books as a young man, but two literary giants forged the path I now follow: **Tom Clancy** and **Vince Flynn**. RIP Gents

I'm over 10 years into my writing journey and many authors continue to inspire me and teach me lessons on a regular basis. Thank you: **Adam Hamdy, Charles Hack, Joe Goldberg, David Darling, Mike Mason, Brad Meltzer, Sam Whitfield, Terrence McCauley, Kyle Steele, Jack Carr, G.P., Dony Jay, Jeff Clark, Ama Adair, Richard Maverick, F.X. Regan, Matthew Leone, Terrance Layhew, Travis Davis, Michael Carlson, David Buzan, Lori Twining, J.B. Stevens, Kyle Mills, John Stamp, Austin Chapin, Steve Stratton,** and **Dr. Jason Piccolo**

Grateful for all the early readers who graciously agreed to read *Supreme Justice* and provide amazing blurbs/reviews and help spread the word. Your efforts and enthusiasm makes a huge difference for the book launch and overall success

Props to **Ama Adair, Mark Elliott,** and **Aida Flick** who helped kick the tires and help find issues with *Supreme Justice*

In November 2024, I took my mom on her 1st trans-Atlantic trip. We visited England, Scotland & Ireland over the Thanksgiving holiday break. Big thanks to **Michael Trott** of **Four Branches Bourbon** and especially his wife **Cheryl Trott** who gave some recommendations including **The Witchery** in Edinburgh, Scotland

⸺◦⸺

Exited to see some of my short stories in comic books now thanks to **Chris Cochrane** and **Machete Comics**. *Bottled Secrets* my three part short story is part of the **Cult Of Machete** comic series ... out now ... www.machetecomics.ca

---

Thanks to **Jonas Saul** at **Imagine Press Inc.** for my copyedits

Appreciate **Marisia Robus** giving the *Supreme Justice* manuscript one final pass before publication

The awesome covers for *The Body Man, Breach Of Trust, Babylon Will Rise,* and *Supreme Justice* were designed by **Momir Borocki**

Blessed to own an Indie publishing imprint, **BruNoe Media Publishing**, and I'm looking forward to everything it will achieve in the years to come

---

Thank you to everyone who picked up copies of *The Body Man, Breach of Trust, Ransomed Daughter, Babylon Will Rise,* and now *Supreme Justice* since I became a published author in November 2021. It's beyond humbling to know my words are resonating with readers worldwide. So far, my books have reached over twenty countries and counting! In January 2024, I put my books on the **Kindle Unlimited (KU)** program, which is part of **Amazon**. Since then, my books have had over *two million page reads* with **KU**

If you read my books please take a few minutes and leave an **Amazon** rating and/or review (plus **Goodreads**). It really makes a tremendous difference to myself and all writers. Thank you for the support, I'm grateful you've given me a chance to entertain you with my stories

Finally, life is a precious gift. You get to choose how you will receive that gift, and what you do with it. Make wise choices

Onward and upward, my friends,

Eric P. Bishop

May 2025

About the Author

Eric P. Bishop grew up in Connecticut, and relocated to the South after college. Moves to the Rockies and the Pacific Northwest occurred before finally heading back East to raise his family. Part of him never left the West, and he is always grateful to make it back as often as possible.

After many years in corporate America, Eric turned his passion for the written word into reality and chased his dreams of crafting novels.

Eric lives in Western North Carolina with his children, where they explore the great outdoors most weekends, all the while he dreams up his next great adventure. He loves to travel and incorporates what he sees around the world into the stories he crafts.

See www.ericpbishop.com for more about Eric, his novels, and pictures of his amazing journey.

"Life's a journey, not a destination."